DOUBLE APEX

JOSIE JUNIPER

FOREVER

NEW YORK   BOSTON

Copyright © 2024 by Josie Juniper

Cover design and illustration by Sarah Maxwell
Cover copyright © 2024 by Hachette Book Group, Inc.

Forever
Hachette Book Group
1290 Avenue of the Americas, New York, NY 10104
read-forever.com
@readforeverpub

First Edition: October 2024

Forever is an imprint of Grand Central Publishing. The Forever name and logo are registered trademarks of Hachette Book Group, Inc.

The publisher is not responsible for websites (or their content) that are not owned by the publisher.

The Hachette Speakers Bureau provides a wide range of authors for speaking events. To find out more, go to hachettespeakersbureau.com or email HachetteSpeakers@hbgusa.com.

Forever books may be purchased in bulk for business, educational, or promotional use. For information, please contact your local bookseller or the Hachette Book Group Special Markets Department at special.markets@hbgusa.com.

Library of Congress Cataloging-in-Publication Data
Names: Juniper, Josie, author.
Title: Double apex / Josie Juniper.
Description: First edition. | New York : Forever, 2024. | Series:
    Frontrunners ; [book 1]
Identifiers: LCCN 2024008739 | ISBN 9781538768976 (trade paperback) |
    ISBN 9781538768983 (ebook)
Subjects: LCGFT: Romance fiction. | Novels.
Classification: LCC PS3610.U55 D68 2024 | DDC 813/.6—dc23/eng/20240226
LC record available at https://lccn.loc.gov/2024008739

ISBN: 9781538768976 (trade paperback), 9781538768983 (ebook)

Printed in the United States of America

CW

10 9 8 7 6 5 4 3 2 1

For Sean—
Regent of my existence, sweetener of my days,
treasure of my soul, content of my heart.
"O King, live forever!"
—your Balkis

CONTENT WARNING

This book contains a few events or references that might be painful to some readers: the illness and death of a main character's family member during the story and nondetailed mentions of past childhood abuse. There is also explicit sexual content and profanity.

1

MELBOURNE

MID-MARCH

PHAEDRA

My focus prowls over the bank of monitors, studying the telemetry. I'm in the zone. My grip on the information is effortless, light, like breathing. When the car is out and data floods in, the numbers become part of me—they flow through, and I react. The rush is gorgeous.

As one of the two race engineers for Emerald F1, I'm part of the brain, the nervous system of the team. Others may be the heart. The bones. The muscles.

And some are just dicks. I'm talking to one now.

"We're close, Cosmin," I say into the radio. "Push push push."

"I thought you'd never ask, dragă," he returns.

My face goes hot with anger. It's his third inappropriate comment this session, despite an earlier warning. I flick a glance at our engineering director, Lars, and he gives me a shrug as if to say, *Cosmin is what he is.*

"You know what?" I tell Lars and our team principal, Klaus, who's on the next chair over. "Good enough for today. I'm gonna check in with Mo."

Klaus nods, Lars offers a little salute.

I take my headset off and force myself to lay it down more gently than fury urges, then stalk away from the pit wall.

People call my dad Mo, short for Morgan—Ed Morgan, team owner. I do too, publicly. It's hard enough being a woman in this job without verbal reminders to everyone that I'm the owner's daughter.

Growing up in a family that owned a NASCAR team before making the jump to Formula 1 eight years ago, I all but cut my teeth on racing slicks. I traveled the United States with my father and NC Emerald NASCAR during the season and had a STEM-focused tutor who traveled with us.

Every swinging dick on this team (as my dad would say) knows I have this job because I'm a rockstar engineer. Mathematics has been my oxygen since I was five years old. I headed for college at sixteen, had a masters by twenty-two, and went to work for Emerald in a junior position the same year. Over the decade since, I've earned my stripes.

I make my way to Mo's paddock office and find him lying on the sofa. The scent of peppermint hangs in the air—he's having another of his headaches. I gently close the door.

"Hey," I greet as quietly as I can while still being heard over the distant scream of engines. "Why don't you go back to the hotel? This racket can't be helping your head."

"I'm fine, chickadee." He lifts the wet washrag folded over his eyes. "Session done?"

"Almost. Jakob got 1'23.081. Cosmin had 1'22.784 when I left."

"*Left?* Why'd you walk away? That's not like you."

I stretch my back. "Ardelean pissed me off. The smart-aleck comments, the nickname. It undermines me."

"Want me to have a word with him?"

"Definitely not. '*Ooh, Daddy, tell the sexist dickhead not to hurt my feeeewings!*' Yeah, *no*. I'll rip him a new one myself when he comes in." I tighten the loose bun in my auburn hair and rake my bangs aside.

My dad re-covers his eyes. "First year with the team, he's testing boundaries. But the kid's fast—slicker than snot on Teflon. Good chance he'll haul our asses outta midfield."

"Hm. We'll see."

My dad chuckles, and I'm happy to hear it until his words follow. "Man, you are *stubborn*. Still won't forgive the boy for not being that reserve driver gal from Team Harrier you lobbied for."

I fold my arms. "I do think it's a missed opportunity, not offering a contract to Sage Sikora when we had the chance. Emerald could've been pioneers in the sport, giving a seat to a woman with that kind of talent, and—"

"*Phae.*"

His tone is weary with a hint of stern, and I feel like an asshole for bringing it up again.

"I admire your grit, chickadee," he says with a sigh, adjusting the washcloth over his eyes as if to remind me of his headache. "But we're not spending over a hundred million bucks a year running this team to make a statement."

A dozen testy comebacks spring to mind, but I know how and when to pick my battles with Edward Morgan. It's so much easier to make Cosmin the target of my anger. Though it'd be a hell of a lot more satisfying if the guy didn't seem to love it so much.

"Bitter pill or not, I trust you to work through these growing pains Klaus says you and our hotshot driver are having and give him your best," my dad concludes. He lifts the rag and shoots a scold-softening, crooked smile my way. "And if Cosmin keeps sassing you, roll up a newspaper and give that pup *your best good smack*."

I cross the room to press a kiss to my dad's cool, damp cheek. "You know I won't let you down. Need anything before I go—water, food?"

"I'm good, thanks. Dim the lights more on your way out."

I'm striding down the hall toward the garage when Lars catches up.

"Cosmin shaved three-tenths off his lap time," he tells me, beaming.

"*What?* No way." I chew at the inside of my cheek. "The douchebag can drive—I'll give him that."

Lars's expression is careful. "Try not to yell at him. *Again.*

For, y'know, the comments earlier. Sometimes you just have to smile and let it ride."

"Don't tell me to *smile*, for fuck's sake. Ardelean's insufferable."

"People love Cosmin. He's a cut-up."

"More like a pervy party clown."

Lars shoves his hands in his pockets, sighing. "Listen, can I be candid?"

"Could I stop you if I wanted to?" I wave an arm grandly. "Have at it."

He clears his throat. "You're being too free with the pro-Sage-anti-Cosmin stuff. Mo and Klaus made the choice, and the ink is dry. But your resentment is like...*a thing*. Everyone feels it. And don't think the press wouldn't have a field day with a 'girls versus boys' war. Race-day radio comms are public, so it'll be more than just the team noticing tension pretty soon."

Our watchful head of communications, Reece—the woman in charge of PR and media relations—has essentially told me the same thing.

I keep my face neutral as I try pivoting to another point of contention. "That's in the past. I'm over it, seriously. It's Ardelean's lack of respect that bugs me. The faux-flirty back talk. It's—"

"Trust me, you need to ignore that. I've already heard people joking around in the garage, saying your annoyance with Cosmin is the result of, uh..."

My jaw goes hard. "I'm not entertaining any *sexual tension* gossip, thanks. I acknowledge that most women find F1 Dracula irresistible, but I'm not one of them."

Since the era of '76 world champion James Hunt, few

drivers have puffed the panties of female fans like our swaggering new acquisition. Last year, Cosmin Ardelean drove for a team that couldn't find its own ass with both hands and GPS, and his pretty face was still *everywhere* in the media.

Lars shrugs with a weak smile. "All right. Don't kill the messenger."

"Copy," I grumble, walking away. "Understood."

I duck into a conference room and grab a bottled water from the mini fridge. When Cosmin's car rolls in, I wait long enough for the fawning to die down and for that dipshit to climb out of the cockpit, and then I head to the garage.

Our new golden boy is talking with a pair of mechanics while combing his fingers through hair the color of blond sand strewn with amber. It's hair most women would kill for. He doesn't deserve it, much like his stupidly long lashes and plump lips with a perfect Cupid's bow. When his hair isn't sweaty and helmet-squashed, it's a tousled dream that'd be in effortlessly beachy waves if it were long.

Cosmin. Fucking. Ardelean.

I sink my hands into the pockets of my black slacks—we all wear the same style of hideous middle-aged-dude pants with the green polo bearing the team's logo—and cross to where the summit is happening.

"Hey there, Legs," I direct at Cosmin when there's a pause to cut in. "I need a word."

He thinks I call him this because he's tall—just shy of 188 centimeters, which is like six foot two. What he doesn't know is that I call him "legs" because in the body of the team, this peacock may be the movement, but he's far from the brains and sure as hell not the heart.

I recognize the PR value in a good-looking, charismatic driver. For the team's sake, I want Cosmin Ardelean to be *so* magnetic that the press can't stop talking to him, guys buy the pricey sunglasses he wears and the beer he drinks, and women douse the men in their lives with Cosmin's cologne. Sponsor cash is what oils the gears in a Formula 1 team.

We all want a championship for Emerald, full stop.

But for my own amusement? I wouldn't mind Ardelean being taken down a few cocky pegs by tripping over his feet and stumbling into dog shit, preferably after asking out the woman of his dreams and being publicly shot down.

His black-flecked blue-gray eyes hold a smug glimmer as he looks over at me. "You like my time? 1'22.486. How's that for a push?"

"Congrats on doing your literal job," I reply, bored. "You guys done here? Let's talk."

"Beautiful."

God, I'm already so sick of how he says that. It's like he learned English with a Romanian-to-bullshit dictionary. Among the things it taught him: "beautiful" is a synonym for "yes," and every woman should have a goddamned pet name.

I stalk toward the hallway. I assume he'll follow, if for no other reason than to stare at my ass, despite the universally unflattering cut of the team blacks.

In the conference room I was just in, a couple of aero techs are talking, gnawing on sponsor-supplied gluten-free granola bars.

"Gents," I announce, "I need the room."

They look confused until Cosmin follows me in, at which point their expressions imply they know why I want to be alone with him. Thanks to the heads-up from Lars, I now have to assume everyone thinks I'm carrying a torch for F1 Dracula.

Great.

I close the door behind the exiting men and turn to find Cosmin with the fridge open, taking his sweet time to search for the perfect water bottle. I refuse to let it needle me, staring at the back of his dumb head until he's done.

He reclines against a table in the exact place I was standing while waiting for the car to come in. It bothers me, his being in precisely the same spot. It's as if he knows. Like he's taunting me, touching me.

He cracks the cap and drinks, Adam's apple dipping, gaze unflinching, a faint smile on his lips.

"Can I help you, dragă?" he asks after a breath.

"Yeah, perfect—let's start with that. What does it mean? Is it Romanian for 'bitch' or something?"

His eyebrows draw together. "What the shit? No."

The accent is not unattractive, I reluctantly concede. His words come out like *Wot the sheet?* and it'd be cute if he weren't a total fuckwad.

"It is like, 'dear' or 'darling,'" he goes on to explain. "A simple word."

"Gotcha. Not appropriate. Unless you're gonna come up with cutesy-pooh Romanian endearments for every *man* on the team, knock it the hell off."

He nods, looking down as if trying for humility. But I notice he also doesn't agree.

"Next order of business," I press on. "Your cheeky sass over the radio? Not cool. I'd like to be able to use the word 'push' without you firing back some junior-high sex joke."

"I only said, '*I thought you'd never ask.*' If you heard something provocative"—he tilts his mouth—"that might be *you.*"

My hands grip the table edge. I notice him notice, and it annoys me enough to hit below the belt.

"Okay, look, you horny cliché. I get that you think you're ten pounds of brilliant in a five-pound sack because of the job you did last season with the bucket of bolts you drove for Team Greitis. Debut year in F1. Huzzah."

I lean in and enunciate as if talking to a child.

"You may be a better driver than I am, but I'm smarter than you. Don't cross me, or I won't rest until your Transylvanian ass gets busted back down to F2. Or better yet, *no one* will give you a seat, and you find yourself hawking protein shakes on late-night infomercials."

I tap the center of my chest.

"*Smarter. Than. You.* I was doing calculus and rebuilding engines for fun when you were still wetting the bed."

For a moment I think I've gotten to him. There's a hardness to those blue eyes. *Points, me.*

He smiles. "I've made a lot of beds wet…" Pushing off the table, he strolls to the door with infuriating leisure. "But not for that reason."

2

MELBOURNE

RACE DAY

COSMIN

My eyes skim the track, the traffic, making micro-adjustments. The engine's roar is the blood coursing through my veins. I'm in the zone, my control firm and organic. I don't fight the car. It's my body and breath. We flow together, and the rush is incredible.

"Ortiz has a botched pit stop," Phaedra tells me over the radio in her no-nonsense tone. "You'll be ahead at pit exit."

"Copy." A jet of adrenaline flares in my chest, like a coal that's been blown on.

Her voice again, smooth and natural, like she's living in my head: "P5 in sight. Bring it home, Legs."

Mateo Ortiz is still in the pits, and a psychological shiver goes over me as I pass the exit. Fifth place sharpens from a hazy mirage to steel-cold reality.

I was not born for this, but I was *made* for it.

First race with Emerald: *TEN. FUCKING. POINTS.*

My teammate, Jakob, landed P9—two points. I like Jakob. Nice kid, though uptight. Twenty-two, already married, and it's certain Inge is the first and only girl he's had. He refuses to enjoy the extracurricular benefits of our career. Absurd. That's like owning a mansion and living in one room. Champagne would only touch Jakob's stern lips if someday it's poured over him on the podium. He's a reliable, top-ten-finishing workhorse—consistently in the points—but not championship material.

For me? The podium is so close I can taste it, with a strong car under me this year.

Communications manager Reece gives me a bracing clap on the shoulder as we walk toward press gathered outside the corral. She has a critical eye and misses nothing. If cool, composed Team Principal Klaus is Emerald's father figure, Reece is a demanding mother who doesn't suffer a fool. Her personality is as direct as her style—short hair, no makeup, quick eyes. She speaks seven languages (including Romanian) and sometimes reminds me of my elder sister, Viorica. They're both nearing forty.

Reece scans the group with her uncanny ability to untangle a dozen comments at once. "That's Natalia Evans," she says near my ear, pointing at a brunette in purple. "New reporter from *Auto Racing Journal*."

I give the journalist in the skirt suit a once-over. "I will talk with her first."

"Don't tempt me to muzzle you, Cos," Reece warns.

"They love when I flirt."

"And *you* love when you flirt."

I flash a grin. "Everybody wins."

The brunette is stunning. Midthirties, tall, hourglass figure, eyes like a cloudless sky, irises ringed in black that matches her lashes. I check her left hand—bare—as she adjusts one earring, fingertips brushing her neck. Subconsciously, she's imagining my hand there. Moving lower. Undressing her.

Perhaps I'll spend tonight between those thighs.

"Cosmin! I have questions," she says, tapping her voice recorder.

I lean on the metal fence and send a wink her way. "I have answers, iubi."

Combing a hand through my hair, I take a drink of water. She watches the straw in my mouth, and as I remove it, I lick my bottom lip. I know the steps in this dance so well I could do it blindfolded.

"Let's move straight to the good stuff," she begins.

I cock one eyebrow. "I'm all for that."

"Excellent. So. First grand prix, double-digit points. You're looking good."

"Glad you noticed."

"Are you worried it could've been luck? Mateo Ortiz had a heartbreaking twenty-three-second pit stop. Akio Ono and Anders Olsson suffered mechanical failure DNFs. João Valle and Drew Powell, taken out by a collision. Was the fifth-place finish your magic, or merely attrition?"

This just got less fun. I may have to spank her for it later.

I drop my gaze with a smile. "That's racing. Sometimes you hunt opportunity down, sometimes it shows up with an apple in its mouth. When those circumstances arose, *I* was the one in the position to take advantage." I lean closer. "It's not the tool, but how well you use it. And I'm an exceptionally skilled craftsman."

She smirks. "Oh?"

"That, iubi," I say, tapping the back of her hand, "is a promise."

Reece touches my elbow, pointing at a short man in chinos. "From the *Herald Sun*," she prompts.

I tip my head in the man's direction, still looking at Natalia. "Everyone wants a piece of me. If *you're* hungry for a second slice, I'm at the Park Hyatt. Nine o'clock in the lounge?"

A figure steps into my peripheral vision.

"Nat!" Phaedra leans over the fence, and she and the reporter hug. "What do you think of our leggy libertine here?" she asks Natalia, giving me a backhand slap to the stomach.

"I think he's going to be disappointed at nine o'clock," Natalia replies. "And your description was spot-on."

I might be able to camouflage my annoyance if Phaedra weren't watching for it like a cat with her green gaze fixed on a mouse's den.

"Aww, Legs." Those naturally candy-pink lips tilt, and her little nose with its smattering of freckles wrinkles. "Did you think you were playing with *her*? Natalia was playing with *you*."

"Clever girls." I give Natalia a level stare. "Shame—I had quite a story to share with you over a bottle of wine."

Her eyes narrow in consideration, and she throws a chummy arm around Phaedra. "These boys do hate to lose, Phae. And you and I were going to hang out tonight anyway. Let's *all* have a drink in the lounge. We're in the same hotel—why not?"

Phaedra looks alarmed. "Hells to the nope. Negative. I thought we were going to binge *Peaky Blinders* and raid the minibar?"

"Just one drinkie," Natalia tells her in a tone like it's settled. "It'll be fun."

She saunters off to interview Jakob, and the *Herald Sun* reporter heads my way.

"It would appear we have a date," I tell Phaedra. Putting my lips near her ear, I add, "Wear white."

She recoils, frowning. "Oh, suck it. Even if I gave two shits what you think, I don't own white clothes—they get filthy. Who the fuck wears white?"

"Good girls who don't mind getting filthy."

"Is there anything you can't turn into a double entendre?"

"You're pouting because I outsmarted you."

She snorts. "You have to get up pretty early in the morning to outsmart me."

"For you," I tell her, "I'd stay up all night."

3

MELBOURNE

PHAEDRA

"Here—it's yours now," Natalia says, shoving a piece of clothing at me when I open the door of my suite. "It'll look amazing on you, but my boobs are too big."

I shut the door and follow her in. "Poor baby. What other problems do you have? You eat pastries all day but can't seem to gain an ounce? You have orgasms too easily?"

"Haha. Seriously though—try it on. I bought it at L'Habilleur when I was in Paris, and c'est très chic, but I feel self-conscious wearing it."

"Cry me a river." I hold it up for inspection. The fabric is heavenly. Soft and clinging, with a deep crisscross front. "I can't wear this tonight. It's white."

Natalia sits on the bed and adjusts the strap on one heel. "Why not? Planning to get sloshed and dribble all over it?"

"F1 Dracula told me to wear white. I'm not letting him think I wore this on his order." I fling the closet wide and peruse my options. "I'm the one who tells *him* what to do."

"I doubt he'd remember he said it. He's like a fountain spraying out flirty comments. Try it on! You know I have a great eye."

I whip off my CAMP SOH-CAH-TOA trigonometry tee and toss it at Nat, who ducks, laughing. She goes to the mini-bar and gets a tiny bottle of Courvoisier, then takes a bowl of chocolate-dipped strawberries from the refrigerator.

"Things are fancy up here on the top floors," she says around a mouthful of fruit. "You know what's in the fridge in my room? Mini Babybels and bottled water." She cracks open the cognac and downs half.

I adjust the shirt, staring into the vanity mirror. It's true I don't own anything white—mostly because I assumed it'd make my pale, lightly freckled skin look weird. To my shock, white is divine on me. The cut of this shirt is magic: my waist looks tiny and my barely B cups are uncharacteristically alluring.

I turn to Nat and hold my arms out awkwardly. "Eh?"

"It's sexy as hell. It'd help if you weren't standing all stiff and pained, like you're waiting to be sprayed down with delousing agent in a Siberian prison."

"You know I'm more comfortable in jeans and T-shirts." I grab the hem of the shirt to remove it.

"Don't you dare!" Nat barks. "You look fantastic. If you schlump down to the lounge in a baggy nerd-shirt and ripped jeans, I will scream."

"I don't wanna play dress up! Especially not around the 'randy rookie'—as they called that oversexed idiot last year."

She lifts one expertly groomed eyebrow and pops another strawberry between her red-painted lips. "You can wear the ripped jeans, but *with* that shirt."

"That's ridiculous."

"Hello—who understands fashion? Moi. The combination of an elegant Paris boutique shirt and jeans that look like you've had them since your teens—"

"I *have* had them since my teens," I cut in.

"—will be very stylish. It says to the world, *I'm refined enough for this gorgeous shirt, yet devil-may-care enough for threadbare jeans.*"

I rotate to look in the mirror again. "Fine. But I'm not putting on makeup."

"A touch of mascara," she asserts. "Your green eyes are one of your best features. Ooh, and a dab of lipstick—those bee-stung lips need advertising."

"I'm not for sale." I pull my shoulders back and twist forty-five degrees, checking out everything the shirt is doing for my figure. "And if I were," I add under my breath, "he couldn't afford me."

Team Principal Klaus is waiting to get into the elevator as Nat and I step out on the first floor. Near him is a starstruck blonde half his age, staring up at him as if a map leading to the Holy Grail is projected on the side of his head.

Admittedly, Klaus is an almost-silver fox. Forty-five,

toweringly tall, rich, obsessive about his workouts. And with that brand of aloofness women find captivating—like he'd be doing you a favor to fuck you.

To the world it seems like arrogance, but I know him well enough to recognize that he refuses to let anyone get close ever since his wife died five years ago. He finds a different girl at every GP and—according to gossip—tells them he can't exchange contact info due to "security protocol."

Hilarious. Maybe Klaus's disposing of women as if they were coffee pods is the last gasp of his midlife crisis, before he gets into model trains or bird-watching. But I'd still put my money on grief.

Klaus gives me what models call a "smize."

"Good evening, Schatzi," he says, using the fatherly nickname he's called me for years. His gaze moves to Natalia. "And?" he prompts, raising his eyebrows at her while the blonde glowers in the background.

"Natalia Evans," Nat says, offering a frosty smile. "From *Auto Racing*."

The blonde clears her throat, holding the elevator door open as it tries to close.

"Have a lovely evening," Klaus directs at me. "Delightful meeting you," he tells Nat before stepping into the elevator.

She turns away and steams off toward the bar so quickly I have to trot to catch up.

"Whoa there, speedy. Where's the fire?" With a smirk, I add, "Oh, *I know*. The fire was six foot five and standing by the elevator."

"I don't know what you're talking about."

"Klaus *is* pretty hot," I taunt. "I saw you giving him the eye."

"Who?"

I grin. "Quit with the act. You looked like you either wanted to murder or devour him—I can't figure out which." I inspect her face. "Have you guys already met? You're blushing."

She stops just shy of the lounge entrance and plants one hand on her hip. "Yes, I've met him. Months ago in Abu Dhabi. And he was very rude."

I give a skeptical squint. "Klaus Franke? Are you sure we're talking about the same guy? He's totally Captain Suave—I can't picture him being rude to you. What happened?"

"He's just..." She presses her lips together, frowning. "Egotistical."

"*Psh!* Girl, you'll have to get used to big egos in this sport. As for Klaus, he owns forty percent of Emerald and could afford to buy his own planet if he wanted to, so the guy might have a little attitude, sure."

"Whatever." Nat sweeps her dark hair over one shoulder with a careless gesture and proceeds into the lounge. "There's your 'randy rookie,'" she says, pointing at Cosmin.

"He's hardly *mine*," I mutter.

As we walk up, he's doing the "turning water into whiskey" trick—transferring the different-density liquids between two shot glasses—for a woman who apparently flunked high school physics and thinks he's a sorcerer.

The woman's pixieish face is framed by a hairdo that should've been left in 2012 along with Mayan doomsday calendars and fingerstache tattoos. Her rapt smile wilts as we walk up. If this is a competition, she knows she can't beat Natalia, who's disgustingly beautiful.

"Ladies, welcome," Cosmin greets us. "This is Abby." He gestures at 2012 Girl, who gives a grudging wave. Swiveling on the barstool, he nods in Nat's direction, telling Abby, "This is Miss Evans. And the woman in white"—he seems to emphasize the color, though it could be my imagination—"is the team owner's daughter, Miss Morgan."

My jaw clenches with the insult.

Really, dickhead? Not your race engineer—just Mo's kid? And exactly why are we being introduced as if we don't have first names, like Depression-era schoolmarms?

Cosmin's eyes linger briefly on Natalia, who's poured into a velvet dress so short that if she dropped her purse, she'd have to kick it home. She looks like a million bucks. And contrary to Nat's assertion that I'm all kinds of edgy in this ensemble, I'm pretty sure I look like a teenager who shoplifted everything from the waist up.

He eyes my shirt, his expression bordering on smug. *He remembers, damn him.*

"Nat made me wear it," I blurt in a tone not unlike the Ally Sheedy goth in *The Breakfast Club*, passing the buck with "Claire did it!" after her makeover.

There's not enough scotch in this lounge to drown the humiliation.

As his gaze drops to my black Converse, I question the wisdom of having insisted on them. But after Nat screeched "You look like a Wookie!" to bully me into submitting to eyebrow tweezing, the shoes were the hill I was ready to die on.

I give Abby a tight smile and motion to the bartender, ordering a double Glenmorangie on Emerald's tab. Cosmin's focus returns to Abby. He places his hands—long-fingered and strong—over the stacked shot glasses, then glides them apart. He's really working it. Which is absurd, because he doesn't *have* to—his angel face alone would get him anything he wants. But he seems to take pure pleasure in Abby's delight at the "magic" trick.

The bartender brings my drink and I sip it, enjoying the singe on my tongue.

Natalia—seated between Cosmin and me—has her phone out and is studying a message. Her lips compress in her thinking way. She darkens the phone and turns it over, then snatches it back up anxiously and rereads the message, like a kid summoning the courage to peek under the bed for monsters one more time.

I crane my neck in an attempt to spy the short text—which appears to be from an unnamed number—and she stuffs the phone into her purse with a growl.

Beside Cosmin, Abby emits a yelp of surprise, giggling as she slips off her barstool and stumbles. He puts a hand beneath her elbow to steady her, then leans to talk with her quietly.

I take another swallow of scotch and eye Natalia, who's digging her phone out as it buzzes with a second message.

"Who's texting?"

"No one," she insists. "Wrong number."

Her tone is too innocent. *I've got her.*

"Oho! I knew it." I make finger guns at her. "It's a guy, right?"

The screen lights up a third time. I grab it before she does, instigating a near wrestling match as she fights to get it back. I wing the phone away and she jabs my armpit.

"Oooh," I purr. "So mysterious."

"Knock it off!" She snatches the phone back. "What's wrong with you? Are you thirty-two going on thirteen?"

The comment stings just enough. "Why are you being secretive?" I snap.

Her look is lofty. "Apparently you don't understand the difference between secrecy and *privacy*. Aren't you supposed to be some big genius?"

"Wow, Nat." I gulp more of my scotch, shaking my head. "Very nice."

It's familiar ground between us, but still a jarring ride. When she's in a bad mood, she'll mock my intellect, and I'll mock her for being selfish or shallow. Fourteen years of friendship and we're like an old married couple. Fortunately, I love her more often than I want to throttle her.

We stare each other down, trying to decide whether to go for blood or laugh it off. Behind her, I see Cosmin get up and walk away with Abby.

"Ardelean!" I call out, grateful for the distraction. "Where are you going?"

Oh, shit. Why do I care?

He turns, holding up one finger to indicate he'll be right

back, and I shrug like it doesn't matter anyway—just curious; nothing to see here.

I sip my drink, watching with conspicuous patience as Nat's thumbs fly over the keyboard of her phone.

"Phae." She puts a hand on my knee.

"Oh, shit. *What?*"

"Don't get mad, but I'm gonna bail. Something's come up."

"What the hell? *No.* Not cool. Don't you dare leave me here with that schmuck."

She surveys the room. "It would appear the schmuck in question has left. You can go back upstairs and watch TV and order room service like you wanted."

"I was planning to do that with *you*," I protest.

She stands. "If I don't see you again before Bahrain in two weeks, we'll definitely get together there. Hold still…" She pinches my cheeks to bring color into them. "You look so cute—like Emma Stone's grumpy cousin. Weaponize it! Talk to other humans." She gives me a side-hug before clicking away on her high heels.

After a few minutes of unsuccessfully trying to look blithe and confident as I sit alone with a drink, I throw back the last of my scotch and stand. I leave a cash tip for the bartender, then head for the elevators.

As I pass the hotel's front doors, I happen to look out at the loading area. Cosmin is holding the back door open on a sedan with the Ola rideshare logo. Where the hell is he going?

He ushers Abby inside, then closes the door before passing

a wad of cash through the front window to the female driver. He raises one hand at the car in a static wave as it pulls away.

Huh.

Normally I'd applaud someone gallantly arranging for a drunk woman's cab ride home, but it was more satisfying to think of Ardelean as a shitbag.

As he turns, I take a stumbling step back, nearly falling on my ass.

He breezes through the automatic doors. "Waiting for me?"

"Hardly. I was going to my room."

He's wearing a suit that shouldn't look good on anyone— jewel green with a peach open-necked shirt and no tie—and before I can stop myself, the scotch on my tongue has given him a compliment.

"Nice suit. Did you get it at the Riddler's yard sale?"

Wait, no. Not a compliment. Remind me never to drink a double on an empty stomach.

He lets the comment go without clapping back, possibly because his phone is ringing. The muffled tone is familiar, and as he pulls it from his pocket, I recognize it's Bowie's "Fame." I struggle to keep my face impassive. Because David Bowie is my favorite musician of all time—I went into full-scale mourning when he died—and this douchebag is not allowed to like him too.

I scowl at the phone, but not for the reason Cosmin clearly thinks.

He thumbs the button to silence it. "I wasn't going to answer it."

"Whatevs—it's fine. As I said, I was leaving. Nat had to go."

"I know." He straightens his cuffs. "I saw her get into a car with someone." Lifting an eyebrow with a mild smile, he heads for the lounge.

Damn him, the bastard knows I'll follow. I trot to catch up. "Wait, do you have gossip?"

He pulls out a chair on a two-top table and invites me to sit, then seats himself across from me. "I don't miss details, dragă."

"Okay, quit being coy. Who was Nat with?"

Playfully following a whorl in the tabletop's glossy wood with a fingertip, he pauses just long enough to be maddening, then angles a sly smile my way.

Where's that rolled-up newspaper my dad mentioned? Someone needs a smack.

He wants me to beg, but I'm not giving him the satisfaction. I fold my arms. *Challenge accepted.*

Face propped on one hand, he stares back. The sight of his strong fingers framing that chiseled jawline is distractingly pretty. *Ugh.*

"Your friend left with Klaus."

My eyebrows jump. "Holy shit. Really? Huh. What did—"

A server interrupts us, bringing a carafe of water. Cosmin requests a few appetizers: nuts, fruit, hummus with bread. Things I routinely eat in the paddock dining room. I'm not sure if it's creepy or impressive that he's noticed.

I gnaw at my lip, pondering Cosmin's disclosure as he orders for us. After the server walks away, I ask, "Did either of them say anything—Nat and Klaus?"

"Not to me. But I overheard an exchange as he helped her into the car. He said, 'I owe you an apology,' and she replied, 'Is that worth more or less than a thousand euros?'"

"What the hell? Weird."

Cosmin pours water for us, then raises his glass. "To a successful season."

"Shouldn't this be champagne?" I tap his glass with mine.

"You've had enough already."

My hand freezes. "Um, excuse you?" As I speak, I listen for tipsiness. Nope—clear as a bell. Mostly. "Based on *what*?"

His smile unfurls and snaps into place like a mainsail. "Based on how much you've been looking at my lips."

I pause only a second before walking to the bar and ordering another scotch. I lean on my elbows while I wait, knowing his eyes are on me. This is why I've kept this pair of jeans, despite their state of deterioration: they make my ass look incredible.

Let him eat his heart out over what he'll never have.

I strut back, drink in hand. Appetizers are on the table. I ignore Cosmin and scoop up hummus with pita, enjoying how the flavor combines with the sweet grapes and booze, then tip a handful of Spanish almonds into my face and crunch like a post-hibernation bear.

He puts an olive in his mouth. I'm avoiding them because I know they're the type with pits, and the thought of spitting the pit out and inciting some crass comment is too much.

I try not to notice the way his lips move as he works the olive around. When he extracts the pit, the motion is so controlled and delicate that it's honestly annoying. I could never look good doing something so fundamentally unsexy.

I take a sip of my water, then poke bits of almond from a back tooth with my tongue. Definitely not looking cool and sexy. Probably a lot more like a sock puppet.

I inspect the grapes, avoiding his eyes. "So, back to Natalia and Klaus. You didn't hear anything else?"

"No. But tonight I had an inkling Miss Evans did not wear that dress for me—the way she watched the door after arriving, as if hoping to see someone." He gingerly sinks his fork into a chunk of melon. "Now we know who, yes?"

Drunk Me is slightly into the way he pronounces "inkling."

Wot the sheet is wrong with me?

Cosmin takes a grape from my fingers. "I also know you wore that shirt for me."

The spite-scotch was a disastrous idea. My brain futilely tears through attic steamer trunks full of bitchy-clever replies.

He holds the grape between his teeth for a moment before it disappears into his mouth. At least I think he does. Though it may be a boozy time lag, combined with anger and my inability to stop looking at his lips.

Points, asshole.

If I were braver, I'd take off this stupid white shirt and mic drop it onto the table before sashaying away. But it'd be just my luck if the press got a pic of that: "Emerald F1 Embroiled in Melbourne Stripper-Frolic Scandal."

I stand and scoop the almonds into one hand and snag a bundle of grapes in the other, exiting without a backward glance.

In the elevator up, I'm gnawing grapes directly off the cluster—every bit the shit-faced Roman emperor—when the random guy who's riding with me chuckles.

"Need somebody to peel those for you?" he asks.

I examine him, a little bleary-eyed. He's definitely admiring the cut of this shirt. His shirt's not bad either, frankly, hugging a torso with weightlifter-y muscles that aren't really my jam, but look good on him.

For a second, I contemplate being a different person for a few hours and letting him peel my grapes and everything else.

The doors open at his floor. He steps out and offers a hand for me to follow.

With my elbow, I prod the close button. Because I'm not that person, and my life won't let me forget it.

4

BAHRAIN

LATE MARCH

COSMIN

My sister, Viorica, looks tired, but I know better than to say so. Last time we had a video call, I made some comment to that effect—purely because I'm worried about how hard she works for Vlasia House, the Ardelean Foundation children's home—and it was lucky for me there were nine thousand miles between us. Rica is quite sensitive about being thirty-seven.

I've learned so much from her over the years. At times this has been painful—she can have a hot temper when provoked, which little brothers tend to do. She was fourteen when our parents died in a car crash and we were taken in by Andrei Ardelean. He was not a good man—cruel, in fact—though he was willing to throw much of his considerable fortune into my education and childhood karting career, starting at age five.

To Viorica he was a monster. I didn't understand the extent

of it at the time; I was so young. Now I know. And though he is dead, I still fight him. I fight his sharp edges, which are part of me. His arrogance, his manipulativeness.

Some days I can't look in the mirror, and I repress a bitter laugh when people comment on my beauty. I only see the ugliness of my uncle's face staring back at me.

I start our conversation—speaking in our native tongue—with a compliment.

«*You have done amazing work, Rica. The garden expansion is beautiful.*»

She rubs the bridge of her long, straight nose.

«*Thank you. But what Vlasia House needs most is a modern heating system—the third floor is so cold in winter—and that will be expensive. We already took such a big financial hit with the new roof.*»

She sips her tea. The video connection is good today—I see the steam rising from her cup. Behind her, she's framed by the tall antique bookshelves in her office.

"Let us switch to English—I should practice," she says.

"Of course."

"The grant we secured last year, though large, didn't go as far as I'd hoped." Her tone is oddly clipped when she adds, "Next week I am approaching a potentially generous new donor."

"Would you like for me to be there?"

"I prefer to manage it myself." Before I can request further detail, she asks, "When do you visit next?"

"Before Baku. But you seem to be changing the subject."

Her scoff tells me my intuition is correct.

"It's something about this donor, isn't it?"

Her nostrils flare in annoyance. "I have it under control, Cosminel," she replies flatly, using the diminutive to put me in my place.

I can't resist goading her a little by pretending to hide an indulgent smile at her sternness. "As you wish."

Her phone rings, and she looks down at it.

《*I must take this,*》 she says, gliding back into Romanian. 《*Good luck this weekend.*》

《*I will do my best. Good night, Rica.*》

I drop my phone on the bed and walk to the window, admiring the bay, the lights of the city on the other side reflected along the edge like neon teeth. My own reflection is faint, as if underwater. Viorica isn't the only one who looks tired.

I change into workout clothes, then grab water, a towel, my phone and wireless headphones, and a pouch of sponsor-supplied energy gel before going down to the fitness center.

I already had a workout earlier with Guillaume, my physio. But when my mind is restless, troubled, I need something less structured. If no one's waiting for a machine, I'll run on the treadmill for an hour, escaping into music.

I incline-run through a Cage the Elephant album—a band my best friend Owen's American girlfriend told me about— thinking of home and Vlasia House, and whether I should take a few days to fly to Bucharest before the Chinese Grand Prix. I'd like to be with Rica for the meeting, to see what is troubling her that she thinks she must hide.

I'm walking back to the elevators when I spot Phaedra coming down the hallway from the women's fitness center. Her hair—a reddish brown that reminds me of the cover of an antique book—is pinned up with damp wisps flying free. Her cheeks are pink from exertion, and the disheveled hair and flush of her face makes me wonder if she looks like this after sex.

She's wearing a long, baggy unzipped hoodie that hangs past her hips like a dressing gown. I wonder if it belongs to a boyfriend. Is she dating? The woman is such an enigma—I know nothing about her, other than the small clues I've hoarded like magpie treasures.

She's staring at her phone, rubbing her neck with a towel. I wait in front of the elevator door. Her shoes bark against the floor as she startles to a stop inches from me.

Standing this close, I notice how short she is—maybe 160 centimeters, five foot three. Her personality makes her seem taller. At this proximity, I see how easy it would be to lift her. Her clean-sweat smell reminds me of hot metal. I want to feel how perfectly my face would fit against her neck. I imagine her salt on my lips, her arms clasping me, slender hands moving up my shirt, fingers aligning in the valley of my spine.

"Good evening, dragă. Nice to see you. What are you listening to?"

She darkens the screen, expressionless. "A podcast."

I could see she's listening to David Bowie's *Diamond Dogs*. My question was merely an opening, a courtesy. Is her overt lie a dare? It's a shame, because I want to ask which is her favorite song on the album.

The nostrils of her freckled nose twitch. "Why do you stink like cough syrup?"

"The energy gel. Not a good flavor—it's meant to be cherry. You want to taste?" I tip my head as if angling for a kiss.

Her look is icy. "You can keep your lips—and your opinions about the flavor of our sponsor's product—to yourself, thanks. You'll pretend it's ambrosia even if it tastes like Satan's asshole. God help us if someone posts a pic of you sucking on anything else."

The elevator arrives, and I open a hand for her to precede me. I push the button for Emerald's floor. The doors shut. I plant my feet, clasping my hands behind myself as if standing for a publicity photo.

A thought rises in my mind: already I'm so used to posing, I've almost forgotten how to be at ease in my body. This might be what every day is like for a woman.

I glance at Phaedra, and her eyes shift away.

"You must be relieved," I say, "that there's a separate gym for women downstairs."

"No. I think it's stupid and backwards."

"Oh?"

"Like, *'Don't worry, li'l lady!'*" she drawls in an American cowboy accent, "*'I'll save you from the dreaded male gaze!'* It's fucking absurd."

I shake my head, perplexed. "Do women want this 'male gaze,' or don't they? It seems you are always complaining about the problem."

"Thanks for your vote of confidence on me being the

spokesperson for all womankind," she says with sarcasm. "No, I don't want men staring. What I resent is *men* deciding I need to be hidden for my own protection in a separate gym. I can defend myself, thanks. If some douche-canoe is gawking, I'll tell him, 'Quit it or I'll stick a fork in your eye.'"

"I'll ask Javier in catering to hide the forks. And I know the slang use of 'douche'—"

"You must hear it enough," she mutters.

"—but why the addition of 'canoe'? This is a small boat."

"It's a more colorful version of the same thing."

"As for not needing the protection of men, I understand your resentment of condescension—"

She snorts. "Really?"

"—but I disagree. It should not be the responsibility of a woman to defend herself from men. The men need to do better."

"It's like you're *trying* to miss my point. Is this a language thing?"

"I went to UK schools, and my English is excellent. How's your Romanian?"

"Also, it's pretty goddamned rich, having a narcissistic play-boy attempt to teach me feminism. You're a complete fucking sexist, and you know it."

"I'm old-fashioned in some respects and quite progressive in others."

"A week and a half ago, you introduced me to that bar bimbo as your boss's daughter, '*Miss* Morgan,' not a god-damned engineer."

"Did you say 'bimbo'?" I scoff. "Which of us is sexist?"

She has the grace to look a little embarrassed.

"And that *woman*," I continue, feeling a rush from the advantage of her error, much like on the track, "had just told me how intimidated she felt about her friends with degrees, herself having none. I introduced you that way to put her at ease, not diminish your accomplishments."

The doors open at our floor. I hold them as we stare each other down.

With an indeterminate noise, she finally steps out. "Super cool," she deadpans. "But you're still missing my point. I don't need rescuing. I prefer to confront things head-on."

"You *are* confrontational. I wonder if you don't look for reasons to be angry."

She plants her hands over her face before giving me a brutal glare through the fingers.

"Stop that shit. Women don't have to *search* for reasons to be angry. It's everywhere—a twenty-four-seven clown fuck. Why the hell would I *want* to be angry?"

"Because it sets your blood racing. But let me tell you this: if I drive angry, I don't drive as well. I wonder if anger is the only type of passion you allow yourself."

The pupils of her green eyes are pinpricks.

"You know what, Ardelean? Go fuck yourself."

Her movements are stiff as she goes to the door of her suite and taps her phone to unlock it. The pneumatic hinge prevents her from slamming it, though she tries.

Back in my own room I feel remorse for my taunting. In

a way, I was giving her what she wanted—she is invested in a certain image of me. But her face comes to mind again, and I'm concerned there was not only pleasurable indignation there but *hurt*.

After a shower, I open my laptop and begin an email.

> To: p.morgan@emeraldF1.net
> From: c.ardelean@emeraldF1.net
> Subject: I am an ass
>
> The heading says it all. Please accept my apology. The comment was uncalled for.

My hands are poised above the keyboard as I consider whether to include more. I type the words to see how they look, to enjoy the relief of freeing them from my fingertips.

> But I think I may be correct. If so, that's a shame. You are fierce and brilliant and lovely, and you deserve every passion.

I immediately delete that and try a different kind of candor.

> I am poor at apologies. I was sensitive and reflective as a child, and my uncle was quite strict. It was my impulse to apologize over every dropped teaspoon, thinking it would spare me his wrath, but I soon learned the abuse was worse if he saw me as weak.

I stop and delete again. Adding my name to the bottom of the initial three sentences, I hit send. In the morning, I find a reply, sent minutes after I fell asleep last night reading Haruki Murakami's *Norwegian Wood*.

To: c.ardelean@emeraldF1.net
From: p.morgan@emeraldF1.net
Subject: You absolutely ARE an ass

All is forgiven if you hit double-digit points again on Sunday.

I wonder if there were secret sentences she typed out and deleted as well.

5

BAHRAIN

PHAEDRA

This isn't a good morning for Ardelean's bullshit. I was already half wrecked when I arrived at the track for Saturday qualifying.

My dad is currently getting a CT scan of his brain because the headaches are worse. When he admitted he was having nausea and balance problems, I flipped out and insisted he go to the doctor.

He grew up a Carolina country boy and thinks the way to deal with illness is to ignore it. He's also worried about rumors reaching the team's sponsors. It practically took a cattle prod to get him on a flight to Switzerland yesterday, but I did it.

Only Klaus and I know why Mo isn't here, and the tension is breaking me.

I flip down the mic on my headset. "What the actual fuck is Cos doing?" I rest one hand over my mouth, watching the monitors, brow furrowed.

Yeah, Cosmin appears to be letting Owen Byrne in the Team Easton car slipstream him.

I bend the mic back up.

"Cosmin," I say. My tone should be enough, but he doesn't reply.

I glance at Lars. His expression is apprehensive, as if he's more worried about the tense interaction between Cosmin and me than our driver's maverick behavior.

"Cosmin," I repeat, stronger. "*Don't* give Byrne a tow."

"Copy."

I wait as they navigate through a chicane and surge back onto the straight, but Cosmin doesn't shake Byrne. Is he offering his struggling buddy an advantage or just doing this to annoy me?

My jaw hard, I shoot a wide-eyed look over at Klaus, both wanting and *not* wanting him to step in and speak to Cosmin over the radio himself. He tends to stay off the comms unless there's a very serious reason. His face is impassive, but I suspect this is a test. And I'm failing.

"Are you seeing this?" I snarl defensively, now mad at both Cosmin and myself for looking like I can't manage him. "If the guy offered a bigger invitation to get fucked, I'd suggest Byrne buy him dinner first! *He. Has. To. Listen.*" I chop one hand against the opposite palm.

Klaus moves to my side to drop an arm around me, then eases off my headset.

"Eyes are on you, Schatzi," he says near my ear, giving my shoulders a squeeze as he leads me away from the pit wall.

It's loud next to the track, so we can't really talk, but there's a visual language we easily convey, knowing each other so well.

Sorry, I mouth.

He taps his wrist, jerks a thumb over his shoulder, points between the two of us: *We'll talk about it later.* I nod, then lift my palms in further apology. He replies with a familiar gesture: taps his chest, levels a flat hand and raises it like an elevator, then taps his forehead.

Your brain is above your heart.

He knows my quick temper, and for years has given me this reminder that I must stay on top of my emotions trackside.

And so my brain plants one boot on my heart and one farther south, where warning earthquakes rumbled last night after I woke up dreaming about Cosmin.

⬛⬜⬛⬜⬛

"And in addition to his insubordination," I complain to Klaus over dinner, "Ardelean is one big swaggering mixed message in a personal sense. He should have the integrity to be a *consistent* piece of shit—if I could unilaterally hate him, it might actually make our communication problem easier. I'd know what to expect!"

My pasta primavera is untouched, I'm talking so much. In the eight years we've worked together, Klaus has listened to me bitch about work, family, men, sexism. Tonight he makes his way through his usual meal of fish and steamed vegetables—knife and fork moving with surgical precision—as I unload, first about my worry over Dad, and now Cosmin.

"One minute," I continue, "he's acting like a gross horn-dog, or being a stubborn dick who *won't listen to his race engineer*, and then he'll turn around and pull some saintly crap like the thing with the drunk girl or helping that lost kid in Melbourne."

"Cosmin has not had an easy life. He himself is likely confused as to who he is."

I snort. "Sure, tough childhood, pampered by some rich uncle. I'm sure Li'l Cos must've been limping around Bucharest with one shoe."

Klaus's fork stalls in transit. "Was money the reason for your happy childhood? No. Your father is very loving. Cosmin's parents are dead. I've been watching his progress since a dozen years ago when Cosmin was in KF1. Andrei Ardelean had a reputation for cruelty. There were ugly rumors."

I fork up a bit of my now-tepid pasta. "What kind?"

"Things a woman should not have to hear."

My fork drops to the bowl with a clatter. "Now *you*, with the patronizing bullshit?"

He takes a careful bite of fish, watching me as if deciding. "It was said that he auctioned the virginity of Cosmin's sister to a group of…*associates*…when she was fifteen." He presses a white linen napkin to his lips, then clears his throat. "And that he personally 'trained' her."

My stomach flops. "Holy shit."

"It may simply be a disgusting tale."

"I doubt a thing like that is cut from whole cloth though."

"He was quick with a fist as well. A young man serving at

a banquet attended by Andrei Ardelean lost an eye to a back-hand slap—Ardelean's ring. A friend of mine was there."

"Fuck." I move the pasta around my plate.

"Schatzi," Klaus says softly. "You're not going to like everything I'm about to say, but I want you to listen and trust me."

My hand tightens on the fork.

"You're one of the best race engineers in the business, and Emerald is lucky to have you."

"I'm not hating this yet," I joke, forking up a bit of broccoli and eating it.

"But your lack of rapport with Cosmin will cost Emerald championship points this year if you can't improve your communication. I'm disappointed in your disinclination to behave like the professional I know you to be."

Even though I was expecting it, his words hit like a cold, slow-motion sucker punch. I stare down at my plate, dragging a noodle back and forth with my fork as I try to decide whether to be apologetic or come out swinging. The sucky thing is, I know Klaus is right.

Before I can cobble together a reply, he continues.

"Of the one hundred two points distributed per race," he says with his quiet intensity, "at least twenty should consistently belong to Emerald. Do we agree on that?"

"Yes," I manage just above a whisper, too nervous to look at him.

He reaches across the table for my hand. "Good. And do you know of the company retreats some workplaces hold? With activities for, hm, 'bonding'?"

A ripple of dread goes through me, and I meet his eyes. "Uh, yeah. They're touchy-feely horseshit. Please don't get all 'holistic racing team' and make everybody do that."

"I don't plan to make everybody do this. Only you and Cosmin."

I withdraw my hand and fight down a sip of water, shooting eye poison at Klaus like one of those spooky toads. "Very funny. Not doing it."

"You *are*. A small trip after the GP—two nights next week in Santorini, Greece. You'll stay in my cottage."

I almost open my mouth to protest again but catch his somber expression. The cottage in Santorini was where he and his wife used to vacation. He rarely goes now, and it's an honor that he's sending me.

I adore Klaus—I can't hurt him by saying no.

"Thank you." I offer a smile that most likely doesn't reach my eyes. "That's...*generous*. There's more than one bedroom, right?"

"It's cottage style, but large. Four bedrooms, in addition to Elena's—she is my housekeeper and an excellent cook."

Klaus sips his wine, studying me. I push my plate away, appetite gone.

"This animosity between you and Cosmin," he says gently, "is corroding the critical bond between driver and race engineer. A racing team is like a family, Schatzi. You know this."

"We *were* like a family back when Augusto and Arvo were driving," I grumble.

"Things change. You are so agile and responsive with new

data, yet you cannot let go of this rigid view of Cosmin. He is equally bewildered by you."

"Did he say that?" There's a twitch in my chest, imagining Cosmin talking about me.

"He doesn't have to. I observe." Klaus swirls his wineglass. "This will be good for you both. I want you to do things together. Walk, talk, have meals, go shopping, enjoy the sights. See each other as *people*. Cultivate the sense of trust that is missing."

"He's gonna do something gross, like suggest we bond over strip poker."

"I've already instructed him to refrain from directing such energy at you. And I'm confident he will be no temptation to you—I've not seen you fancy a blonde."

"You talked to *him* first? What the fuck?"

Klaus holds up a hand. "Only because there was a convenient opportunity."

"What did he say?"

"He was reluctant, but I won him over."

Klaus holds out a hand again, and I allow him to clasp mine. He gives it a squeeze.

"You have made a lot of sacrifices for your work. Few could be more devoted to Emerald's success than you. Please—make one more small sacrifice."

I squeeze his hand back. "Fine. But if Ardelean tries to put the moves on me, I'm sacrificing *him*—by throwing him into a volcano."

███████

I expect Cosmin to be a pain-in-the-ass seatmate during the flight to Santorini—hogging the armrest or making stupid jokes about the Mile High Club—but he's unusually subdued. I suspect the disappointment of Sunday's final-lap disaster has him in a state.

He'd fought his way from eighth place to third and had just rounded the final corner. The team was losing its collective mind over a podium finish. Aaaaaaand something went wrong with the energy recovery system, which would have given Cosmin the power boost he needed. They're pulling it apart now, determining what went wrong, as we sit in first class with mimosas.

Troubleshooting analysis is a huge part of Formula 1. F1 cars have distinct designs, team by team, built from the ground up. The diversity in design and the upgrades implemented throughout the season mean there's a lot more that can go wrong…and things are certain to do exactly that. The dance floor is always moving under us.

Cosmin's been reading about the car's computer system on his iPad since we took off an hour ago, making notes, cross-referencing. I guess that's one way we're alike—he wants solutions rather than comfort when things go pear shaped. He took one sip of the complimentary in-flight cocktail and hasn't touched it since, he's so focused.

I hijack his glass after mine's empty. "Cheers," I tease, lifting it.

He offers a neutral grunt, swiping the screen to turn a page.

"Leave that to the IT wizards," I say with a sigh. "You're not gonna find something they don't."

He doesn't look up. "Perhaps not."

"The car's fuckup may not be software related."

"It is."

I sip the cocktail and study his profile. That wavy golden-caramel hair is flopping over his forehead, and he holds one hand on his mouth, glowering at the screen, head thrust forward at an angle.

His skin is naturally sun-kissed, weathered enough to be mature, but looks like he's never had a pimple in his life. Annoying. His nose is long and straight, with perfectly curved nostrils that make him appear perpetually alert. Even his stupid ears are handsome.

"How do you know it's the software?" I ask.

"Were it purely mechanical, I'd have felt it. But I can't feel ones and zeros."

I lean my chair back a few inches. "Hm. I suppose we'll find out."

After the second mimosa I'm loose and happy. I didn't think I wanted a vacation—however brief—when there's so much to be done at the beginning of the nine-month grand prix season. And I even *less* want to be stuck in an Ammoudi Bay cottage with this prick. But the champagne is telling me it might be entertaining; at the very least, Cosmin will say or do stupid shit that'll make great stories to tell Nat.

I link to the Wi-Fi to text her.

I still haven't mentioned to her that I know who her mystery caller was in Melbourne. I've left opportunities wide open, hoping she'll confide in me, but so far she's said nothing. I'd be lying if I claimed her withheld trust didn't hurt my feelings. I'm in an awkward position with both Nat and Klaus now, owing to what Cosmin told me in the lounge that night.

Klaus is a dead end for Natalia—that much is certain. Not only does he avoid relationships, but he has a special distaste for journalists. I guess if she manages to crack his reserve, at least he won't be another married shitbag, lying his ass off about a forthcoming divorce—Nat's had too many rides at the Cheatin' Hearts rodeo already.

She means well. She's not an Evil Other Woman, just an optimist too quick to believe the same tired lines.

I tap out a message:

> Hey, girlfriend. You'll never guess what I'm up to. Jetting to Greece with F1 Dracula.

Three dots appear immediately.

Nat: OMG I KNEW YOU HAD A THING FOR HIM

Me: Wtf? No. I was pulling your leg. Sort of. I am in fact flying to Santorini with him, but not for amorous purposes. It's a work thing.

Nat: Oh boo. How many people are going?

Me: Just us. Klaus is making us "bond" because my palpable loathing is fucking our radio communication. We're gonna do trust-falls and talk about our feelings, haha

Nat: Maybe build a shelter out of sticks like on Naked & Afraid.

Me: Ew gross nope

Nat: That guy's hot as hell. You're totally gonna do it.

Me: You know the ruby earrings I inherited from my Gramma Dorothy? The ones you say I should give you because they'd look amazing with your hair? If Ardelean gets between my thighs, the earrings are yours.

Nat: I feel sorry for you potentially losing a family heirloom, so I'll give you a way out: if you don't have sex with him before Silverstone, you keep the earrings. You've got three months. YOU WON'T MAKE IT.

Me: You're on, bitch. I'm going to nap a little before Santorini. Love ya.

As I click my phone dark and drop it in the seat pocket, I hear a chuckle.

Fuck.

He was reading the text exchange over my shoulder. My face goes five-alarm hot.

And there's his familiar smirk.

"It's okay, dragă," he says, his voice smooth and dark. "When you lose those earrings, I'll buy you a new pair." He leans back and closes his eyes. "And a matching necklace. You'd look lovely in pearls."

6

SANTORINI

COSMIN

When Klaus told me about the planned trip to Santorini, outwardly I was all scorn, but inside, I was jumping like a kid at a funfair.

I excel at hiding my emotions, though Phaedra sees me as a heart-on-my-sleeve extrovert. Everyone does, aside from Viorica, who understands all too well how we had to perfect the skill of constructing a seamless costume, growing up with Uncle Andrei. I'd have chosen one better fitting, given a choice, but life necessitated the one I wear—like a magician's cloak, made for misdirection.

We step off the plane, and I clothe myself in the carefree façade. When I insist on carrying her bag, Phaedra is annoyed and attempts to snatch it back. I swing my duffel bag over a shoulder and switch the handle of her rolling suitcase to my other side. With my free hand I tap her nose with my forefinger, as if she's a sulky child to be cheered.

"Let me be a gentleman." I head for the building, and Phaedra strides to catch up.

"Yeah, so, suggestion? Don't *boop* my nose again, ever. You won't be able to shift as well, driving with half a finger."

She has on a pale blue tunic that compliments the red glints in her hair. The neck is untied, strings flipping in the breeze. From this angle I spy her freckled chest and one smooth collarbone. She catches me looking and ties the strings. I open the door for her grandly, and she pauses, scowling, before walking through.

"Let's please keep a low profile and avoid any press, like Klaus said," she tells me. "I know it doesn't come naturally to you. But seriously, none of your usual swanning about like you're the second coming of Sex Jesus. Try being somebody else."

"The point of this trip is for us to get to know each other."

She rolls her eyes. "I've already seen everything a person needs to know about you."

A rattle of pain vibrates in my chest like clipping the rumble strip on track. On its heels, anger. *Fine—I will remain a caricature. I was a fool to think this might ever be more.*

Still, I want her.

I've wanted Phaedra Morgan for months. Her volatile nature inflames me, her intellect captivates me, and her seeming imperviousness to my charm is an irresistible challenge. I cannot resist pushing her buttons, trying to spy the cracks in *her* façade. She wears a mask as much as I do, for her own reasons. I suspect we are more alike than she thinks—connected, yet invisible to each other, like the hot and cold sides of Venus.

If she's close enough for me to smell her skin and hair, my lust is ungovernable. And not in my usual easygoing, hedonistic way. Instead, it is an agony-colored, thwarted lust the likes of which I've not felt since I was fourteen—a boy wanting every woman but allowed none.

Now I can have every woman, but want only one.

I crave those plump lips sliding against mine. I long to pick her up and plant myself deep, holding that round ass and pulling her against me. I'm greedy to hear the sounds she'd make. Her voice snaps me to attention like a dog.

Sometimes she'll emit a small moan—out of frustration, or on the tail of rare laughter—and I imagine the sound is a result of something I'm doing...a vocalization escaping her iron control as my tongue teases her.

I push the thought away, lifting her suitcase to clasp it in front of me, trying to make the move look natural while I order my cock to stand down.

A tall, unsmiling woman with salt-and-pepper hair approaches us.

"I am Elena. I have your car." She turns and walks toward the parking lot. Phaedra and I exchange a look.

"She's apparently a great cook," she tells me in a loud whisper.

"Hopefully more of a cook than a conversationalist."

Mutual conspiratory smiles thaw the air between us, and

my heart lifts. Elena marches toward a blue Alfa Romeo Spider.

She hands me the keys. "It belongs to Herr Franke and has only two seats. My sister will pick me up here. I will visit with her and return to the cottage in three hours to prepare dinner." She takes a sheet of paper from a wicker handbag and passes it to Phaedra. "The directions."

"Oh! Huh." Phaedra unfolds the page. "Paper directions." She glances at me and lifts one corner of her mouth. "I didn't know that was still a thing."

Elena gives a curt nod before returning to the airport building.

I put our bags in the boot and offer Phaedra the keys. "Would you drive?"

Her coppery eyebrows lift. "Really?"

"You're an excellent engineer—I assume you drive well too."

A smile twitches on her lips. "Oh, quit sucking up." She takes the keys from me, turning back the cuffs on her shirt while walking to the driver's side. "Buckle in, pretty boy."

It's meant as mockery. But I'll take it.

The cottage is seashell white with low, rustic archways, stained-glass windows, and mosaic tile floors. Upon arrival, we chose bedrooms, Phaedra placing her bag in the smallest because it's farthest from mine. She napped for a few hours, and I recharged in my own way—changing into workout clothes and running on the three hundred steps from Ammoudi to Oia.

After that, I took a long shower during which I admit to a certain amount of *reflection* on Miss Morgan's charms, imagining her hand rather than my own.

The flinty Elena proved to be an unparalleled cook. Phaedra and I filled ourselves with spanakopita, stuffed grape leaves, htipiti and bread, olives, dates, and shared a bottle of pinot noir on the back patio, which overlooks the Aegean.

The sunset is breathtaking, and I admire it now while lounging on a chaise, watching the candy colors melt into the sea. I've almost nodded off, lulled by the music of the waves, when Phaedra returns from her room, where she went to change after dinner.

I straighten when I see her outfit: the shirt is the same, but she now wears an ankle-length orange skirt. A loosely woven blanket is draped over her shoulders, serving as a shawl in the evening chill. Her feet are bare, and I can't help staring at them.

"What?" She drags the other chaise farther from mine before sitting. "Don't gawk like a weirdo."

I emit a small, helpless laugh. "I've just never seen you in a skirt."

She yanks the fabric down to cover her legs. "Blame Elena—this is the only thing I have with an elastic waist."

"What about pajamas?"

"I don't wear pajamas." Her eyes are closed when she says it, but fly open as she realizes what she's let slip.

"I don't either." My voice comes out lower than I expected.

She peeks at me before fussing with the skirt, drawing up her legs.

"I, uh, talked to Mo," she says, clearly reaching to change the subject rather than lingering on the point of our respective sleep-nudity. "He's gonna be in Switzerland a few more days. He's—" She chews at her lower lip. "Meeting with someone."

I'm unsure why she's telling me this. I assumed Ed Morgan was away on business, but there's a tension to Phaedra's tone. I sense she wants me to ask for details.

"Yes? New sponsor?"

"No, no." She flips one hand, as if I'm badgering her. "It's nothing."

In the shadows of a fading sunset, I covertly study her expression. Her brows are pinched, and it may be a trick of the ruddy light, but she looks teary.

The awareness falls around me, weighty and frightening, that she could easily have stayed in her room after the meal. But she's come out to sit with me, the man she hates, and is angling to confide something.

The responsibility feels overwhelming. Every week I climb into a twelve-million-dollar car and feel less pressure, even knowing I may put it into the wall. Phaedra's trust seems more fragile and valuable.

"The meeting," I venture. "Not business?"

She shakes her head, watching the sea, twisting one of the ties on her shirt around her finger tightly. She unwinds it and her hand drops, dangling alongside the chaise.

"It's...it's a d-doctor," she falters, just above a whisper.

I pause as I contemplate what this could mean, then capture her hand and lean in to place a kiss on her knuckles.

"Your father will be all right, dragă. He's well cared for."

She pulls away—though gradually—before meeting my eye. "I hope. Mo says Dr. Brunner is one of the best."

"Of that I am certain." I offer a reassuring smile. "But I meant he is well cared for by you."

When I come downstairs at nine the next morning, Phaedra is in the kitchen, pouring out the last cup of coffee. She's wearing khaki shorts and a strappy tank top that shows off the curve of her shoulder blades. Her feet are bare, and her hair is twisted up, secured with a gold clip shaped like a leaf.

"Is there more coffee?" I ask, coming up beside her.

She smells like soap, but her hair is dry and has the pleasant sugary-musky scent of being unwashed. I ache to slide my arms around her, our bodies parallel as I stroke her narrow little waist.

"There is if you make it," she says with a playful smirk.

It encourages me enough that as she walks away, I catch her hand and reel her back.

"Cruel woman, stealing the last cup."

She tries to hold it away and my hand sweeps up her bare arm.

"Quit!" she commands with a laugh. She sidesteps and bumps the counter. "Oh my God, Ardelean, let go..."

I wonder if she doesn't mind the way we're pressed close. Her color is high, pupils wide in their halo of green.

"Let me have this cup," I coax. "I'll make more for you."

"Maybe don't roll out of bed at nine if you're desperate for caffeine. I've been up since six, you lazy schmuck. Besides, I already drank out of this one. It's officially mine. Claimed."

We both go still, and I'm looking down at her from a foot above, our bodies aligned. She's breathing fast, and my gaze drops to the curve of her breasts. Her full lips are rosy, and she moistens them. A dart of concern folds between her brows.

"What are you doing?" she asks.

I shift my hips. "Admiring you." I gently manacle her wrist and draw it closer. Her fingers are around the mug, and I cover them with my own. Our hands joined, I lift the mug and take a sip. "Officially mine. *Claimed*," I echo.

Her direct nature regains control of our moment of runaway lust. She shakes her head.

"This isn't a romantic getaway, Ardelean. It's like an extended conference room meeting, minus the headsets."

"I know." I allow a hint of teasing in my tone.

"We're just supposed to, y'know, chitchat. Get comfortable."

"I'm very comfortable." An electric surge of blood flow moves my cock, and I suspect she feels it.

"Cosmin," she whispers. "*This*"—and to my shock, she pushes her hips against me to illustrate her point—"can't be what we bring back to the team. It's not what Klaus intended."

I lightly run a knuckle down her upper arm. "We are supposed to build trust. What better way?"

"The nonfraternization guidelines exist for a reason: no dating team members, journalists, investors, or sponsors. The rules are clear."

She pauses, searching my eyes, and I think she's going to step back, but she remains pressed close.

"You weren't there when it happened," she continues, "but three years ago when Reece started dating her wife, who was an Emerald systems tech at the time, Colette *had to quit her job*, for fuck's sake."

I sigh. "Yes, but—"

"We stick to the program, got it?" She lifts the coffee mug, resting it against her lower lip for a moment, but doesn't take a drink. I wonder if it's to make sure I don't initiate the kiss we can both feel.

"No flirting—it's too risky," she insists. "We're supposed to, like, just talk about movies we love, watch Premier League over beers, tell each other our favorite colors. Friendly shit like that."

She edges away from me, and my body is in mourning. I caress her shoulder, a ghost of a touch. She freezes.

"I told you, dragă. My favorite color is white."

I'm afraid the moment will be lost forever if I don't give her something by which to remember it. I brush my lips along the curve of her shoulder.

"And some day, when you admit you wore that white shirt for me...I will reward you."

7

SANTORINI

PHAEDRA

At first, I think our cover is blown—there are so many eyes on Cosmin as we walk the narrow, cobbled lanes of Oia. Can there be *that* many Formula 1 fans in this tiny Greek town? Then I notice: it's all women. The attention is because of his beauty, of course.

Your brain is above your heart, Schatzi. Klaus's presence is in my mind like an Austrian Jiminy Cricket, cautioning me to behave. So my brain scolds my heart, which is crouched like a defending tiger wanting to scratch out the eyes of the women leering at the man who had me weak-kneed and wet a few hours ago.

True, I don't typically go for blondes, but Ardelean is kinda killing me today.

As we explore Oia's shops and kiosks, I watch him, and I watch *women* watch him. He's wearing a white dress shirt turned up to the elbows, untucked over jeans with rolled cuffs and—oh, God help me—gray Converse.

I almost always wear Converse myself, and I'm a sucker for a boy who wears them too. I'd wonder if he bought them recently to impress me, but they're scuffed and creased. His outfit is effortlessly adorable: from the waist up, like a sexy best man at a wedding after a few drinks; from the waist down, solid indie cred.

He's examining an outdoor table of small ceramic boxes, their glaze blue as the surrounding sea. His wavy, long-on-top hair is nodding against his forehead in the breeze, and as he combs it back with his fingers, I imagine him raking *my* hair. Grabbing a handful. Pulling just enough...

Well, shit. *That* little daydream escalated quickly.

I'm doomed.

My common sense says Cosmin and I are both so intense that things would be *fucking amazing* for about a week, followed by wanting to murder each other, and the team would implode. Remembering he's a smug asshole isn't really helping.

He buys a ceramic box, and at another table deliberates over sets of hair combs.

"I need your help," he tells me. Gesturing at two, he asks, "Which would look better with this color hair?" He points at his own.

"Well, aren't you a pretty princess!" I tease.

"So amusing. It's for my sister, Viorica—she looks like me. But a little gray too."

I take two combs and hold them near Cosmin's head.

"This one looks great," I say.

My fingers are so close to his hair, longing to plunge in and feel it. I hope my heartbeat isn't visible through my thin shirt.

He buys the set and an old-fashioned hand mirror.

Halfway through the shopping district, we pass a confectionery. A mouthwatering scent wafts out, and a rosy-cheeked matron stands next to the doorway with a tray of samples.

She doesn't speak English, but Cosmin tries French, which she knows. He says something, opening a hand toward me, and the woman raises her eyebrows and nods, smiling.

"Hey, no fair!" I laugh. "What's the big secret?"

"No secret," he says, almost shy. He picks up a sample—a piece of something that looks like fudge with bits of cookie—and holds it near my mouth. "I referred to you as my beautiful friend."

Klaus was right, all the times he's said there's something magical about Santorini. Because in the space of twenty-four hours, Cosmin *is* sort of my friend.

In my chest, there's a jolting collision between the apprehension that it won't last after we rejoin the team in China, and the apprehension that it *will*.

I open my mouth and he puts in the candy, touching my lower lip. He takes a piece himself, and his long, golden lashes flutter closed in a way that's unnervingly suggestive as he savors the candy. They open, drowsy with pleasure.

"What do you think?" he asks, focusing on me. "Like heaven, yes?"

I discreetly lick chocolate from my back teeth. "Hell yeah. It's way good."

Cosmin asks the woman a question and she laughs, her eyebrows lifting in shock. She grins and nods, taking the tray inside.

"What did you ask her?"

"I'm having ten kilos sent to—" He pauses. "To family in Romania." He drapes an arm around me and leads me into the shop.

I nearly shove my foot directly into my mouth by commenting that he doesn't *have* that much family but withhold the observation as I realize he must be sending the candy to the orphanage-type-thing he and his sister fund.

His relaxed joy at choosing the gift touches me, I have to admit. He isn't even trying to boast about it.

Okay, okay. Points for the peacock.

Inside, I gesture at a glass case where there's a long roll of the biscuit-fudge.

"Says here it's called 'mosaiko.' We could look it up online and get a recipe for free. Ten kilos'll cost a fortune."

He shrugs. "This will make everyone happy."

I watch as he gives the woman a shipping address, then runs his credit card for 285 euros plus another seventy for shipping and proceeds to round it up to 450 euros "with a tip." The woman is falling all over herself with gratitude and sends us off with a gift bag of sweets.

"You made that woman's day," I say, as we wander down the lane.

He tips the open bag toward me, and I shake my head. He fishes out something covered in nuts and pops it in his mouth.

"Good," he says around the candy. "Perfect day for everyone."

My heart gives a giddy kick, and I look away. "I don't think she expected a tip, especially such a generous one. You're a big tipper."

"I'm a big *everything*," he assures me with a wink.

I roll my eyes. "I knew you couldn't resist being a neanderthal for a full day."

"Hmm." He puts the side of his thumb in his mouth, sucking a smudge of chocolate. "Maybe I'll throw you over my shoulder and carry you back to my cave."

▚▚▚▚▚

I lean chin in hand on the patio table as my eyes flick to the pieces, then to Cosmin.

I move my king again. "It's a draw."

"Perhaps not." He moves his piece.

My king scoots to the left. "Um, except it *is*. Let's call it."

"You could still make a mistake."

"Not gonna happen."

He sighs. "I don't like to lose."

"A draw isn't a loss."

"Nor a win," he murmurs, staring at the board.

"And that's okay! Just have fun."

"Winning is fun. And I am hoping to distract you into

an error." His eyes narrow in a conspicuously bedroomy way. "I'm told my eyes are magnetic."

I snort. "You're told shit like that too often, Ardelean. Which is why you're an insufferable prick."

He sits back and studies me. "You still think this after two days together?"

"Not exactly. But it's your public image. How the world sees you."

"Everyone loves a rascal." He lifts his wineglass and finishes the last sip.

I almost don't say it, but I've had three glasses of wine to his one, and it slips out. "Do *you* love you?"

He wavers in the act of setting the glass down. "Why would you ask that?"

"Why would you answer a question with a question?"

He fiddles with the cuff of the hoodie he's wearing, as if picking a bit of lint. "Not that question."

"You mean you don't want to *answer* that one," I state.

"Correct." He offers a stiff smile. "Ask a different one. But you must answer it too."

I take a slow breath through my nose and purse my lips for a gusty exhale.

"Okay, way to make it difficult—like when my mom would let me cut a treat in half with my sister, but Aislinn got to choose first."

There's a musical clicking from a wind chime made of oyster shells. The shushing of the ocean rises and falls below us.

I peek at him. "What are you afraid of?"

"Hm. I don't like this question better."

"Come on—what kind of softball do you want me to throw: '*How big is your dick?*' Be real or this is pointless."

"You want to see?" he jokes, hands going to the button on his jeans. He pretends he's about to stand up.

"Cosmin!" I laugh.

He settles in the chair again, and we watch each other.

"All right," he says. "I'm afraid of…like in the book with the little people and the dragon—the Hobbit book. The dragon—"

"Smaug," I insert.

"Beautiful. Yes. This dragon has one missing scale. He's afraid someone will shoot him there—the only weak point." He rubs a hand through his hair. "So, that's it. My fear."

My brow furrows. "I don't think that's how it went. The dragon isn't 'afraid someone will shoot him there.' He doesn't know he *has* a missing scale."

"It's how I remember it."

"That's very telling. And you're being deliberately vague, not saying what the 'missing scale' is. Your real fear."

He shrugs with a blithe mock frown. Reaching for the stem of his empty wineglass, he rotates it, then slants a look at me. "Your turn."

I give a small huff of laughter. "You get what you give, dude. I'm not planning on baring my soul here: I'm afraid of spiders."

"Everyone is afraid of spiders."

"Hey, you set the tone. Wanna try again?"

I can't tell if he's thinking or pouting in the silence that follows. Part of me is angry, and I'm not sure why.

Dammit, we did what Klaus instructed. Shared meals, went shopping, watched TV with popcorn, had drinks, talked about superficial shit, got more comfortable. Cosmin's favorite food is cheese. Favorite book is Nabokov's *Pale Fire*. We both love Bowie.

His favorite color is white.

I stand, and with a flick of one finger, tip over my king. "You win. Now it's not a draw."

I go into the cottage and head upstairs to get ready for bed. In the morning we'll go to the airport. Everything back to normal.

Fine, whatever.

I'm practically seething as I brush my teeth, scowling at my reflection. Why am I so pissed? What did I expect? I didn't want to do this stupid "bonding" thing in the first place.

I walk out of the en suite, hands occupied with braiding my hair for sleep, when I see him standing by the dresser.

"What the fuck are you doing in my room?"

He points at a ceramic box. "Leaving this. I chose it for you." His lips press together, as if they're fighting back more words.

I want to walk over, but I resist, folding my arms as we stare each other down.

After a long moment, he relaxes his shoulders with a stifled sigh.

"Perhaps I cannot speak every fear," he continues, "but

today I feared if I admitted this is a gift for you, you would tell me not to buy it. And tonight, playing chess, I was afraid of the night ending. This is why I didn't want a draw. It makes the game *over*."

The way he says this sends my heart skidding as if running on ice.

I walk to the dresser, and he takes a step back to give me space. I glide a hand over the cool lid of the box. The blue-gray glaze is the color of Cosmin's eyes.

I smile, my throat tight. "Thank you. It's lovely."

"So is the woman who now owns it."

I'm not aware of my body sending the invitation, but he reads it nonetheless. In the fraction of a second as he moves toward me, I'm expecting an old-movie-level fierce kiss—my head wrenched back, mouths pressed hard.

Instead his arms drape around my waist as if they've always been there, like part of me. Like my own ribs. His forehead leans into mine, and I watch those long, gold eyelashes drop again, like when he was eating the chocolate.

I'm the one who tips my head to capture his mouth. And dear God, the curve of that full lower lip is everything I imagined tasting. Our mouths are closed but soft, searching new angles, touching as if our lips are eyes, scrutinizing each tiny detail to commit to memory. Because I think we both know: a memory is all it can be.

His hands fan out, and he presses me against his pelvis. I feel him hard, wanting, and I flood with electric heat. He's everything I'm missing—the need is overwhelming.

He's not moving, but some part of me can feel the way he *would*, if I let him in: the hot rolling of our hips, the wet juncture of our bodies as his cock fills me, sweaty skin and the jab of bones and a rhythm pushing us toward ecstasy.

I'm absolutely twitching inside, and it takes every bit of pragmatism I possess to pull away—I've never been this turned on, though we're touching so lightly, so cautiously.

His breath is shaky, which is surprising. He smiles down at me.

"No? Afraid of losing those earrings to Natalia?"

"I'm afraid of losing more than that," I admit in a whisper.

His hands drag up my back, down my arms, catch me at the waist, and slide up again, searching. His thumbs drift across my braless breasts, and my nipples are so tight they ache. I'm torn between not wanting him to leave, and hoping he'll exit quickly so I can get under the covers and finish what he's started.

He cradles my neck, those teasing thumbs feathering along my jaw before he brushes one final kiss across my hungry lips. He steps back. I force myself not to glance down and sneak a glimpse of what I'm missing.

Laying one hand on the dresser to balance myself, I close my eyes, laboring to calm the throbbing above and below my waist. I hear his footsteps as he heads for the hallway, but I don't open my eyes—if I see him leaving, I know I'll stop him.

His voice slips around the corner. "Good night."

8

CHINA

MID-APRIL

COSMIN

Santorini was a terrible idea, and I'm irrationally angry with Klaus. The kiss was a terrible idea, and I'm (rationally) angry with myself. I can't stop thinking about Phaedra, even when unconscious.

I'm a light sleeper—the need to remain vigilant was terrorized into me as a boy. Uncle Andrei was creative in his training, and fond of saying *A man must be prepared to respond with ingenuity and vigor at all times.*

Since Santorini, every time I surface to consciousness from sleep, Phaedra is there—some disintegrating dream image, anywhere from the pedestrian to the powerfully erotic.

Which is why I fuck everything up days after the trip to Greece.

Upon our return, I'm gracious and appreciative with Klaus,

praising the beauty of Santorini, the charm of the cottage, the cooking of Elena. I make a point of being scrupulously professional with Phaedra in front of the team. Gone are my little taunts and libidinous jokes. But inside me is a monsoon of confusion.

Being near her after the kiss is torment. The strategic brain I usually apply to racing is consumed with looking for ways to have Phaedra Morgan, now that it's clear my desire is reciprocated.

There must be a way to make this work without impairing our driver/race engineer rapport.

It's not until the night we arrive in Shanghai that I force myself to acknowledge the irresponsibility of flouting the rules. Could I in good conscience risk a job that supplies Vlasia House with its most reliable income? I wrestle with this question while standing outside the door of her hotel room, which is diagonal from mine.

My knuckles feel the undelivered knock in the same physically prescient way I feel the car. Music is playing inside, and I try to picture where in the room she is sitting, what she is wearing, the expression on her face. Those eyes, which can be stormy and serious and lively. The way she pushes those plump lips out and wrinkles her nose when she's annoyed, or presses the tip of her tongue against the center of her upper lip while concentrating. The sound of her voice—crisp and smooth, like elderflower soda.

I have every symptom of adolescent lovesickness.

The elevator at the end of the hall dings.

Someone from the team could see me standing here. I pivot and walk to my own room and lie on the bed, holding a lens to the microscopic fault line of panic I feel. It's rare for me, but unmistakable, twisting in my gut like the animal fear of fire—its power and unpredictability.

She is the fire. If I have her, it burns everything else in my life.

Those months of juvenile provocation, knowing how much it made her dislike me...how did I not recognize that an intuitive part of me was doing it out of self-preservation?

It's safer to let her despise me.

This is in the back of my head the next morning when I turn Phaedra Morgan's fire into ice—slower, but equally destructive.

▚▚▚▚▚

I've left the television on, so when I hear a noise as I'm getting out of the shower, I assume the morning news is the source.

I sling a towel around my waist and walk out of the bathroom to find a petite housekeeper standing near my bed with her back to me. She twirls around in alarm, clutching the open water bottle that was on my bedside table. She drops it, and water splashes out in a small arc.

She's young and pretty—hair an inky bob, pink lips, skin the golden color of milky tea, eyes like varnished ebony—and blushing furiously.

She drops to her knees, scrambling to retrieve the water bottle, and in her coltish awkwardness loses her balance. One arm flies out and she grasps the bedcovers. Glancing at her own hand on the tangled sheets as if it doesn't belong to her, she snatches it back, seemingly mortified at having touched something so personal.

"Good m-morning," she says in a tentative near whisper, rising and setting aside the bottle. Eyes roaming over my bare chest, she adds, "You need more towels?"

Amused, I ask, "It's a bit early for cleaning the room, isn't it? Seven o'clock?"

She wrings the hem of her apron. Her soft brows draw together, and as she meets my gaze, a glossy sheen washes over her dark eyes. Her confession spills out in a tumble of words.

"I knew you would be gone later. You are my favorite driver, and I wanted . . . to meet you." She sags onto the foot of the bed, covering her face. "Will you have me fired?"

"Of course not." I turn the television off and sit beside her. "It will remain our secret."

She sniffles, and a tear slips down her cheek. "You won't report me?"

I stretch across the bed to get a tissue, then hand it to her. "No. But you must make a promise: don't try this sort of thing with anyone else, should you wish to meet a guest of the hotel. You could be hurt, gambling on the mercy of a stranger behind closed doors."

She peeks at my bare leg where the towel has parted. I stand and go to the closet to choose an outfit, then step around the corner into the bathroom to put on my trousers, leaving the door open. "What is your name?" I call to her.

"Mei."

"Do you have tickets to the race, Mei?"

There's a long pause. "I . . . cannot afford to go."

I lean out to look at her as I button my shirt. "Not a problem. I'll get you a pass. Hold on one moment."

She stands nervously in the doorway alcove while I gather things and put them in my twill messenger bag. I tap my notes on my phone and open the door for her to precede me. "Now, your full name, please."

"Zhang Mei," she tells me, stepping into the hallway.

There's no cleaning cart visible outside, and I gently tease her, "You could not have given me a new towel anyway, could you?"

She shakes her head with an embarrassed smile.

I follow her out and close the door, staring at the screen as I type with my thumb. "There. We're all set now—your pass will be at the front desk."

Standing on tiptoe, she quickly kisses my cheek. "Thank you! It was a pleasure to meet you." The words come out in a rush. She ducks her head, hustling down the hallway toward the elevator.

Behind me, a door clicks shut and I hear a harsh chuckle. I turn to see Phaedra, dressed for a workout, draping headphones around her neck. Her hair is twisted on top of her head with small tendrils hanging, and I want to hold her face and kiss the bitterness off her naked lips.

But then, maybe this is a good thing—as long as she dislikes me again, there's no danger the spark of our feelings could grow.

I adjust the strap of my bag and saunter over. "Why the sour look, dragă?"

"Very classy, Formula Fuckboy," she deadpans, eyeing the lipstick on my face. "You had to ask her name *afterwards*? Nice of you to give the cleaning staff a complimentary dicking down. Personally, I just leave twenty bucks on the dresser."

"There's enough of me to go around."

She flips her hand at me. "Whatever—you're not my problem until you're in the car. Have a swell day." She starts toward the elevators, then pauses. "I'm sure you think I'm jealous, but that's not what's bothering me."

"No?"

"Nope. It's the fact that I saw *shame* on that woman's face. It doesn't speak well of you. Implies you used your playboy patter and 'seduced' her. You've heard of consent, right?"

I lift my hands, conceding. "You will choose to believe what you wish. But maybe you're also a *little* jealous. Because of Santorini."

There's a flash of wounded anger before she replies. "The kiss meant nothing. Not to me, because you're not my type. And not to *you*, because that shit is just your nature—might as well ask a dog not to piss on a fire hydrant."

She walks away, but before she reaches the elevator, I call out.

"You're forgetting something, dragă."

She turns but continues walking backward, arms folded.

I grin. "You kissed me first."

9

CHINA

PHAEDRA

Pardon the bad pun when I say *F1 Dracula sucks.*

One thing hate is really good for: I haven't had such an energetic workout in weeks. I run like Forrest Gump on Adderall and lift weights like the Jaws of Life heroically prying minivans open.

Every time I get mopey remembering the look on Cosmin's dumb sexy face when we kissed—

It was tender and cautious and passionate, oh my God...

—I bring up the image of him sending that housekeeper out the door at seven a.m., asking her name like a goddamned afterthought. Next thing I know, I'm back in beast-mode, flexing as if in the grips of 'roid rage.

I need to get my head straight, because I've invited Natalia to meet me for breakfast, and I'm going to call this game of chicken we appear to be playing and just straight-up ask her about the Klaus thing. I let it slide in Bahrain, trying to give her space, but we're not going another grand prix weekend without talking about it.

When I've finally hit the wall, I go to toss the squeezy pouch for my protein gel into the trash and accidentally throw my towel in instead. I consider digging it out, but the bin is deep and gross looking. This is why I have the hem of my shirt pulled over my face—mopping up sweat—when I wander into the elevator and lean against the wall.

Someone else steps in and the doors shut.

I yank my shirt down and Natalia and I stare at each other in shock. I'm almost positive she says "Oh crap," but my head-phones are still in.

I pop one earbud out. "You're hella early. Like by ninety minutes."

With a nervous smile, she shifts the strap of her Prada bag. This is when I notice she's dressed far too fancy for eight thirty in the morning—a gauzy, high-neck halter dress and heels with gladiator laces.

"Surprise!" she sings, lifting her hands with a jazzy wiggle.

"Why'd you say 'Oh crap' when you saw me?"

"I didn't."

"And why are you so dolled up?"

She rolls her eyes. "I'm dressed normal. Jesus, just because I don't share your depressing 'I slept under a pile of leaves' fashion sense?"

My eyes narrow, because I know she's throwing insults to set me on the back foot. Mentally, I hear an echo of

Cosmin's words in Melbourne: *Miss Evans did not wear that dress for me.*

Lying to me is becoming a habit for her, and that in itself makes me far more uncomfortable than whatever's going on with her and Klaus.

Trust has historically not been easy for me, growing up so nomadic, in a sporting world where uncertainty is the rule. Nat was my first—and is still my *only*—truly close friend. This recent dynamic is worrying. I'm both dreading and clamoring to clear the air between us.

"Okay, well." I lift the neck of my shirt and mop my face again, just to briefly hide. "I hope you're not starving, because I have to shower first."

"No problem." She holds up her phone. "I'll just answer some emails."

The doors slide open at my floor, and we step out.

"You look like a high-buck call girl in ancient Rome," I say.

"Oh, for heck's sake. Thanks, but not really."

I lead her to my door, and as I'm opening it, she's already on her phone. She passes me and when I try to peek at her screen, she wings it away.

"Nat..."

"What?"

"You're hiding something. Don't make me tackle you."

She darkens the screen and drops the phone into her purse. "It's just a message from my editor." She plants a manicured hand on her hip. "Now go clean up."

I take a shower, bathroom door cracked an inch. When

I'm done washing, I leave the water running to fake her out, then wrap myself in a towel, easing the door open to sneak up on her.

She's sitting on the foot of my unmade bed, typing, thumbs flying. Before her peripheral vision warns her, I spot the contact name at the top: *Charcoal Suit*.

"Aha!" I crow.

She shrieks, and the phone flips out of her hands and spins to the carpet. "What the crap is wrong with you?"

"You're not dressed up for *me*, you lying monster."

She dips to retrieve her phone, giving me a bland smirk. "Aww, were you hoping I wore something special just for you? Are you in wuuuuvvv with me?"

I bite back a snarky retort about how I could never fall for someone with half my IQ, but for one thing I'm not supportive of the IQ scale—it's fundamentally flawed—and for another it's too mean-spirited, like bringing a howitzer to a BB gun fight.

I go into the bathroom and shut the water off, then return and sit beside her on the bed.

"Nat, you left the Park Hyatt in Melbourne with Klaus. I know because Cosmin saw you guys."

Her composure wavers for a moment, then returns. "So what? We *talked*—that's all," she says with a careless wave. "Walked a little and had a conversation. He apologized for having been rude that time I mentioned."

I scoff. "And that's all?"

"Jesus, Phae. *Stop.*"

"Fine, whatever. But then why have you been lying to me? Are we friends, or not?"

"That's a dumb question for an alleged genius."

I don't bother pointing out that she's not *answering* my "dumb question." I force myself to articulate my biggest worry.

"Okay, look. You've only had the job at *Auto Racing* a few months, and when you took it, we both thought it'd be this endless slumber party for you and me, traveling to the same cities and hanging out a ton. But you seemed to like me more when you were in New York working for the literary magazine and barely ever saw me in person."

"That's ridiculous."

"Is it?"

I wait, and her silence speaks volumes.

"Are you, like…sick of me?" I prod.

"No! You're kind of a jerk sometimes, but—"

"Um, *hello*? You can be a total Regina George yourself. And now you're lying too."

She gets up and goes to the closet as if to find me something to wear, sliding the hangers side to side with no real aim.

"Holding back isn't the same as lying," she grumbles. "And I have a good reason: you're judgmental. I'm an adult, and not stupid. I have a danged MFA from Queen's U Charlotte."

"You *are* smart, which is why it kills me to see you making the same mistakes over and over. It's dangerous to keep believing the tired lines of all these thrilling married douchebags."

She wheels around. "*Klaus. Isn't. Married.*"

"He also isn't emotionally available!" I cry, flipping both

arms up in exasperation. "And you obviously have a crush on him."

Nat's eyes narrow. "I wonder why you care so much. Do *you* have a crush on him?"

"Oh, for fuck's sake. *No.* He's like my cool uncle, and you know it. You're also stonewalling me right now. What are you hiding?"

She flops onto the bed with a grumpy sigh. "Okay, I slept with him once last December in Abu Dhabi."

My mouth drops open. "He was that rando you mentioned—the one-night stand?"

"I neither confirm nor deny," she replies primly.

"Nat, you can't get involved with Klaus. I know I told you about what happened with the woman from *Chalk Talk*. There was an actual lawsuit, for fuck's sake. He *hates* journalists."

She delivers a smug look. "I don't think he hates this one."

"Nat..."

"Let me effing enjoy a simple flirtation!" she almost shouts. "This isn't your business, Phae! Can you see now why I never want to tell you anything? You're so superior."

I recoil as if slapped. "You '*never* want to tell me anything'? Seriously? Wow." I spring to my feet and go to the closet, yanking a shirt off a hanger. "Wanna know what your problem is?"

"Oh, *this* should be priceless."

"You pin your hopes to bullshit. Like how you pay a hundred bucks for your tubes of miracle face cream with, like, seahorse jizz or whatever in them. Same ingredients as my giant bottle of Dollar Store hand lotion, most likely."

I wrench the shirt over my head.

"Christ almighty," I growl, "did you pretend to believe in the Easter Bunny until you were sixteen just so you could keep getting baskets of free candy?"

I don't know why I'm taking the gloves off now, but I'm too mad to hold back. I'm unpleasantly reminded of all the times Aislinn tattled on me when we were kids, running off screeching, *Mama, Phae's being spiteful!* I had no way of explaining then—or even understanding myself—why it was worse to let Aislinn have her way than to ruin it for myself.

I know I'm fucking this friendship, but I can't seem to rein it in now that I've started.

"Nice to know what you really think of me," Nat bites out, getting to her feet and grabbing her purse. "You just think it makes you sound smart to be cynical all the time."

This is the point where I should apologize, right? Stop her from leaving?

"I'd rather be cynical than delusional!"

*Wow. **No.***

Fuck my stupid noise hole. Is this like throwing the last oatmeal cookie to the birds so neither Aislinn nor I can have it?

Holy shit, Morgan, shut up! I warn myself. *What are you trying to win?*

"Really helpful, Phae," Nat snaps. "No wonder everyone says you're so brilliant." She slings her purse on. "You know what? I take it back: *I am sick of you.*"

With that, she strides to the door and flips it open, then walks out. And because I'm a piece of shit who perversely can't resist making it worse, I run after her, sticking my head out and shouting down the hall, "I hope you mean it, because I'm over your bullshit!"

She lifts a hand and flips me off, and she's only ever done that as a joke, so it really hurts. I shut the door and sit against it, head in my hands.

My dad is sick, I suck at my job, I'm falling for a man I can't have, and my best friend has dumped me…

I say it to myself again and again—twisting the knife enough to let the tears leak out—and then cry for everything I can't fix.

10

AZERBAIJAN

LATE APRIL

COSMIN

Race week in China was already shit before the grand prix. Phaedra was cold, and even the perennially unflappable Klaus seemed out of sorts.

Team owner Mo went to the States for a "family situation," and there was gossip in the press about what that might mean. Then, nine laps into the race, my right rear driveshaft hub broke, and I had to retire. Jakob came in eleventh, just outside the points. No one was happy.

This weekend will be different. The Baku City Circuit in Azerbaijan is quite long—over six kilometers—and thrillingly fast, with gorgeous technical bits that play to my strengths. I qualified in fourth and Jakob seventh. A podium finish is within my grasp.

During the morning meeting on race day, Emerald's chief

strategist suggests a daring plan, unlikely to be implemented by other teams. Based on today's weather report—taking heat, wind, and even angle of shadows into consideration—he lobbies for starting the race on hard compound tyres.

Most teams will start on soft compound tyres and switch to hard later, employing one pit stop. A few other teams may start on mediums and switch to hard. Computer simulations suggest this bold alternate approach could put Emerald at a serious advantage.

As the strategy is discussed, there are nervous sideways glances amongst the team members in the room.

Phaedra speaks up.

"I see the potential advantage," she allows, her tone cautious. "Switching to soft tyres later in the race would be great when the shadows cool the track and there isn't as much worry about the rubber degradation. In the meantime, we'd get some good data seeing how everyone else performs on them. But"—she massages the bridge of her nose—"at this circuit, there's a *massive* probability we'll see the safety car. This is Baku, so there's a high crash risk. I mean, it's only worse in Monaco—we all know this, right?" She lifts her hands and looks around the room in an appeal for agreement.

About half the team members nod in concession; some glance at Klaus, as if wondering whether to commit to an opinion.

He hasn't weighed in yet, and I'm not the only person who's noticed an odd tension between him and Phaedra this past week. I even overheard a mechanic joking about it, saying,

"The Fellowship is broken! We'll never make it to Mount Doom now."

"If so," she continues, "we're royally fucked. Might as well pass out pillows of lube to the other teams. They can enjoy it along with their less costly pit stops while the safety car is out."

"I assure you, Miss Morgan," the strategist asserts, "it's worth the risk."

"Perhaps you'd like to see the data, Phaedra my dear?" Klaus puts in mildly.

He's looking at a tablet, not at her. His tone says the offer, rather than being an invitation, is rhetorical, meant to imply that her question is unwelcome. It's also the first time I've heard him directly address her as anything other than Schatzi.

She fixes him with a look of disbelief. "And perhaps *you'd* like to walk back the condescension."

Klaus lifts his gaze, so slowly it borders on careless. They lock eyes, the air between them thick with tension.

"It's windy as fuck today," she goes on. "With decreased grip on the hard tyres, Cos and Jake are already going to struggle with braking points. Did the simulations take into consideration *exactly* where the wind will be channeled through building gaps? Are the gusts going to hit them in—"

"Respectfully," Klaus interrupts, "it's what *your father* pays Wilhelm to determine." He nods toward the chief strategist.

Highlighting the fact that Ed Morgan owns the team is a card dealt from the bottom of the deck, and out of character for Klaus. I can't imagine what's instigated this hostility. I wonder whether Phaedra said something negative about Santorini and Klaus's feelings were hurt.

"Oh, *apologies*," she tells him with heavy sarcasm. "If I'd known I was expected to be only 'seen and not heard' today, I'd have dressed up fancy."

Several people in the room develop a rapt interest in their coffee cups. Jakob unwraps a protein bar with the careful silence of someone trying to eat candy in a theater during a deathbed scene. Anything to avoid Phaedra's calmly murderous expression.

After an uncomfortable silence, she looks at me. "All right then. So. What do you think, Legs? Jake?"

Jakob pauses mid-chew, then shrugs, eyes wide at being put on the spot.

"Gotcha. And how 'bout you?" she asks, lifting her chin at me.

I take a slow breath. "It's a bold plan and partially contingent on luck. But isn't that life? I'd love to hear the commentators gasp and chatter when they see the Emeralds roll out on white sidewall tyres." I grin. "And if we pull it off, we're gods."

A tiny smile flickers at the corner of those sweet lips. It's the first I've seen directed at me in over two weeks since the housekeeper incident in Shanghai.

She claps her hands together. "I'm sold."

I'm excited to see if the gamble pays off. But more than anything, I am delighted to see Phaedra smile at me again.

After I pass Anders Olsson, Phaedra's voice in my ears is calm.

"Clean, Cos. Nicely done. P2. You've gone purple in sector one."

"Copy."

I can't believe our luck in avoiding the safety car. It's almost unheard of here because the long straights necessitate a low-downforce setup, and due to the high number of ninety-degree turns on a street circuit, there's heavy braking. A street circuit also means minimal run-off area, so a mistake is likely to buy you an appointment with the nearest wall. It's a demanding combination.

I feel like I'm flying, outside and in. I've ramped up my aspirations since Ortiz retired with a gearbox problem and Ono had what Phaedra refers to as a "four-way clown fuck of a pit stop"—nearly forty seconds when they brought out mismatched tyres.

A podium isn't enough anymore. Now I plan to take down Drew Powell and fucking *win*.

"Box this lap," Phaedra says. "Let's get the softs on."

The expression "man plans, and God laughs" would not be inaccurate to describe what happens next. My own pit stop is at least a *three*-way clown fuck when the left front tyre's wheel gun malfunctions. The tyre gunner is struggling and crosses his arms in the air to indicate a problem.

Fortunately, there are two wheel guns for each tyre, allowing for just such a failure, and it's swapped out. We're past twenty seconds and cold steel seems to settle in my gut as I acknowledge even a podium has likely slipped away.

My brain pivots to points—*any*.

I get the signal and speed away. But something is amiss. Did I imagine the mechanic's posture and arm movement, glanced in my periphery, indicated a problem?

As I surge out of the pit lane and onto the track, I can feel it. Something's off.

"What happened back there?" I ask Phaedra.

"One moment, Cos. Lars is talking with the crew chief." It's only a few heartbeats until she's back. "The wheel's not fitted correctly. You need to—"

"Fuck! What the shit?" I snap. "All right. I can bring her around." I see the shimmy now, and slow down.

Cars are blasting past me, and I've received the black-and-orange flag indicating a mechanical problem. Seeing flashes of the wheel as the tyre starts to dance free, I realize I can't make it to a run-off area without endangering everyone. I pull over.

Despite a potentially brilliant strategic choice, we were undone by a simple mechanical error. It's maddening.

"Yellow flag," Phaedra tells me. "It's not your fault, Legs."

The other cars whip past, orderly under the virtual safety car.

Merry fucking Christmas, guys, I think, releasing my harness as the track marshals trot out to meet my twelve-million-dollar paperweight.

After a race, all I want to do is take an ice bath, rehydrate, and sleep for at least ten hours. (Sometimes with company, but no such luck in Baku.) Viorica texts me Sunday night as I'm lying in bed, listening to music and doing meditative breathing.

《Don't reply now,》 she writes in Romanian. 《I know you must be exhausted. So sorry about the race. I am glad you're safe, as always. There is information I need to share about the donor. Please call tomorrow.》

I flick the table lamp on and call her.

"I did not mean to wake you," she says.

"I couldn't sleep. And I'm curious about this donor information."

Viorica makes a reluctant humming noise. "We should speak in the morning. If we discuss this now, I'm concerned you may not sleep."

"It's better to tell me, so we can deal with it. Now you have me worried." I pile pillows behind my back.

"First let me say this: he's offering a quarter-billion leu."

I suck in a breath. "A quarter *billion*—with a *B*? That's fifty million euros."

"Yes. And with that money we could finish the children's villa. All twelve houses, the adjoining school, and an on-site medical clinic."

I pick up a glass of water from the bedside and sip. "For you to sound apprehensive, the attached conditions must be troubling."

"Yes. The man is...Grigore Lupu."

My hand clenches the glass so hard that I must consciously set it down or risk injuring myself. The water's surface tremors like a storm.

Neither of us has spoken this man's name in a decade.

My sister's captor. The man who abused her innocence when she was a girl of sixteen and our uncle sold her to him.

My gut boiling with rage, I flip over to Romanian in a burst of profanity. «*Fuck his mother's Easter, that worthless shit-shoveler!*»

"Cosmin!" Viorica scolds, aghast.

"No. Absolutely not. We don't take five bani from that dog."

"Listen, *please*."

"It's out of the question. Unacceptable. I'm making good money already, and if all goes well, I could have a substantially bigger offer in two years when my contract is up."

"You're getting two million. Even though you live modestly and send most of it to Vlasia House, and will surely command more soon, it could take a decade to amass the sum Grigore would give us immediately."

"Rica, *no*. We—"

"Think of our dream," she cuts in. "Twelve adjoining houses in the villa, each with a housemother and six children in residence. Raised like *families*, not like forgotten, lost children."

"Why does this villain wish to give us the money? What does he want?"

Her sigh crackles over the line. "He wants to make amends."

"Some things, Rica, cannot be forgiven. You should know this better than anyone."

She emits a bark of laughter. "A quarter-billion leu to forgive. You would withhold this money from the children because you won't pardon someone for a wrong done to *me*?"

She pauses, and her next words are cold as iron. "*It's not your place.*"

"I apologize," I mutter.

"He is in his seventies now and feels remorse."

"Bullshit." I scrub my face with one hand.

"*Cosmin.*" Her tone is hard. "You must trust me."

"Many of the associates of Uncle Andrei weren't honest businessmen. If we entangle ourselves with this man, it could end up defying the purpose of having used our inheritance to start the foundation."

"Do *not* lecture me—"

"We're protecting children who've lost their parents as we lost ours. Sparing young girls the horrors you suffered. You'd take a payoff from the monster who victimized you?"

She huffs out a sharp sigh. "I don't wish to discuss this anymore. Are you coming home before the Spanish Grand Prix?"

My sister tends to change the subject when she knows I'm right, so I don't press further. The money would have been useful, but I'm relieved she's letting it go. As the emotional turmoil catches up to me, I sag like a puppet whose strings have been cut, draping a hand over my eyes.

"On Wednesday." There's silence on the line for a moment. "I apologize for being so adamant about this donor," I say. "Thank you for your patience with my temper."

"Yes. We needn't say more."

Once we hang up, I turn out the light and stare at the shifting parallel lines of city glow on the ceiling as the AC agitates the vertical blinds. Putting in my headphones and listening to soothing music doesn't help me to calm.

I reach for my laptop and type out another of the emails to Phaedra I've been writing and saving to my draft folder, unsent.

> I tell myself it's not possible to miss something I've never had, but I do. I miss the win that slipped through my fingers today. I miss the childhood denied me.
>
> I miss you.
>
> You make me feel poetic, which is why I will never send these letters.
>
> "Your eyes are like the green vines nodding in the shadows on the patio in Santorini. Do you recall the split tree on the hillside, how I pointed out your hair was the same color as the heartwood, when we were overtaken by that rainstorm?"
>
> Only a fool speaks like that.
>
> But I would be a fool for you.
>
> Good night, dragă.

11

BARCELONA

MID-MAY

COSMIN

I nearly managed third place at the Spanish GP. It would have felt like a podium if the twelve points I won had earned a smile from Phaedra, but her brief thaw at Baku was just that.

In the two weeks since, she's avoided me aside from work. I tell myself this is for the best. When Jakob and Inge invite a small group to spend an afternoon on the fifty-foot yacht he bought Inge for their first anniversary (the lovestruck fool spent half his year's salary on it), I accept only because I know Phaedra will decline.

To my surprise, when I board the shuttle bus taking us to the marina, Phaedra is sitting at the back, her freckled nose buried in a hardbound copy of the newest Julian Barnes novel. She's wearing a man's blue oxford shirt, unbuttoned with sleeves rolled to the elbows, and a white bikini top beneath.

I wonder if it's tied with a simple bow, and what it would be like to pull the string and free her breasts and hold their warmth in my hands.

The time we were caught in the rain on Santorini, her thin shirt clung to her and I noticed she has a large tattoo on one shoulder blade. I hope to see it in detail today if she removes the shirt to sunbathe.

Her unadorned green eyes meet mine for a moment, then refocus on the page. As I make my way up the aisle, I greet Reece and her wife, then Jakob's race engineer, Alfie, and his wife—a woman I've never met, who is introduced to me as Georgie. Based on the woman's volume, and the way she grips me when we shake hands, I suspect she had cocktails with breakfast.

I sit sideways in the seat in front of Phaedra's, resting my arm along the back. "An unexpected pleasure, dragă. Typically you avoid such gatherings."

She touches her tongue with one fingertip and turns a page. "As long as no one gives me shit about reading all day, I might as well get some fresh air. Plus Klaus wants to talk."

I tap the edge of the novel. "Which of Barnes's books is your favorite?"

Her glare is suspicious. She tucks the cover flap into her page and closes the book. "You've read his stuff?"

"I'm fond of postmodern writing. I've not read that one yet—perhaps you'd lend it to me when you're finished."

"Stop doing that." She sits back, squinting.

"Doing what?"

"Liking what I like. It's creepy."

I laugh. "It's a coincidence. We simply enjoy many of the same things."

"Yeah, I'm not buying it."

The van starts up, and Jakob and Inge climb aboard, merry and chatty and looking very young and in love. The door closes and Phaedra's attention snaps to the window.

"No," she breathes.

I follow her eyes. Klaus is still outside, staring at his phone, and the van is moving. Phaedra puts both hands against the window like a child realizing she's being taken to the dentist. The strains of Elvis's "Big Boss Man" jangle from her phone, which she fumbles from a straw beach bag.

"Klaus, why aren't you on the bus? Should I ask the—"

I can hear the rumble of his voice leaking from the phone. She's taut as a bowstring and after a long moment of listening, wilts dramatically.

"Okay, fine. Sure, bye."

I raise questioning eyebrows. She stuffs the phone back into her bag.

"He claims," she says crisply, "to have 'an urgent matter requiring attention.'"

"Klaus has many responsibilities."

Phaedra emits an unladylike snort. "He faked me out, pretending he wanted to talk. He was getting rid of me. I suspect his 'urgent matter' is a certain lying blue-eyed brunette journalist with a compelling pair of 36C tits."

The bitterness in her delivery surprises me.

"Have you and Miss Evans quarreled?"

She ignores my question and plows on. "But I can imagine—given your penchant for predawn tumbles with random-ass hotel maids—you think some tawdry hookup is a perfectly good excuse to flake last minute on plans, right?" She whips her book open again and the cover flap cuts her finger. She yelps and the book tumbles, hitting the floor in a flutter of pages.

I thrust one hand into my messenger bag as I grasp her wrist with the other to prevent her from putting the wounded finger into her mouth.

"Don't," I instruct softly, withdrawing a canteen of water. I take a clean handkerchief out and moisten it before passing it to her.

"Thanks," she mutters, dabbing the fingertip.

I duck to retrieve the book, then move to join her. As I set the book on her legs, I'm surprised to see she's wearing a short skirt. One of my fingers ruffles the fringed hem and she smacks my hand with a little growl.

"Keep your hands to yourself, Formula Fuckboy."

"You're wearing white," I can't help pointing out.

"It's the only color in my size they had in the hotel's boutique." She checks whether the cut is still bleeding, then stuffs the handkerchief into her beach bag. "I'll wash it and give it back later."

"That's not necessary." I hold out a hand.

"Yeah, no. I'm not giving you a handkerchief with my blood."

"Afraid I'll cast a spell on you?" I tease. "If I haven't already…"

"Your confidence would be impressive if it weren't so annoy-ing." She puts the book into her bag and folds her arms. "What kind of anachronistic freak carries handkerchiefs anyway?"

"'Anachronistic,'" I repeat. "You think I'm old-fashioned?"

"I'm pretty sure cotton hankies went out with Jell-O salads and Benny Goodman."

"And yet—as you saw—they're useful on occasion." I give her a wink.

"Okay, the wink made it gross. Now I'm assuming you mean something sexual, and *no*, please don't elaborate if that's the case." She rummages through her bag, pulls out a pair of oversize sunglasses, and puts them on before leaning back. "Now leave me alone, please."

Under the guise of watching the scenery, I examine her face for a minute. There's a slight tremble to her lower lip.

"I'm correct, yes, about you and Miss Evans?" I venture. "I've not seen you in each other's company for—"

"Think you're pretty clever, figuring that out?" she snaps. Her brows crumple above the sunglasses. "Zero points for reading the room, dude."

"I apologize."

"It's none of your damned business." Her throat dips as she swallows hard and turns toward the window, jaw clenched. "Just because I lost Nat and might lose my dad too doesn't mean I need a new friend. You can fuck right off."

This is the moment I realize Ed Morgan must be dying.

I wish the fact that Jakob is a nondrinker meant the bar on the boat would not be fully stocked, but he and Inge are consummate hosts and cocktails flow freely.

Georgie has finished her second espresso martini before noon and insists upon sitting next to me even after I manufacture a pretense to move. Phaedra is on a lounge chair nearby, reading.

"How many languages do you speak?" Georgie purrs, her bottle-tanned face propped on one palm. I've removed her hand from my thigh more than once. Her fake lashes are applied imperfectly, and I try not to focus on the crooked left one.

"Five, but only three well—Romanian, French, and English."

"Debatable on English!" Phaedra pipes up. Despite the insult, I find myself gratified that she's listening.

"You know," Georgie says, dropping her voice, "I looked up *one* little sentence in Romanian." She trails a fingertip down my arm and delivers a clumsily rendered line: «*I want to go to bed with you.*»

This is of course the moment her husband returns, handing her a third drink. "What's that, my love?" he asks.

"She said," I tell him smoothly, "that she is sleepy."

"Ah! My clever girl." He leans to kiss her cheek.

Inge appears in the doorway leading to the deck. "The picnic is ready!" she announces in her musical voice. "Can some of you transport things to the tender so we can go to the beach?"

"Of course, liebling," Jakob replies, pushing to his feet from a deck chair.

Alfie and I follow. As I'm toting a basket and emerge from the narrow stairs, I catch up with Reece.

"I'd like you to make my excuses to remain behind," I say discreetly. "Headache, perhaps?"

"Has all my scolding about optics finally got through to you?" she teases. "Good call. We don't want anyone thinking you're encouraging that woman's behavior." She takes the basket from me. "Back downstairs with you until we're gone."

I loiter in the kitchen, waiting for the group to depart. The tender roars off, headed for the beach.

Minutes later, I hear the unmistakable sound of crying.

12

BARCELONA

PHAEDRA

I blame the stupid fucking banana for my breakdown.

I ask Inge if I can stay behind and rest in one of the bedrooms, because of (fake) cramps. She ushers me into bed with a cup of herbal tea, then comes back minutes later, offering a plate containing a sandwich and a banana.

"The potassium is good for cramps," she assures me, pointing at the fruit.

After she gently pulls the door almost closed, I lie on my side staring at the plate, listening to the chattering and footsteps as the group leaves. It's a relief not to have to go. Too much smiling, pretending I'm not frozen with terror inside. For that matter, I can't take much more of watching Alfie's cougar wife slobber over Cosmin.

The tender buzzes away, and silence descends. I stare at the plate on the bedside table, thinking about my dad.

Chondrosarcoma in the base of the skull. Massively rare.

He FaceTimed me a few days ago to deliver the news. I knew it was bad when I opened the call and my mother was on-screen as well, not just leaning into the frame in passing to say hello like we usually do.

She's not interested in racing—the main focus of Mo's life and mine—only in the "stuff" Emerald has provided. So I never know what to talk with her about, and we're a little awkward. Mo is "my person," and Mama is Aislinn's—they're far more alike, the kind of people who use hair spray, count calories, and iron their clothes.

More like Natalia, I guess. It hurts to think about her right now too.

When Mo brought up the coming transition during the call and wanted to discuss business—whether he might offer Klaus the chance to buy the Morgan family's 60 percent, or whether I should become "head honcho" when Dad "crosses the bar"—I slapped my hands over my ears like a little kid and shouted, *Don't!*

Not being able to talk with Nat has made everything harder. I realized I was equally in the wrong because I also hid something from her—I didn't tell her about the kiss in Santorini with Cosmin. So I broke down and texted her the week after the Chinese GP, and twice more since then.

No reply. Looks like she wasn't bluffing about being sick of me.

On the team, only Klaus and Reece know about Dad's cancer. And Klaus has been odd—stiffly courteous or terse in a way I'm not used to. I've always claimed I don't want special treatment due to being the owner's daughter, and I guess this is what that looks like. Yay.

I know there's a chance his shift in mood toward me is because he and Natalia are cozy now, and she made me sound like a monster. But I also wonder if my father's illness is bringing back, for Klaus, the pain of losing his wife, Sofia.

I'd been hoping to have a heart-to-heart today on the boat and talk it all out, but no such luck. I've never felt more alone.

But back to the freak-out over the banana...

When I was a little kid and traveled with Dad and our NASCAR team, despite spending my days in an earsplitting environment, I was afraid of thunderstorms. Whenever there was a storm at night, I'd fall asleep to him singing that "Yes! We Have No Bananas" song. It made me laugh, and I'd relax. Worked every time.

I want to be little again. I want to be happy.

I want to feel something other than numb or terrified.

I allow myself the luxury of a messy, all-out sobfest, alternating between blubbering and hoarse whimper-singing.

"*We have an old-fashioned toh-mah-toe...*" I croak through tears. "*A Loooooong Island poh-tah-toe...*"

The cabin door sweeps open, and I shriek. I grab the first thing handy, throwing it at the intruder before scooting back against the pillows, arms knifed out like I'm doing kung fu.

The banana bounces off Cosmin.

"Why the fuck are you here?" I shout.

"I could ask the same." He picks up the bruised fruit and

hands it to me before sitting on the bed. "I assumed you to be at the picnic."

"I'm not in a picnic mood," I mutter, swiping tears and tangled hair from my face. Holding the banana on my palm as if it were a dead pet, I feel my lips tremble. "You ruined it."

"It was you who wielded this formidable weapon," he replies with a hint of a smile. "Shall I look in the kitchen for another?"

I throw it at him again. "It doesn't matter!" I wail. Curling on my side, I turn away and cover my eyes. "*Everything's* ruined!"

I mewl out small miserable noises and the bed shifts as Cosmin scoots closer. I feel a warm hand on my hip, resting there as if anchoring me. The mattress dips as he lies beside me, fitting his body against mine.

I stiffen. "What are you doing?"

"Comforting you."

"I don't want your stupid comfort. You're not the right person."

"This is true." He works an arm under my neck and the other loops around me. "But I am the *right now* person. It will have to suffice."

He smells really good, damn him.

His hands are large. I've looked at them plenty of times, but still, I turn one over, pressing my thumb into the palm, prodding the firm muscle there, following the arc pointing to his wrist. His arms are bare, shirt rolled to the elbows like mine.

He's wearing tailored linen shorts, so his knees touching the backs of mine are skin-on-skin warm. His hard chest shifts against my back as he breathes, and a flutter of something electric goes through me.

"Cosmin…"

"Hmm?"

I tip my ass subtly against him. "How long is everyone going to be gone?"

"Long enough that you can cry all you need to and sleep." He holds me closer.

I turn over and crumple a pillow beneath my neck, watching him. He does the same. He's not wearing the expression I imagined. I'm waiting for a sly grin, a raised eyebrow. But he only combs a bit of hair away from my face.

"I look like shit," I tell him.

"Nonsense. You're lovely."

The threads of black in his blue-gray irises are like road maps. There's a faint vertical dent in his full lower lip and I remember what it felt like to kiss him. It might've been the last time my heart beat hard for any reason other than anxiety.

It's kicked up now in a rhythm like someone executing a few cautious shimmies on the dance floor, but afraid to let go entirely.

I edge my feet toward him, and he gives my ankles a space to tuck between his. The arrangement is natural, like a thing we've done for years. I toy with a button on his shirt, freeing it from the hole.

His eyes narrow. When I slide a finger into the shirt's

placket, he scoops my hand up and delivers a kiss to my knuckles before placing my hand on my own hip and giving it a pat.

"You're good at two things," I tell him, "and I've only seen you do one of them." Reaching for his shirt front again, I flick another button free. "I need the other one now."

"You'd be angry with us both tomorrow." He skims a finger down the bridge of my nose. "Also, I'm good at more than two things."

I close in and kiss him. For a mortifying moment his lips don't move, but as I'm about to pull back—my cheeks hot with embarrassment—he opens and touches my upper lip with his tongue. His hand slides into my hair and draws me closer as the kiss intensifies.

I suck his lower lip and give it a nip, and he lets out a soft groan just before the hand that was in my hair drags down my back and splays over my ass, holding me in place as he presses his pelvis against mine. I equally want to push my ass back into his hand and shamelessly mash my crotch against his, so I end up sort of doing both, and the undulation makes Cosmin pull in a gasp through his nose.

"I don't think this is what you really want or need right now," he insists.

"Bullshit." I twist open the rest of the buttons on his shirt. "And you want it too."

"Of course I do." He responds to my next kiss with a faint moan, then pulls back and looks at me seriously. "But we both know why it's a bad idea, no?"

"It's a *great* idea." I give his lower lip a small bite. "I want you to make me feel good for twenty minutes—that's all I ask."

"You're worth more than that."

"Cool." I part his shirt and stroke his smooth, rock-hard chest. "I'll take thirty."

"That's not what I mean." He traces my cheekbone with a knuckle.

I brush his hand away like a gnat. "You're a total man-whore twenty-four seven, but now that I'm asking for it, you're getting all emo?"

"Fiery girl. So intense," he murmurs with a pensive smile.

"Here's intense for you: I want you to *fuck the life back into me*," I demand through clenched teeth. "Then we can forget it happened. Are you game or not?"

The look in his eyes goes savage. He rises on an elbow. The hand he still has on my ass digs in hard enough to hurt, but dear God it's wonderful to feel something, anything.

"It's not a *game*," he growls an inch from my lips.

I reach between us and jerk open the fly of his shorts. The fabric of his boxer briefs strains across a cock huge and hard enough to make me weak in the knees. I yank the elastic away from his skin, plunging inside and grabbing him with a single possessive jerk.

His eyes glitter. "*No.*"

"You mean you're not going to fuck me?"

My harsh whisper is somewhere between furious and taunting. I expect him to pry my hand off that massive hot steel piston and walk out, but instead he kisses me so passionately I accidentally bite my own lip and taste blood.

"I mean, draga mea," he tells me, pushing my skirt up, "that we're not going to forget it happened."

The next minute could best be described as "a tussle," in a way that I previously thought was purely for artsy nineties films where people hate-fuck, and there's no soundtrack aside from angry panting and the noise of thread popping as clothes are wrenched out of the way.

Ardelean is a goddamned beast and it's exactly what I want. Everything else in my life mercifully blurs like scenery outside a white-knuckle car ride as we claw our way to operational nudity—close enough to get at the parts we need.

The oxford shirt I'm wearing hangs from one arm and my bikini top has been whipped off and tossed. My skirt is twisted at my waist, panties torn free at one side—forcefully enough that the fabric left a welt on my hip. Cosmin gasped an apology into my mouth when I yelped, and my reply was something like "*I don't fucking care—get your cock in me.*"

He rises to his knees on the bed, and I wrestle off what he's wearing from the waist down as we kiss in a frenzy. He collapses on his back to kick his clothes free before springing on me like I'm a prey animal. I thump against the wall while reclining, and Cosmin cradles my head in a way that feels too sympathetic—any tenderness now might bring my sorrow back in a smothering avalanche.

"Don't be nice," I snap, lunging for his mouth again.

He makes a noise of assent and I'm relieved he understands.

Grabbing the backs of my knees, he hauls me toward him. Two long, hard fingers thrust into me, and he pauses, watching my face. I think he's testing to see how deep I am, and a wicked smile curls on his lips.

"Beautiful," he murmurs.

How did it used to annoy me when he said that? It's the hottest fucking thing I've ever heard.

I splay my legs and grind on his hand. His fingers stroke inside me, faultlessly rubbing my G-spot, and a deep, sweet ache spreads. With his thumb he lightly strums my clit. I'm getting so wet the bedspread is going to be wrecked.

"Are you fertile?" he asks. "If so, there are other ways I can please you."

"No. I have the implant." I'm impatient to feel his cock in me, and I arch against him. "Don't slow it down, don't slow it down. Keep the momentum, Legs. Let's do this."

With his free hand he captures my foot and presses a kiss to it. "Rapacious girl. You're so used to giving me orders. Do you want to put on a headset and tell me what to do by radio as I fuck you?"

His fingers slide out of my pussy. He takes off his shirt and reaches for a pillow, tapping my hip to lift so he can place it beneath me. He kneels between my thighs and pulls me over his lap, reclined with my legs spread.

"You're made for me inside," he says, his eyes dark with lust.

Grasping himself, he slides back and forth through my lips, and I bring my knees up and wriggle closer, desperate to be filled. He pushes in a few inches, then withdraws, aiming the head of his cock—now drenched in my wetness—at my clit, drawing slick circles around me. Two fingers of his other hand glide back into my pussy and I twitch in invitation.

"So deep inside, but so tight," he murmurs. "You can take all of me."

"I fucking need it. Don't be a tease."

"I'm going to watch you come first." His fingers inside me are doing something that feels like a figure eight, slow and hypnotic. "You made it clear you want to use me."

My eyes lock with his in alarm, but there's no bitterness in his expression. He takes my hand and wraps it around his cock.

"So, use me," he concludes. "I'm your toy."

I'm stunned at how unashamed I am. We're strangers in this respect, and something about that risk is thrilling. At the same time, I'm oddly at ease. Though the porthole windows are small, it's broad daylight and we can see each other down to the last freckle and scar. My legs are smooth, but my girl bits are only trimmed—strawberry blond, lighter than the hair on my head.

"Your little pink cunt is perfect," he tells me, as if he knows I'm self-conscious about not being shaved.

His delivery is surprisingly not lascivious, but falls somewhere between matter-of-fact and affectionate, and I'm pleasantly shocked he uses a word I never do.

I hold him in place and churn my hips to slide him against me. My clit is throbbing—it feels like every bit of blood in my body has converged between my legs. Cosmin's gorgeous eyes are low lidded, studying me. His plump lips are parted, helpless in thrall, trapped by the sight of what I'm doing. I feel stunningly powerful.

"How are you so confident I'll come?" I can't help taunting him.

I'm keeping a poker face, but holy hell, I'm nearly there already. A mischievous part of me wonders if I can discreetly get myself off and pretend I didn't, just to deny him the satisfaction of pleasing yet another woman in an endless parade.

Hand wedged between us, he adds another finger and sweeps my tight, wet walls, massaging and watching my face for feedback. "Because, draga mea, I know how responsive to input you are."

My insides pulse as if trying to swallow his fingers, and I whimper, the peak creeping closer. My knees tremble as I scale the final approach, and I relax them.

"Ah, sweet one," he says with a knowing smile. "Trying to hide it from me. That's your plan, yes?" He opens his slippery, probing fingers, stretching me inside.

My breath is coming in tight little gasps now. "You don't always win…"

It's a relief finally to let myself enjoy how hot he is, and my gaze devours him. His shoulders are golden epaulets of lean muscle, the tilt of his head on that strong but elegant neck is arrogant in a way that turns my blood molten.

His tongue touches his lower lip and those stormy eyes narrow. "No. But something tells me I will today."

His fingers withdraw and he splays them against the outside

of me, pressing into my pubic bones on either side of my labia. I gasp as a rushing feeling descends—not just the onset of orgasm, but something else.

What the actual fuck is that? It's as if everything settles into place, like landing gear on an airplane.

My eyes go wide, searching Cosmin's face. If there's ever a time his cocky smile is welcome, this is bizarrely it—that smug tilt of his full lips sends me over the edge. A *whoosh* of something heavy and gorgeous, inevitable, with the gravity of a roller-coaster plunge, rides in on the wake of the regular orgasm I'd expected.

The gearhead nerd part of me dimly thinks of the word "turbocharged" and the overwhelmed woman part of me cries out, writhing against his hand as I drop back and fling my arms out to grab the bedspread.

Before the spasms pass, he stretches on top of me and fills me with his cock. I let out a surprised noise almost like a bark of laughter, a joyous "Ha!" and whip my arms around him, seizing his ass with greedy hands, forcing him closer.

"Yes—oh God, *that*...pleaseyesohmyfuckinggod," cascades out of me, delirious. "Do it hard," I order him. "I don't want to feel anything but *this*." There's no part of me that isn't grabbing him like the last parachute in a plane going down.

His hands wring my hair, and the pain is sharp but delicious. He's holding me in place, his hips slamming in an exquisite arc—not just chasing his own lust, but in a motion clearly engineered to herd me toward ecstasy again.

His tense breaths carry a hint of a growl each time we

collide. There's nothing tender here, no mercy in the way I buck against his thrusts, the way my nails rake him, the unintelligible raving that spills from my bruised lips, right along with the sweet juice he's gouging out of me with his perfect cock.

Whatever witchcraft he's used on my pussy is working, because I'm probably a half minute from another climax, and that has literally never happened during a missionary fuck. I'm not sure if it's his imposing size, the slight curve that seems to hit everything just right, the smell of his skin, the savage music of our mingled groaning and panting, the smacking of sweaty skin.

Through my fog of arousal, a flutter of anxiety appears like a lighthouse in the distance, the dim warning beam telling me: *This sex is too good not to want it again. I'm doomed.* I don't realize I've babbled it aloud until Cosmin slows, fixing me with a fevered look.

He crushes my mouth with his, and the sore spot I bit earlier flares.

"You're right," he says. "We're both doomed. I claim this castle, and I will write my name in every fucking room of you."

The words storm past the walls in my heart with the same heat I feel in the blissfully aching territory below the skirt rumpled around my waist.

Cosmin grasps my wrists and locks them over my head, and my legs encircle his waist just so I can keep holding him. The words I want to say are hiding behind my kiss-ravaged mouth. *Yes, absolutely fucking **yes**, we're going to do this forever.*

But I'm as scared from the neck up as I am turned on from the neck down. Wanting him this much is terrifying.

How did I ever think we could do this casually?

Electric tremors roll up my thighs like warning thunder and my eyes squeeze shut. I thrash my head to the side, my hair a tangled pool beneath me.

He shifts gears with my body, using the same unerring timing he has behind the wheel, grinding against me slow and steady and slick, with almost the motion of wiping fog off a mirror.

I feel his lips touch my earlobe, biting it, then saying quietly, "Closing your eyes won't conceal you, sweet girl. I'll find you anyway."

My eyes snap open, and I can feel I'm glaring, my face doing something unexpected and possibly homicidal.

"Fuck you, Ardelean." I drop my trembling legs to the bed as a lush warmth blooms from a pinpoint, right where he's rubbing me. There's no reeling it back. It opens into a chasm that drowns me in sudden pleasure. "Fuck you!" I cry over the white roar of climax.

"*No*," he throws back at me. "Fuck *us*!"

He releases my wrists and his arms move behind my neck, holding me hard like a rag doll as he pounds into me, saying against my neck, "*Us...us...us...!*" with every thrust. My insides are soft and twitching with aftershocks.

With a broken, stifled cry that's half euphoria and half like grief, he buries his face against my neck and tenses, shoulders rigid, arms like cables around me. I can feel him jerk and pulse inside me, and instinctively I smooth my hands down his back and clutch his ass, pulling him closer in that moment, greedy to claim every bit of him.

His hot breath gusts against my neck, and he's murmuring something in what I assume is Romanian. The same series of words, three times, each sentence a little quieter until he sighs, kissing my shoulder and lifting his head to search my face.

There's no way I look good—I was crying before we even started this insanity.

He shifts half off me, propping up on one elbow, and a pang of loss ripples through me as his body withdraws. Usually I have all the afterglow tenderness of a nineties gangsta rap song and can't wait to eject a guy the second he's done, but as the heat from Cosmin puddles beneath me, his absence feels lonesome.

Clarity returns, and I realize what I just yelled at him. A shiver of mortification falls. I cover my eyes with a hand. "Sorry for cursing at you. I don't know why I got angry."

"I understand."

His lips brush mine, and I keep my eyes open purely for the enjoyment of seeing him. This close to his face, now that we're not tearing each other apart, I can see his simple details—the delicate skin of his eyelids, the dampness of the raw-honey-colored hair at his temples, the way his cheek dimples as he lifts one corner of his mouth in a smile that I'd almost think was shy if he weren't a narcissistic douche-canoe.

He kisses me again, whispering something so quietly I doubt it's even meant for me.

"*What?*" I whisper back.

He runs a thumb along my shoulder. "You're so beautiful."

"I'm going to have Doc Bartosz check your eyes so you don't put my fucking car into a wall."

He bites my shoulder, laughing, and pulls me against his chest in a little-spoon embrace. Sprawling an arm out, he grabs a pillow and tucks it under our heads. His heartbeat against my spine is slowing already, owing to his conditioning. He traces my engine tattoo with a fingertip.

"It was my hope to see this today," he says, "but the manner in which it happened was unexpected."

"Ford flathead V8, in honor of the first thing I rebuilt entirely on my own when I was a kid. Ten years old. I'd already rebuilt a Slant-6 and a Chevy small-block with Mo, but the flathead was all me."

His lips on the nape of my neck send shivers across my skin. "I wish I could have known you then, as a child."

"I'd have just told you, 'Buzz off, little towheaded fucker.'"

"You still do," he teases.

I close my eyes and laze into the strange-yet-familiar feeling of Cosmin kissing my tattoo. Thinking about working on engines with my dad, the pain returns, a jab that sinks in deep.

"Mo's dying, Cos."

I can't believe I've said it in plain words—a statement, not a question—let alone to the Randy Rookie.

His arms tighten around me. "I'm so sorry. He's a good man."

"Did you know?"

"When we were on Santorini, I determined he was ill. This morning on the bus, I understood the extent of it." He rubs his lips feather-light against my neck.

This morning on the bus seems like a million years ago. I glance at the paper cut on my finger, as if it might be healed, proving the time between before-Cosmin and now-Cosmin must be longer.

Eerily, he says exactly what I'm thinking.

"Only a few hours have passed." He draws my hand back and kisses the paper cut. "But, like the old song: *What a difference a day makes*, no?"

Another wave of fear dashes over me. Did I really let Cosmin Ardelean in, or was he always here?

I turn over to face him. I wonder if he assumes my frown owes entirely to sorrow over my father's illness, or if he can read me so well that he knows I'm freaked out about the sex.

I rush in with words before he can see too much.

"Do you believe in an afterlife?"

His gaze angles away. "I cannot say I have *belief*, but I have hope. Not only because the thought of seeing my parents again is pleasing, but...I would like to think my uncle is in Hell."

Cosmin is so unguarded right now that a shimmer of tenderness sneaks up on me despite my efforts to repress it.

"He hurt you?" I venture.

"He hurt my sister far more. That I will not forgive." He pulls me close, as if afraid to make eye contact. "I did not know the extent of it until after my uncle died—Viorica kept the worst from me."

My hand is on Cosmin's waist, my thumb sliding along a ridge of muscle, and I can't believe how natural it feels to be with him like this. The vibration of his low voice, where my ear rests against his chest, seems as much a part of me as my own heartbeat.

He combs his fingers through my hair. "She's a better sister than I deserve. A truly excellent person."

I think of Aislinn and am envious of Cosmin's admiration for Viorica. Aislinn and I have never been close. I was gone for most of every year when she was little, and either harassed or ignored her when I *was* around. As adults we have nothing in common.

Remembering that Cosmin's bond with his sister owes much to having been raised by an abuser, I feel guilty for my envy. My childhood was overall a joy. The image of my father's smile comes to me, the sound of him saying *Oh, my chickadee* in his quiet drawl...

He's leaving me. I'm going to be alone.

How will I do this without him?

I can't be dating one of the drivers if I head the team. If my father passes the mantle to me, faultless professionalism is expected. He trusts me. I could never risk destroying his legacy.

And if Klaus buys Emerald? The indulgent "uncle" of just a few weeks ago might have gently reprimanded me or even turned a blind eye to a little mischief—especially if he's breaking the rules by dating a journalist—but Team Principal/full owner Klaus Franke would likely fire my ass. Part of me already has a paranoid suspicion his recent emotional distance could be seeding the ground to force me out.

I peek at Cosmin—his eyes closed, relaxed—and anxiety over what I've done sweeps in on a wave of post-orgasmic clarity.

Oh God. How do I undo this disaster?

13

MONACO

COSMIN

It wasn't the bedspread that gave us away—Phaedra put that in the washing machine and told Inge she got blood on it. It was Reece noticing my words as we exited the boat.

When we got back to the hotel, she came to my room.

"I'm not best pleased I have to ask you this—it's frankly not in my wheelhouse and I should be handing it directly to Klaus, but I thought I'd give you the benefit of the doubt in case I'm mistaken. Did you have sex with Phae this afternoon? And don't lie."

I offered what I hoped was a confused smile. "Why would you ask that?"

"Cosmin!" she snapped, eyes flashing. "On the dock you said, 'After you, draga mea.' The 'mea' implies you think she's *yours* now. Also: washing the duvet? I'm not a fool."

As I lifted a bottle of pomegranate juice to my lips, buying a moment's time under Reece's hawkish gaze, I could still smell Phaedra on my hands. "There's no cause to bring anything up with Klaus."

"Because you didn't do anything, or—"

"Because it's a private matter."

"It's not a 'private matter'—it's in your bloody contract!" She clapped a hand over her forehead. "You utter knobhead! What were you two thinking?"

When I went to the door of Phaedra's room an hour later to tell her of the conversation with Reece, there was no answer. That evening, Reece texted me that Phaedra was on a flight back to the States to see her father. For the next week she stayed in North Carolina and attended meetings remotely. I went to Bucharest for a few days to spend time with Viorica.

Tomorrow Phaedra will rejoin the team in Monaco. I've been here since last night, staying at the apartment my friend Owen shares with his American girlfriend, Brooklyn.

She's the daughter of a man who amassed a fortune producing reality TV programs. Smart, beautiful, excellent taste in music, and with a joyous, extroverted heart. I rely on Brook to introduce me to new bands. She and Owen have been together two years and have a passionate and loyal (though unconventional) relationship.

I'm lying on the bed in the small guest room, reading over some of the emails I've written but not sent to Phaedra this week. The lights in the room are off, but there's ambient light from the large window looking out on the Boulevard du Larvotto and the sea.

A tap on the open doorway pulls my attention to the bright rectangle framing Brook. Her long blond hair is curly and has streaks of turquoise and pink. She rarely wears makeup, her chief adornment being the sleeve of vintage-style tattoos covering her right arm.

"Trying to sleep?" she asks.

"No, please come in." I darken my phone and set it aside, and Brook sits on the edge of the small bed.

"I made a kickass couscous salad if you're hungry," she offers.

"Thank you. Perhaps later." I roll onto my side and prop my head on one hand. "I'm being a poor guest. My apologies for appearing distant. I've been preoccupied."

"Yeah, no shit," she says with a small laugh. She takes her phone from her pocket and taps the screen. "I made you a gloomy playlist. Suspect you need it."

My phone chimes and I open and peruse the link.

"That L.A. Witch song," she continues, "'Baby in Blue Jeans' is basically auditory heroin. Angsty as fuck."

We sit in companionable silence while I scroll through the new songs.

"You're free to tell me to MYOB," she ventures, "but you've got the 'moping about a girl' look. For a guy who has his dick in everything, it surprises me."

My eyebrows lift in amusement. "I'm not as promiscuous as you assume, iubi."

"Uh-huh, sure."

I consider whether to change the subject, then decide to unburden myself.

"I've made a misstep with someone I care about deeply. Phaedra Morgan, my race engineer."

Brook chuckles. "Haven't met her, but I'm a fan since the thing last year with that clueless old scrotum who owns Team Coraggio. Don't know if you heard about their online pissing match. He said snarky shit about 'lady engineers' and she fired back that he should stick to what he understands, '*like tax evasion and horsie-tail butt plugs*.' Y'know—because of that leaked video of him at the sex party."

"Beautiful," I say with a laugh. "That's my fierce girl."

"*Is* she your girl?"

The smile fades from my lips. "Likely not."

"That's why you've got 'a face like a slapped arse,' as Owen says."

"Yes." Quiet descends, the only sound the drone of the video game Owen is playing in the living room. I peek at Brook. "I ended up in bed with her."

"Uh-oh."

"She hasn't spoken with me since."

"Oof." Brook waits a beat. "Are you in love?"

I sigh. "There's a saying: Mă faci să visez în culori—'You make me dream in colors.' It's how she makes me feel."

Brook takes from her pocket a tin of the anise candies to which she is almost addicted, chooses one, and pops it into her mouth. "You should tell her."

"I don't have confidence such a thing would be well received."

"Why? Because she's a badass, you think she doesn't want

to hear schmaltz like that? Lemme tell you a secret: I'd rather get dental surgery than watch *The Notebook*, but I still swoon when Owen says romantic shit." She leans toward me and drops her voice. "None of us is immune. *Tell her.* Say it in Romanian, an inch from her ear."

"Hm."

"But if she doesn't feel the same way about you, obviously don't mug yourself."

I think of Phaedra's demeanor on the boat. She was businesslike when she got up to wash the bedspread, and insisted I go up on deck and pretend to have fallen asleep in a lounge chair. When the group returned and we went back to the marina, she retreated into her novel. On the shuttle bus to the hotel, she ignored me.

I assumed this was a temporary but necessary deception, especially when I caught her sneaking a sorrowful look at me in the hotel lobby as we all crossed to the elevators.

Now I'm not so sure. Eight days of silence seems to tell a different story.

Wednesday afternoon, I take a chance on going to the hotel where Phaedra and a few others on the team have rooms. Much of the reason I'm staying with Owen and Brooklyn is that I told Reece I would avoid Phaedra in nonwork environments. In exchange, she agreed to drop the issue and say nothing to Klaus.

But I can't endure another sleepless night picturing Phaedra, remembering her scent, her moans and whispered urgings, those hypnotic green eyes.

I have to see her.

After I knock at her suite, there's a minute of silence before the door opens. Phaedra's auburn waves are piled on her head, and she's wearing a thick hotel bathrobe too long for her short frame. Her lips part. She wrings a handful of the robe's fabric closed at the neck—likely bare underneath. The scent of lavender and mint swirls around her.

I lean against the doorframe. "May I come in?"

"No." Her bare feet shift on the champagne-colored carpet, one resting atop the other. "I was taking a bath." She points a thumb over her shoulder. "Gonna get back to it. I'll see you at the paddock in the morning."

Her eyes drift over me, then snap away as if she's caught herself. I wonder if she's thinking the same thing I am—remembering what I look like without clothes.

"Draga mea," I say quietly, "I'm not of the opinion that men are owed an explanation when women spurn them." I spread my hands. "Still, I would ask."

"Don't be Captain Melodrama. You're not *spurned*. I'm just avoiding you. And we both know why, so there's your Scooby-Doo mystery solved."

"What is 'scoopy do'?"

She rolls her eyes. "Romania stopped being communist before you were born. You're telling me they didn't let you have Scooby-Doo?" She crosses her arms. "It's an old cartoon about a stupid talking dog and a hippie. Like, fighting crime and shit."

I lower my head and smile, then look at her through my eyelashes. She scowls, impervious to the attempt at charm.

"If you invite me in, we can look it up—a video of this police dog cartoon."

"It's... no, it's not a police dog. For fuck's sake. I'm explaining it wrong." Down the hall, a door opens, and Phaedra gasps. "*Shit!*" she whispers, grabbing my shirt and yanking me inside. "Did you pass anyone in the hallway?"

"Only staff."

"Oh, jolly," she deadpans. "I'm assuming no hot maids, or you wouldn't have made it this far—you'd be in the nearest broom closet, finagling her into a knee-trembler."

"I do not know this word—*finagle*." I raise an eyebrow. "But 'knee-trembler' is familiar."

"What a shock. I'll bet you got the rest from context." She presses her ear to the door, listening for people in the hall.

I sit on the corner of her bed. "Thank you for inviting me in. I'd like to talk."

She crosses to the window, tying her robe tighter and peering down at the expanse of Monte Carlo. "It was hardly an invitation," she stage-whispers with annoyance. "I just don't want anyone to see you. Reece promised not to rat me out to Klaus if I stay away from you."

When she perches on the armrest of the love seat near the window and adjusts the robe to cover her leg, I stare at its smooth curve, the slender ankle, the high arch of her foot.

"Ah. She spoke with you as well."

Phaedra nods, twisting the bathrobe tie. "Look, dude. I

appreciated your, uh, *support* in Barcelona. Good times. But with the announcement that Mo's on 'family-related sabbatical,' eyes are on me. Our, uh, *afternoon* on the boat was fun, obvi. But..." She chews her lower lip and shrugs.

"Do you have feelings for me, draga mea?"

"Like it matters," she says immediately, her voice gruff.

I stand, closing the distance between us. When I touch Phaedra's chin to coax her to look at me, she doesn't flinch away.

"Your comment about 'maids' when I arrived implies you're still angry about Shanghai." My thumb brushes her lower lip. "But I have kept a secret from you."

Her green eyes are dark, and I'm drawn to the rise and fall of her chest, a pale sliver of freckled skin at the open V of the robe. I undo her hair and arrange the long waves over her shoulders.

"I led you to believe that woman had been in my bed, but she hadn't. She was simply a shy fan who took a bold risk to meet me before I left in the morning. She became embarrassed and cried. I felt sorry for her and arranged for her to have a race pass. End of story."

Phaedra has her hands lightly on my waist; I'm not sure she's aware of touching me.

"I kinda believe you. But it might be because you're standing super close and smell incredible." She touches her upper lip with her tongue. "You should probably leave."

I bend to kiss the crown of her head. "Should," I echo. My lips alight on her brow. "Could," I add. Next, I slide my fingers through her hair, grasping her as I kiss the corner of her parted mouth. "But *won't*. Because your roaming hands are asking me to stay."

I pause with my mouth a centimeter from hers. We're so close, our focus jumps back and forth to settle on each of the other's eyes like birds testing branches.

Her mahogany lashes drop closed as I claim her lips, touching the upper one with my tongue where I just saw her do the same. Her right hand moves, fingers closing around the contour of my cock, leisurely stroking through my jeans. My rumble of encouragement vibrates into her mouth as our tongues explore, hot but unhurried.

"I have to taste you," I murmur against her.

"You *are* tasting me."

With a wicked smile I pull my shirt off, then glide my hands down the warmth of her neck and skim over the robe. I tug the knot on her belt free before sliding inside.

"*Everywhere*, sweet one," I clarify.

Her skin is soft and dewy from bathwater, and the lavender-mint scent rises with her own earthy-bright heat. I push the robe off her shoulders and straighten to take in the sight of her nakedness where she's perched on the arm of the sofa. The sparkle of moonlight and boats on the inky sea frames her from the window behind.

"You're at precisely the correct height," I say, kneeling, "for me to savor." I push her legs wide and place a kiss on the inside of her thigh. "I've been imagining this for months." My whisper-light kisses move like footsteps tiptoeing to paradise.

My hands stroke her ankles, the taut calves, the humid hollows at the backs of her knees.

As I trace up her thighs with my knuckles, she shifts toward me in offering. Her hands tangle into my hair. I brush both thumbs along her pink lips, flirt with her already glistening opening, then coast back up to expose her wet and swollen bud. She's shaved underneath now, though the front is still a downy trapezoid the color of new pennies.

Stroking the recently denuded skin, I glance up. "Expecting company?"

She narrows her eyes with a sardonic half smile. "Oh, shut up and don't be smug. I wasn't expecting 'company' other than the battery-operated type."

The thought of Phaedra doing this makes my cock lurch. With a helpless groan I make contact, my tongue sliding a lazy circuit around her clit, lingering in areas that cause her hands to tighten on my hair.

I find a spot that elicits a tense whispered "Yes! Oh fuck…" and bathe it with the flat of my tongue until she pushes against my face, gasping. She tastes like salt and heat, the sweet muskiness of cantaloupe mixed with a dark richness like walnuts. I can't resist gliding a path down to her entrance and pushing my tongue inside. A small, hoarse sob escapes her.

"More," she begs. "*Don't stop.* You're really good at that."

"Confess, draga mea." I slide two fingers into her and find that shy little patch like a firm, sticky sponge saturated with her lust. I rub and glide, physical memory directing my hand into the motion that made her twitch and moan last time.

"What am I confessing?" she manages, throwing her head back. She releases my hair and digs her fingers into the sofa. "Anything. Just tell me where to sign. I did it. Guilty."

I give her several long, slow licks, then tease the spot I've noticed she loves most while my fingers rock inside her. She's so delicious it's driving me mad.

"No *false* confessions," I warn. "Just this: Whom did you think of while you pleasured yourself?" I return my tongue to her, then suck her clit before pulling away again. "Whose face, voice, tongue, cock? Whose name spilled from your lips when you came?"

I renew my teasing ministrations, finding the precise rhythm that makes her beg me not to stop. As she gets closer, I can only catch a few syllables of what she's deliriously saying under her breath—broken shards of words, riding atop her panting.

Her thighs are tense, and her toes point into the carpet like a ballerina. Her hands providing leverage on the sofa's arm, she pitches her hips in tight little thrusts, as if bobbing on a quick current. Her eyes are squeezed shut, her nipples pink caps on the lightly jiggling mounds of her breasts.

When I draw back, she groans in dismay. I know she's seconds from the edge, and inside her, my fingers define a lemniscate—the infinity symbol—against her hot walls. "Pentru totdeauna," I whisper.

Forever.

My mouth covers her sweet cunt and she whimpers with

relief, then goes silent in concentration as my focused caress leads her to the tipping point.

Her hands dive into my hair again and she allows herself one unrestrained sob of ecstasy before perhaps realizing that too much noise could give us away. Her legs jab straight as climax thunders in, and she strangles her cry into a discreet moan, shuddering against my hand and my lips.

"It was you," she gasps, the words rough. "I thought about you...*always*, dammit..." Her eyes open and settle on me.

"Such an obedient girl." I stand and tip her flushed face to kiss me. "Are you always so well-behaved? Mmm?"

I pull her to her feet into my arms. My cock is aching, crushed in my tight jeans, and she presses against me hard.

"I think you may be a bit bad," I say as she drags my head down to kiss her.

Her mouth is ravenous against mine. "I am now," she manages through the slick warring of our lips and tongues. "And it's your fault." She snags the waist of my jeans and pulls me toward the huge window. "You make me want to do terrible things."

Planting her palm on the center of my chest, she shoves me against the cool wall perpendicular to the window and drops to her knees, wrenching my fly open. I help her, stepping out of my clothes and pushing them aside with my foot.

Her hands coast up my thighs and torso. She pauses, staring straight up into my eyes, arms stretched high in a posture so like supplication that I want to tumble her to the carpet and fuck her like a raging beast. Her pupils are splayed dark as mountain lakes ringed by trees, lips plump and abraded pink from kissing. A cascade of coppery-chestnut waves falls around her shoulders, parting over her tits.

From this angle, the jutting curve of her ass is bewitching. Her hand fits perfectly around the girth of my cock, and she begins to stroke me, one corner of her mouth lifting in a smirk.

"You look stunning on your knees," I growl.

"The view's about to get even better."

With that, her mouth closes over me. I tip my head back with a hiss between clenched teeth, and one of my hands moves to the top of her head, fingers twining in the silken locks.

I watch her plunging up and down, my cock glittering and those plump lips sliding. I'm riveted by the way she blends the use of her lips and tongue and hand. She's incredible—so skilled. Suddenly I wish to destroy every man she's touched this way. Her mouth and hands belong only to me, now and always.

My hand tightens in her hair. I'm too close—I have to stop her before I'm unmanned.

"Numai mie îmi aparține," I murmur under my breath, half delirious.

She runs the tip of her tongue around the ridge of my cock, massaging the sensitive underside before pausing. "You said the same thing on the boat. What is it?"

Her lower lip is shining, and she sucks it into her mouth for a split second, eyes locked on mine. The gesture is both so erotic and so natural that a stab of need tears through me. I pull her to stand, dovetailing our fingers.

"It means," I tell her in a harsh whisper, switching places with her as if in a dance, "you belong to me, *only*."

I crush her lips in one fierce kiss before rotating her and trapping her against the wall, turned away from me. She gasps, and her palms flatten on the wallpaper—a geometric sage pattern with radiating threads of gold. Where her hands land, it appears electricity is shooting from her fingertips, and it seems fitting.

Yes, this wallpaper will be burned into my brain—I know it when I dip my knees to angle myself at her opening and she arches back, her posture begging me to ram my cock home. As I do, it wrings a cry from us both, and Phaedra's hands slip up the wall an inch with the force of my entry.

Her hands move again and again, fingers tensing, as I slam into her. I brace one palm on the wall and she clasps my wrist hard. With my other hand I reach around and caress down her belly, settling two fingers on her clit, slowing my thrusts, kneading and stroking her outside while I churn up a storm of tension inside her. Her snug walls squeeze me, and that round ass I've been watching for months is pure bliss to smack against with my hips.

We're beside the large window, and Phaedra swings one leg out and rests her foot on the windowsill, opening herself wider. One of her hands settles over mine as I rub her slippery clit.

I deliver a small bite to the side of her neck. "Do you want to take over?"

"No," she breathes, her eager body alternately grinding against my fingers and sheathing my cock deeper in herself. "I just want to be with you while you do it. *Fuck*, it's so good…"

"Beautiful, beautiful," I whisper into her shoulder as her legs start to tremble. "Fall apart for me."

Her hand atop mine adjusts subtly, showing me exactly what she needs in this position. I follow her lead and she lets out a low, breathy moan, rocking against my hand as I drive into her with the short, sharp thrusts she seems to want right now.

"I never got the chance," she says in a delirious whisper. "I'm taking it now…"

"Whatever it is," I reply, my lips against her neck, my fingers sliding in a motion Phaedra guides with her own, "you deserve it, sweet girl."

There's a flutter inside her, and she clenches around my cock. The hand she has on my wrist against the wall digs into me.

"Anything, draga mea. Name it and it's yours."

"A secret!"

She pushes her ass back against me hard as she comes, her hand flying up and covering the breathy whimper that spills from her. As silent shudders pass through her, I cup her breasts, squeezing their warm weight, feeling the pebbled nipples at the center of my palms.

With a few more wild plunges, I shower her inside, groaning into her neck, doing my best to stay as quiet as she was herself.

Together we go still. I sweep her hair aside and give the back of her neck one last little bite, then stroke down her ribs and waist. She follows me with her hips, emitting a note of disappointment, as I withdraw.

I turn her around and cradle her face in both hands, pressing my lips to hers for a long moment, both of us content just to be touching.

When we part, she reaches to push hair off my forehead. "Did you mean it, Legs?"

I'm not sure to which part she's referring, but I answer honestly, "I never say things I don't mean."

"You'll be my secret? I missed out on all that stuff like sneaking around with boys, making out in cars. I didn't go to high school—I just had a tutor. My first boyfriend was a glorified business arrangement, in my twenties. There have been no scandalous secrets in my life."

She trails off and looks at the carpet, then goes to flop face down on the bed.

I join her and sprawl out too, smoothing a hand down her back. "Talk to me, lovely."

She props on a hand and studies my face.

"It makes me a hypocrite to ask. I've spent months criticizing you for being a sleazy ho-bag, and now that you fucked some stellar O's out of me, I'm like, 'But could you be my sleazy ho-bag?' I'm actually starting to, uh, like you as a person." She rolls her eyes, and I'm not sure which of us she's mocking. "It seems shitty of me to exploit your nature for kicks."

"That's all it could be—'kicks'? Fun and games?"

She looks away. I suspect we're both remembering that moment on the boat in Spain, when I told her it wasn't a game.

"Maybe we could just go for it and keep it discreet," she suggests quietly, eyes focused on tracing a curve on the bedspread with her fingertip. "But if that makes you feel *objectified* or whatever, I can handle a no thanks."

I roll onto my back and put my hands behind my neck. "Are you hoping both that I will say yes and I will say no?"

"I acknowledge it's completely reckless, Cos. But if anyone could keep it casual, it's a womanizer like you. And...I need the distraction right now."

I recognize the truth in what she's saying. And I certainly cannot begrudge her a "distraction" during this painful time, however much her words may sting.

If I'm to win her, I must be in the race.

Timing. Strategy. Tenacity. Focus. Every moment, hunting for the opportunity for advancement.

And so—despite having told her moments ago that I never say things I don't mean—I toss the words between us like a dice roll.

"Certainly I can keep it casual." I lean across the empty space between us to kiss her. "Consider me your scandalous secret."

▀▄▀▄▀

The Monaco Grand Prix is nearly a hundred years old, and if it weren't already considered the crown jewel of international motor racing—the most prestigious, glamorous, and iconic event of the Formula 1 calendar—it wouldn't exist, due to its demanding and dangerous track layout. It's the only circuit with a race-length exemption...260 kilometers, rather than the minimum-required 305 kilometers.

A street course, it's narrow, winding, and bumpy, with elevation changes and corners "as tight as a nun's budget," as Owen says. It also has a tunnel section, in which the light-dark-light change is a blinding adjustment, and downforce on the car is temporarily altered due to the aerodynamic properties of the enclosed space.

Despite the slower average speeds at Monaco, racing incidents and the resultant presence of the safety car are common. There's almost no room for overtaking on the track, so qualifying in a strong position and executing clever pit strategy are critical. It's a highly technical race...and highly unforgiving.

Since Wednesday night, Phaedra and I have spent every possible stolen moment in each other's presence. Interestingly, we devote nearly as much time talking about the upcoming race as we do making love (a term she loathes, but which I cannot help using in my head). Our communication is curiously relaxed now that we've settled on our agreement.

"We should've been having strategy meetings naked all along." She laughed as we lay tangled together Friday night, sweaty and drifting on a tide of post-sex bliss, chatting about the upcoming qualifying session.

"I think," I replied, rolling her beneath me again, "this is a brilliant but impractical plan. Though I confess, many times in meetings, I've pictured you in nothing but the headset."

Race morning, Sunday, there's anxiety over the weather, with possible intermittent rain approaching. A street course is already tricky for grip—the surface isn't the same as on a track engineered specifically for racing, and road traffic means the presence of dirt and oil. Throw in a bit of rain and things become perilous. The tunnel section also complicates tyre choice, as it stays drier inside while the main part of the track is wet.

In the morning meeting, the team discuss multiple permutations of what could happen. Klaus notes—with an expression both approving and a bit sly—that Phaedra and I seem to be quite in tune, jumping into each other's sentences with intuitive ease. She does a convincing job of claiming it's nothing more than the result of an accidental, impromptu meeting over coffee yesterday, during which we discussed the race.

Already, after only a few days, I can read her expressions better for having seen them unguarded in bed. On the tail of Klaus's praise, I spot immediate—though subtle—signs of her relief. The coolness I've noticed in their dynamic since the Chinese GP appears to be thawing.

I've qualified third on the grid. In the reconnaissance lap, Phaedra and I discuss adjustments to the three systems that combine to supply rear braking. The balance feels excellent, but factors such as tyre degradation and the changing weight of the fuel load will cause this to evolve during the race. The right touch is essential. If things are off, understeer causes the car to feel lazy and unresponsive; too far in the other direction creates oversteer that could send me into a spin. The brakes are nearly as important as the steering wheel in controlling the direction the car is pointed.

A one-stop strategy is best in Monaco—it's imperative not to lose track position on circuits with such slim opportunity for overtaking. I'm starting on soft compound tyres and will make one stop to switch to hard compound for the rest of the race. This could change, should there be significant rain.

As the race begins, I maintain position through the scrum of the first corner. Phaedra is calm and encouraging, delivering periodic updates on weather radar along with her invaluable engineering input. Things are going beautifully until lap 21, when the beginning of rain asserts itself. Within three laps, a sprinkle becomes a steady drizzle.

"How long might this last?" I ask Phaedra.

"Could be twenty minutes," she replies easily. "How's it feel? Lot of chatter about switching to inters. Thoughts, Legs?"

It's probable the drivers ahead of me will watch and wait too, pushing a decision as late as manageable.

Phaedra and I discussed many possibilities last night. Aside from the team's plans A, B, and C, we bandied about our own informal plan D (as one might imagine, there were plenty of jokes about that particular letter of the alphabet).

The rain gets heavier in the next sector of the track, and before I reply to Phaedra's question, she speaks again: "Powell's boxing for inters."

"Radar?"

"Not ideal."

I creep through the hairpin at what feels like a snail's pace, round turn 8 and head into the tunnel, where the dry track buoys my optimism. I brace for the flare of bright sky as I emerge. The light quality, in that moment, feels more relevant than the weather forecast—the difference between theory and experience.

I tell Phaedra, "Feeling confident."

"Understood. Ollson boxing for inters now as well."

"Copy."

I'm questioning my gut feeling—the rain is quite heavy. But something tells me to wait longer and see if I can stick to a one-stop. My soft tyres are at least better under the current track conditions than mediums would have been.

In another lap I'm more certain this is the right strategy. I suspect other teams will regret having panicked. I'm feeling my tyre degradation, but the rain is clearing.

"Were we correct?" I ask Phaedra, knowing she'll understand my meaning.

She chuckles warmly. "That's plan D for 'damned straight,' Legs."

On lap 31, I box for hard tyres. The rain has stopped and a dry line is forming well. For several laps, the grip is still so precarious that my stomach is in my throat, but my unease dissipates as conditions improve and Phaedra tells me Olsson and Powell are making another pit stop. Suddenly I'm in first place—the car and my spirit both flying, a win in sight *on my sixth race with Emerald.*

For the next twenty-three laps, I lead the race.

I'm a force of nature.

Though my focus is 100 percent on the dozens of details rushing at me simultaneously, in the background of it all, a foundational pulse thrums through me: the presence of Phaedra.

We're an unstoppable combination.

A good drive already has the intense flow-state exhilaration of falling in love. The only thing that could top it is falling in love *during* a race.

Shooting out of the tunnel on lap 54, I'm headed for Nouvelle Chicane—about to lap João Valle—when disaster strikes.

He makes a pointless, jerky move as I'm alongside him, sending us careening in two directions like colliding billiard balls. A shuddering slam brings me to a halt, mind spinning, the hiss of adrenaline in my ears, loose tyre bouncing across the track in my peripheral vision.

"What the *fuck*?!" I shout, staring at the scarred barrier in disbelief as what's happened catches up to me. My heart is tripping in my chest. I smack the steering wheel with one hand, swamped with grief over the perfect win my race engineer and I were reeling in together.

"You're okay, Cos?"

"I'm *not* fucking okay!" I snarl. "That halfwit daddy's boy sent me into the wall! What was he trying for with that shit? Harrier told him to get out of my way, yes?"

"Race stewards are looking into it," Phaedra says, her voice smooth and certain.

My teeth grit in frustration. Behind me on track, cars edge past the sprawl of post-wreck detritus. I force myself to breathe slowly.

"Just glad you're all right," Phaedra adds, conspicuously neutral, though I can hear the tension in her tone.

I shake my head, eyes squeezed shut, mourning the loss of my victory.

So damned close…

"We had it," I groan. "We fucking *had* this one."

"Next time, Cos," she tells me. "We'll get it next time."

My eyes open as it connects with me, what she's said:

We'll get it next time.

We.

After the final-lap debacle in Bahrain just two months ago, she said, **You'll** *get it next time…*

I can't help a little smile inside my helmet as I climb out of the car.

14

MONTRÉAL

EARLY JUNE

PHAEDRA

Along with a photo of my grandmother's earrings, I emailed Natalia this message last night:

> You win, Nat. I fucked him before Silverstone.
>
> I'm sorry I hurt your feelings. There's no excuse. I miss my best friend. I promise I'm not saying this to be manipulative, but my dad is sick, and I'm scared. Please call me. I want to apologize in person. (And give you the earrings—they're yours, fair and square.)

Cosmin had to fly to Bucharest again a few days ago, and whatever the reason was, it had him in a bad mood. He flew in to Montréal yesterday and was completely wiped out after a seventeen-hour flight with a layover in London. When I saw him, I told him it wasn't a good idea to meet up for a shag.

"You need sleep way more," I said. "You look like death warmed over, and frankly, I'm not damaging my product."

The comment was meant to be lighthearted. But the look he gave me—patting my cheek with a weary smile and closing the door of his room, leaving me awkwardly standing in the hallway—held a bitterness that didn't seem entirely owing to lack of sex.

The next day, members of the team—Cosmin, Jakob, and a handful of engineers including myself—all do the track walk. The on-foot lap is a Thursday-of-race-week tradition, ninety scheduled minutes allowing drivers and their immediate team to discuss circuit features and changes, track surface, and other small details in a relaxed, hands-on way.

I've been nervous about seeming chummy with Cosmin ever since we decided to throw caution to the wind and become clandestine fuck buddies. I study the track with a serious scowl, hands stuffed in the pockets of my team blacks, and allow Engineering Director Lars to walk between Cos and me as we stride around the course.

At the Ponte de la Concorde corner, João Valle passes us, riding a kick scooter. Owing to the tangle at the Monaco GP between Cosmin and Valle, there are still hard feelings. It wouldn't have been so bad if Valle hadn't later caught wind of Cosmin's radio outburst.

When the "halfwit daddy's boy" comment made it to Valle, several witnesses said he shot back something in Portuguese that roughly translates to "fuck that motherless nephew of a Balkan thug," and...yeah. Not pretty. It hasn't escaped my notice that the thing Cosmin hates most is being mentioned in the same breath as his uncle.

Public apologies were exchanged and we all jetted off to the next continent, but today is the first time the two have been near each other since a grudging handshake in Monte Carlo.

Lars and I glance at Cos, watching for a reaction when Valle wends around us, showing off by doing a tailwhip like some middle schooler.

An impish smile perks up on Cosmin's face. "Playtime for you, João?" he calls out. "Quite jolly on your little toy. But racing is a man's game."

My shoulders stiffen when Valle makes a U-turn and heads back. He's stupidly good looking, and being absurdly wealthy— the eldest son of Brazilian sugar money—doesn't hurt his prospects in any sphere. He's a mediocre driver whose finest asset is the fat checks Papa Valle writes to Harrier. João's girlfriend is an Italian model who towers over him at nearly six feet. The kid leads a charmed life and is so frivolous that he makes devil-may-care Cosmin look as grim as a mortician by comparison.

"Are we going to have words, Ardelean?" Valle asks.

"*No*," I immediately reply for him.

"There have been words enough," Cosmin says. "We both know what happened in Monaco."

Valle's angel face is sullen in a way that would be a sexy pout if I found short, pretty-boy billionaires attractive. "It was a suspension issue," he grits out, his tan, muscular hands strangling the scooter handles. "Responding to adverse situations is your job. Or do you expect only a smooth path? Maybe fairies fly before your car and sprinkle the way with rose petals?"

Cosmin combs a hand through his hair and even in this moment of tension, I remember the feel of it last week when I was riding him and tangled my fingers in it when I came. I hope I'm not blushing.

"Are you offering?" Cosmin returns. "I'll get you a little pink basket."

"You're careless," Valle warns.

"And you're boring. Cară-te." Cosmin dismisses him with a flip of his hand.

He so often murmurs in Romanian mid-fuck that just the sound of it gets me wet now, and my nostrils flare as I huff out a sharp sigh, annoyed at my own weakness.

Lars glances at me—I think he assumes I'm about to say something about how the "suspension issue" excuse is bullshit. The crash was entirely the fault of Valle being a dipshit with no feel for his car.

"Yes, you are *so* cool," Valle sneers. "Estás a meter água." He kicks off to ride away.

"Give my regards to your girlfriend," Cosmin calls after him, and my stomach drops.

Rumor has it Valle's not the only man on the grid to have scaled that leggy peak—she and Cosmin supposedly had a one-nighter last year at Monza.

Valle's foot drops to the asphalt with a bark of shoe rubber and I'm sure there's going to be a fight.

"Jesus wept, Ardelean," I hiss. "Lay off before we have—"

Lars puts a hand on my arm, which frankly pisses me off, because not much makes me stabbier than men shushing me.

In my periphery I see Valle ride off, going for the moral high ground, or maybe mentally having acknowledged that Cos is eight inches taller and could paste him.

I yank my arm away, and my eyes go back and forth between Lars and Cosmin. "I was trying to prevent a scene," I snap.

"And now you are creating one," Cosmin replies smoothly. *"Excuse me?"*

"Rein in the temper," Lars states, his eyes flicking past me to where a group from Team Coraggio are drawing near. "Hide your feelings and let's get back to work."

I'm already seething when the barb Cosmin throws out next becomes the last straw.

"Miss Morgan is well practiced in hiding her feelings—she can be bloodless." His eyes shift from Lars to me when he adds, "But she is selective in applying this skill."

A chilly smile flits over his features before he continues his saunter down the track.

What. The. Actual. Fuck.

Bloodless? Is this selfish shitbag pouting, calling me cold or emotionless or something because I didn't put out last night? He can't seriously be offended that I joked about him being a product, can he?

With everything I'm going through, I'm appalled he'd be so self-absorbed. And borderline name-calling me in front of another team member? What a prick!

I hate him a million times more than I did months ago.

The Coraggio people have caught up, passing us with a critical side-eye. I know open bickering between members of any team becomes potent fuel for paddock gossip. But in my head, a haze of fury obscures every thought other than how I'm going to make it hurt the most when I tell Cosmin this shit is *so over*.

Ardelean is ruining my day. In the background during everything I do—the meeting, running analytics, the press conference—it beats in my head like distant drums: *How. Fucking. Dare. He.*

I'm dealing with so much already with the Mo situation, and Cosmin knows it. His piling on is the emotional equivalent of throwing someone a bowling ball when they're drowning. Over the course of the day, my nice, solid, satisfying anger disintegrates into bewildered hurt.

Klaus is walking into the paddock's dining room as I'm walking out with my food, and when he drapes an arm over my shoulders, I'm almost shocked—it's the first time he's been affectionate with me in weeks.

"How are you holding up, Schatzi?"

I swallow a bite of sesame noodles. "Hey, stranger. Thought I'd lost you."

He rumbles out a chuckle and follows me to an outside table where I sit and stab at my meal, sending him a nervous glance.

"I've always been here," he assures me, reclining into a chair.

"Have you?" I take a bite. "It's not like I need a nightly tuck in and bedtime story," I mumble around the food, "but you've been so, um, *businesslike*."

He sweeps a glance around us to see who's sitting nearby before lowering his voice and saying, "The situation with Edward is very difficult for me. I'm not handling it well, and perhaps it has made me distant."

He and Mo are best work-friends, and he's also the only person who calls my father Edward. Mo calls Klaus "Klausy," and occasionally "K-Dog," which is such boomer hilarity that I can't even.

"Understandable," I say nonchalantly.

I'm tempted to add, *It also has plenty to do with my apparent-ex-best-friend Natalia*, but this isn't the place to get into that topic, *or* Mo's cancer, which still isn't public knowledge. For that matter, I need a sense of where Klaus's head is on a possible Emerald acquisition.

"Wanna get dinner tonight?" I offer. "We should probably chat."

"I have a prior commitment." His dark eyes skate away.

I can't resist baiting him. "Ooh, is that a blush, Herr Franke? You generally have no problem owning the parade of F1 fangirls rolling through your bed like chocolates on an *I Love Lucy* assembly line, so I can't imagine why you look sheepish. Something you wanna tell me?"

One dark eyebrow lifts, and it's all we need: he knows I know, and in the space of just a few heartbeats, our connection links up again, crackling to life like an open comm channel.

"Dinner tomorrow instead?" he suggests with a smile.

I shrug as if the relief isn't killing me. "Sure, cool."

He reaches across the table for my hand. I pause mid-chew, then lay my fingers over his palm, tentative as a child surrendering a shoplifted item.

"I want you to be happy," he tells me, looking into my eyes in a way so significant-feeling that it freaks me out. I don't mean romantic—Klaus has never gone there, period. It just seems he's trying to tell me something indirectly.

I poke at a sesame seed in my molar, brow furrowing as I study his lean, handsome face and glittering eyes. My stomach drops as a horrible thought occurs to me: *Is it too late? Is the deal done, and Mo hasn't told me?*

"What do you mean?" I manage, my nose prickling with the threat of tears. "Are you firing me?"

His open-hearted laugh—something I haven't heard in a while—is the best sound, and my shoulders relax as I crack a smile to mirror his.

"Ah, Schatzi. *No.*" He closes one eye and shakes a finger at me. "You're a pessimist. Kind words are not always the sugar hiding a bitter pill."

15

MONTRÉAL

PHAEDRA

I'd take kind words *or* bitter ones from Nat at this point, but by day's end there's still nothing. Silence.

The fact that she doesn't bother replying despite my mention of Mo being sick settles a cold realization in my stomach: I need this friendship more than she does. All these years I've thought I was the alpha and she was the sidekick—the arrogance of being a child prodigy!

Humility is a bitch.

I've been back at my hotel room for a half hour and have changed into sleep shorts and a tank top. I'm pacing, drinking Glenmorangie and soda while eating a barge-size bar of salted-caramel-filled chocolate and keeping an ear out for Ardelean, who has the suite kitty-corner from mine.

When I hear the elevator, I walk to the door and press my

eye to the peephole. Seconds later a blond blur passes, and his door opens and closes.

Reece is staying just down the hall. I don't think she's in her room yet, but I can't risk any chance of her seeing me knocking at Cosmin's suite, especially half-dressed. I shoot off a text to him.

Open your fucking door.

The read receipt pops up, and I hear his room click open a moment later.

Dropping my phone on the bed, I charge into the hall and beeline to where Cosmin stands in his doorway. He's opening his mouth to say something when I smack his chest hard with both palms, letting out a furious sound between a growl and a screech, teeth clenched. He stumbles back, hands raised, and I follow him inside, delivering a harder shove.

"What was that bullshit this morning?" I demand, hands fisted at my sides. "'*Bloodless*'?"

He takes a deep breath and releases it in a nervous chuckle.

"Don't you laugh at me!" I snarl, shooting my arms out to slam into his chest again. "This isn't funny!" Another punch-shove.

He snatches my wrists as I'm preparing to double slug him again. "Stop that this instant."

Baring my teeth, I kick his ankles while wrenching to escape. I'm apoplectic with indignation that he's holding my arms—despite the hypocrisy, since I'm basically punching him—and muttering inarticulate fragments as my bare feet jab him.

"Don't you . . . Motherfucker, I'll . . . What are? . . . Okay, that's it, you son of a . . . *grrrrr!* Let me go . . . I will *end you!*"

I get frustrated enough at the restraint that I pull his arms closer in the hopes of delivering a bite.

That seems to be a line in the sand for Cosmin when he spots my intention, because he barks out "Hey!" just before ducking to flop me over his shoulder like the caveman he joked about being when we were in Santorini. Except this caveman isn't playing a sexy game.

He strides to the bed, and I yank his shirt up in back to get at bare skin. The "red mist" has descended, and I'm not sure how to dial it back. It's as if everything that's ever hurt me is going to be punished through Cosmin, and I'm beyond caring whether that's fair.

I manage one good rake, though my fingernails aren't long.

"Ai de pula mea!" Cosmin gasps. The hand he has wrapped around my left ankle tightens reflexively, and I explode into rage, flailing like a lunatic, loose hair roiling around me. I only dimly register the very real possibility that I might fall and be injured.

"Control yourself!" he orders, doing his best to get a better hold on me, like a juggler whose bowling pins are escaping him. "Bloody stop, dammit!"

I'm thrashing so much that his hand connects in a smack with my bare thigh as he tries to adjust his grip and prevent me from falling. I yelp and choke out a sob, tumbling to the bed.

His arms are extended to guide my landing, his face drawn as if he's in pain too. He reaches to touch my knee and I unsuccessfully kick at him with a screech.

"Are you all right? I'm so sorry, dragă—I didn't intend to strike you."

I stand on my knees on the bed, twisting to inspect the back of my thigh. Swallowing tears, I rub the spot as I glare at him. "You asshole, is this how you are?" Suddenly I see a place to twist the knife. "Go ahead and hit me, like your uncle hit you and your sister. Are you just like him?"

Cosmin blanches, taking several steps back until his feet run into a dresser. His hands flatten against it, posture like a burglar who's been caught in a searchlight.

I open my mouth to apologize, but my anger won't let the words past the lump in my throat. A sigh deflates him, and he walks to the sofa and sits, cupping his face.

I pivot to sit on the edge of the bed. "Don't you dare," I growl. "Don't make me pity you after you hurt my feelings this morning and embarrassed me. This isn't even Steven."

His hands slide off and he looks at me, his wavy hair—the same color as the caramel in the chocolate I was just eating—disheveled, eyes bleak. "Who is he?"

I blink at him. "Who is who?"

"Steven."

"Oh, for fuck's sake." I stand and walk to the mirror. "You're being cute and clueless about English because you know it's a weakness of mine when you do it." I scrutinize the faint pink mark on my thigh.

"I didn't know you found that attractive," Cosmin says, tired. "You seem impatient when it happens." He stands and pulls his shirt off. "And with many other things."

I'm torn between suspicion and guilt, recognizing the truth in what he's saying as well as the resignation with which he delivers the words.

I *am* impatient. I lash out without thinking. I go for the thing I know will hurt most. I throw the last cookie to the birds so Aislinn can't have it either. I take potshots at Natalia. *Fuck.*

"Why are you undressing?" I demand, changing the subject. "Don't get any fancy ideas, Legs. Not happening."

"I'm taking a shower. I'd just arrived when you texted." As he passes me on his way to the bathroom, I see the twin claw marks on his lower back, one deep enough that it's bleeding.

"Oh, fuck, Cos." I stand up. "You're bleeding."

"It's fine."

He rounds the corner and I hear the water go on. I sit on the bed. My eyes drift over the objects on his bedside table: a glass bottle of water, cordless headphones, a novel called *The Baron in the Trees*. There's a bookmark tucked inside, and I pick it up to snoop.

The bookmark is a child's colored-pencil drawing of a Formula 1 car—Emerald's—with sponsor names written as if copied by someone who can't read. It's long and thin, so the young artist has filled the space behind the car with "speed lines" and billows of smoke. I flip back a few pages and peruse what Cosmin might've read before sleeping last night.

Minutes later, the water turns off and I hear him brush his teeth. He comes out, a towel around his hips.

I hold up the bookmark with a weak smile. "Hopefully the smoke isn't prophetic."

He merely nods, going to his suitcase and taking out a pair of blue pajama bottoms, giving them a shake before stepping into them, turned away.

"I didn't expect you to be here still," he says, speaking over his shoulder.

His profile against the soft glow of dusk in the big window is striking, and my heart twists, sad for everything we're doing wrong.

He comes to the bed and props a stack of pillows against the ornate headboard before sitting as far from me as possible. I watch him sidelong. Ugh, his stupid torso is a work of art and I don't want to love looking at it. His neck is strong, shoulders broad, chest and stomach defined by polygons you could set your watch to. His skin is smooth and naturally golden.

After only a few weeks wherein we've managed a dozen covert fucks, my fingers already remember the lines and textures of him like the words to an old song. It's as if my hands are touching him right now, the thumbs feathering over his exactly right non-weird nipples (why are most guys' nipples so gross? Cosmin's are perfection) and gliding up to follow the long darts of collarbone, then resting on the hard, teardrop deltoids of his shoulders. I glance away before he catches me staring.

"So," I venture. "Who's supposed to, like, say shit first? How does this work?"

He rubs a hand over his face. "I hope you'll understand I would prefer not to talk now." His nostrils flare a little as he levels a cool gaze at me. "As you're so fond of pointing out, we are not dating. No discussion is necessary."

My embarrassment is acute, and I scramble to my feet off the other side of the bed. "Fine—suits me. Enjoy your evening."

"Wait..."

I fold my arms, and after a long silence where he doesn't continue, I look back.

"Give me a moment." He lifts his hands and hovers them near his head. "I have many things in my mind. Please stay."

I woodenly lie down. He has all the pillows, and the way my hands are clasped over my chest as I lie flat and rigid makes me look like I'm preparing to be sacrificed.

He grabs a pillow from behind himself. "Here. Lift."

I comply, and he inserts the pillow beneath my head. Another tense minute goes by, punctuated by the thin sound of traffic horns below and faint chuckle of a distant helicopter.

"You're apparently not going to apologize for making me look like a twat this morning," I say. "Sorry you got your nose out of joint over not getting laid last night, but calling me 'bloodless' for *not servicing you* was selfish and rude. And I was joking about the 'product' thing. Christ, Cos—my dad has inoperable cancer. Maybe give me a break if I don't express everything perfectly all the time?"

He scoots down and turns on his side, mashing a pillow beneath his neck. "My comment wasn't about the lack of sex. I was hurt. What I truly wished for last night was someone to talk to. My trip to Bucharest was difficult. A bit of compassion from you would not have been unwelcome."

A ripple of shame goes through me.

"But at my door," he continues, "you felt compelled to point out—once *again*—that I'm essentially a business asset whose cock you like when you're bored."

He's absolutely right, so of course I go on the offensive, because I am—as my mother once said—borderline feral and don't know how to play nicely with others.

"We're not *friends*, Cosmin."

His jaw clenches hard enough that I see the muscle twitch. He rolls onto his back, jamming his hands behind his head. "Yes. Thank you for clarifying."

"And when I'm '*bored*'? That's not accurate."

He scoffs. "My mistake—the term you used was 'a distraction.' Iartă-mă, te rog."

My eyes narrow. "I'm gonna assume that was something insulting."

He lifts his head and pins me with a look of disbelief. "You're a very suspicious woman. You're *closed*. Like a fist." He lifts a hand and squeezes to illustrate his point. "It means 'forgive me, please.' Though it was meant with sarcasm."

"Yeah, no shit."

"You once thought the same thing about 'dragă,' asking me 'Does this mean bitch?' You are maddening! You expect the worst of everyone, and fool that I am, I align to your expectations because you make me fucking crazy. Why am I so—?"

He shuts his mouth in a firm line and retreats into silence.

I roll onto my stomach and prop on my elbows. "Why are you so...?" I prompt.

His critical gaze touches on me before cutting away. "I refuse to give you compliments while the sting of your insult lingers."

"What about *your* insult?" I retort, sitting up straighter. Suddenly the rest of what he said catches up with me. "Wait, what? *Compliments?*"

"Never mind."

I rest my chin on my folded arms, watching his chest rise and fall. *Aaauuuggghhh, this is so goddamned stupid. It's easier if we just fuck.*

I do want to ask him what happened in Bucharest. But if we start doing that "talking about feelings" shit, it's like a relationship, and that's not our agreement.

Hoping to switch gears and entice him into a nice, straightforward "let's not get all angsty" fuck, I say, "You know what we should do right now?"

I allow the question to hang, arranging my expression into something provocative.

He rubs his eyes, missing my artless attempt at seduction. "Yes. We should apologize."

"For fuck's sake." I shake my head. "Okay, fine. I'm not good at this though. And I suspect you're no better. We're not relationship people."

He rolls onto his side again to make eye contact. "This is an assumption of yours."

"Oh, really?" I say with a smirk. "You're suddenly the 'marry' in the 'fuck, marry, kill' game?"

"I would love to marry one day. Are you surprised?"

Actually I am, and for a moment I fall silent, trying to read his expression. Deciding there's absolutely no way I'm going there, I scoot closer and lower my voice. "Let's get the apologies out of the way and do what we do best."

I reach over him and grab the bottled water, unscrewing it and drinking some so my breath doesn't smell like scotch. When I set the bottle down, I curl over his hip to peek at his back. The deeper scratch is still bleeding slightly.

I return to my spot on the bed, cross-legged, and look him in the eyes. His mood is hard to decrypt—there's suspicion, hurt, a sober watchfulness. But also lust. Those gray-blue eyes are dilated black as new tyre rubber in the rain.

"I'm sorry I clawed you," I begin. "And also that I said the thing about your uncle."

My focus angles down at one of my hands, and I press my thumbnail into my knee, jabbing little crescents into my skin and watching them fill in.

Cosmin puts his hand over mine to stop me, and I meet his eyes. I take a deep breath.

"And I'm sorry I suck at being friends and didn't talk with you last night." I shake my head. "This'll sound like bullshit, but I'm *not well socialized*, Cos. I have very little skill with compromise or *human* mechanics. I'm awesome with machines and data but shit with people."

His hand is still on top of mine, and he moves his thumb rhythmically, caressing my knuckles. After a lull stretches out for a minute so seemingly eternal you'd think it'd fallen into a black hole, he lifts my hand and kisses the fleshy base of my thumb.

"Thank you for that. Not only the apology, but sharing some of yourself. It is a rare thing." His hand glides up my bare arm. "I cannot apologize enough for accidentally striking you. Please forgive me."

"Iartă-mă, te rog," I whisper.

He encircles the point of my elbow with a fingertip, then his caress glides up to my shoulder and down into the V of my strappy tank top.

"Also I apologize for using the term which spurred your anger," he adds. "'Bloodless' was an unfair word."

My eyes drift closed, enjoying his touch shimmering across my skin.

"Draga mea."

My eyes open, and he cradles my face with a speculative expression.

He presses those gorgeous, pillowy lips together, moistening them. "I would like to propose an alteration to our arrangement."

"Um..."

"You say we're not 'relationship people.' But we have just navigated apologies after an argument. We are improving our relationship skills."

I open my mouth to protest, and he lays two fingers over my lips.

"What if we practice with each other? Behave as if this were more than sex?" He scoots closer, eyes shining. "In the privacy of our time together, we can pretend to be in love. Fall asleep together after sex, instead of running away. Fight and make up. Compromise." He brushes my lips with a soft kiss. "Make love sometimes, rather than fuck."

My pulse dances at the term "make love," which I've always thought was the hokiest shit ever, but hearing it in his lilting accent makes it sound *very different*.

I'm not hating it. And that terrifies me.

I scowl. "Pretending to be in a relationship is the same amount of energy as being in one. I don't wanna work that hard."

"It's practice." He kisses me again. "Tomorrow, we practice on track. Tonight, in bed."

His hand is cupping my breast, teasing the nipple with his thumb through the cotton. With the next kiss, his tongue coaxes my mouth open and sweeps inside, stroking. I feel the strap of my tank top slide down, and I move my arm to give him room to bare my breast. A little zap of expectant pleasure surges between my legs.

"What would, um—?"

My words are absorbed by his intoxicating kisses. Dear God, this idiot is a great kisser—he has something like the tactile version of perfect pitch. Our lips slide and tease, delivering small bites and licks, and dammit, I've completely forgotten what I was going to say.

The words come back to me and I grab them.

"What would...the next step be...if I agree?" I ask between kisses.

He sucks my lower lip, then pulls away, smiling, and stands to remove his pajama bottoms. I try not to stare at his jutting cock, but it's rather majestic, to be honest, and I know what he can do with it. I rise onto my knees and eagerly remove my clothes too.

"The next step," he tells me, lying back down and gathering me into his arms, "is I make love to you." Sketching a path of kisses down my neck, he strokes my back, over the curve of my ass, along my thigh, grasping behind my knee to bring my leg up to rest on his hip.

"Sounds like you're doing all the work," I say just above a whisper.

His hand slips between us and he places it over me, two fingers resting at my entrance and his thumb stroking my clit in languid circles. I gasp and tip my hips in encouragement.

"It will be an effort for you, I think," he says, gently mocking. "I know how you are. Always fierce. You want hard, fast. A sexual blitzkrieg." His fingers sink into my wet heat, and I moan. "Impatient girl. If I take you on the scenic route, can you relax and enjoy the view?"

Those strong, elegant fingers slide in deeper, curling to massage the little patch of pure bliss that harmonizes with what he's doing to my clit. His mouth goes to my nipple and he lightly sucks, rolling and stroking with the tip of his tongue.

The scenic route is sounding pretty awesome on one hand (no pun intended), considering I want him to do this approximately forever. But unease shivers through me, because the scenic route is also a long time to be in a car with someone.

What if you run out of things to say? What if conversation gets *personal*?

A memory of Santorini—being annoyed when he wouldn't tell me his fear and I accused him of being evasive—swims up, and I wonder: *What changed?*

He kisses my lips again. "So beautiful...so beautiful," he's murmuring against me, and I'm simultaneously swooning and calling bullshit, because this guy has reputedly banged half the runway at Paris Fashion Week, and I'm, y'know, I guess *cute*, but short and grouchy, with a big ass and the foul mouth of a longshoreman.

He starts a trail down my body, and everywhere his mouth touches is like something in one of those fairy tales where flowers sprout from the hoofprints of unicorns. My skin is alive, tingling.

"Tu esti sufletul meu pereche," he whispers, and I have no clue what he's on about, but frankly he could be ordering pizza in Romanian and it'd still make me weak in the knees—the knees he parts and settles between.

He presses an almost reverent kiss to my clit before he spreads me gently with his thumbs and applies his tongue and lips to the task of bringing me *almost* to climax three times. Again and again, he lets my arousal partially retreat like a cat toying with a mouse until I whimper and mock beat his shoulders.

"Don't be evil!" I wail as he kisses my inner thigh. I'm twitching hard inside, and it feels like a river of silver glitter is rushing through me. "Let me come, dammit..."

He sits up and takes my hands, pulling me upright onto my knees and turning me to hold the headboard.

My legs are humming with pre-orgasmic tension, and I'm dying for him to get his cock in me. I close my eyes, waiting for him to grab my hips. Instead, he nudges my knees wider and slides under the archway I'm creating, his head inches from my pussy.

"Lower, sweet one," he instructs. "Let me taste that lovely cunt."

My inhale snags in my throat, both lust and embarrassment surging through me in a wave. I look down at his passion-splayed pupils, the shine of his lips, already wet from licking me to the edge of control.

His hands grasp my thighs in encouragement, and my muscles tense. There's nothing I want more than to settle over his mouth and have him finish what he's started, but I'm too shy.

"Cosmin," I falter.

"Mmm?" He lifts his head to deliver one tempting stroke of his tongue, then reclines with a sultry smile.

"I don't, um, I don't know about this. We should just do it the regular way. Right? I don't want to suffocate you or something."

He chuckles. "You won't. I promise."

"But it, uh, it seems impolite? Like, sitting on *a person*."

His left eyebrow goes up. "But *this* person very much wants you to. I'm aching to see those sweet tits bounce as you ride my face." He kisses my inner thigh. "Do you not wish to, or have you simply not done this before?"

Clearing my throat, I swallow hard. "I haven't. I kind of thought this was mostly made up—one of those sex things people say they do, but no one actually does."

He squeezes my ass with both hands, then eases two fingers inside me and slides his thumb against my clit, waking up the hunger in me that was retreating from sheer nerves.

"You can be adorably innocent." He brushes my clit hood up to gingerly glide over the nerve, and I gasp. "I look forward to showing you all those things you think are 'made up.' I assure you, draga mea…" He lifts his head again to sweep me with a long, hot lick. "People actually do them all."

"Oh God." I'm so turned on I'm afraid I might drip right on him, and when I clench my pussy it sends a wave of tingling everywhere.

"Now come here so I can taste you."

The edge of command in his voice strips away my reticence, and I widen my knees to get closer. My hands are white-knuckled on the headboard right until his mouth claims me in a way so unlike anything I've felt before that I'm stunned silent.

He's *everywhere down there.* Holy hell. His tongue is inside me, then plowing through my labia, then stroking my clit with flat, insistent licks, then doing something swirly and intense as if he's overcome, madly devouring every inch of me.

For the first minute I think, *This is awesome but it's not going to get me off—there's too much happening*, then the pre-climax steamroller starts barreling down from some side street where it had been parked.

It's not like the usual buildup; it's coming from a deeper place. The focal point is my clit, but there's a bright energy concentrated in my entire pelvis, like a hidden room behind my navel where a party is raging.

I don't even realize I am, in fact, riding his face. Not until he groans in ecstasy and I register the undulation of my hips and the fact that I'm deliriously mumbling encouragement, my thighs trembling, one hand now planted behind me, digging into his chest while the other grasps the headboard, which knocks on the wall as I writhe against his mouth.

"That feels so good, I don't...Yes, I want...Oh God please...That's fucking amazing, never stop...ohgodohgodohgod Cosmin, I'm..."

My pleas wrench off as a staggering orgasm rolls through me. There's nowhere my body can hide from the euphoria, right down to my flexing toes as I let out a shriek that I can only hear at half volume owing to the rushing white noise in my ears.

His hands caress my ass, my hips, soothing me as I settle back down to earth, shuddering. My legs are so weak I feel like I might collapse, and my eyes are squeezed tight.

He shifts from beneath me and I smack my other hand onto the headboard, breathing hard. His arms cradle me, laying me on my back, then kneeling beside me, he runs his hands reverently up my torso and stops at my face, smoothing my cheekbones with his thumbs.

"You're stunning, my sweet girl."

He kisses my lips, and I reach for him, pulling him on top of me. We merge so naturally, his cock filling my soaked pussy, drenched inside and out. The lavish wetness between our bodies creates a lush sliding as he rocks into me. Almost immediately I'm climbing the peak a second time, fingers seizing Cosmin's muscular ass, pulling him deeper, my legs splayed shamelessly as I pant and moan.

"Go hard, go hard," I beg. "I'm nearly there again..."

His hands sweep behind my head, and he kisses me deeply. "No," he whispers.

My eyes snap open, annoyed.

"*There* you are," he teases before giving my lower lip a bite.

What he's doing is perfect—he's hitting everything just right, and the long, lazy strokes are like the best kind of massage. It's an orgasm-inducing version of the relaxed bliss of having someone brush your hair.

My body's practically lighting up from the inside, exuding a golden glow matching the color of Cosmin's eyelashes where the lamplight gilds them. It's as if we've been tuned to the same frequency, and—because apparently I'm such a nerd that even sex isn't invulnerable to my mathematical musings—I'm seeing sine waves coast up and down, gliding the way his hips are.

His kissing is so focused and artful, I'm legit impressed at his multitasking. We've never kissed this much while his cock is in me, and I'm feeling at once treasured and *very, very exposed*. I turn my head away and put my forehead against his shoulder. The hot, wet friction of us is killing me.

"Ochii tăi sunt frumoşi," he murmurs, using his thumb to gently turn my head to face him again. "Look at me with those beautiful eyes, sweet girl."

I peek at him and all but drown in his vivid, stormy-sky gaze.

"Is that the 'lovemaking' part—talking?" I ask, so vulnerable in his embrace that I can't *not* mock a bit.

I have to punch holes in what I'm feeling just to release the pressure so I don't say one of the mushy things swirling through my brain. Meanwhile, imminent climax is gathering throughout my body, a net sweeping up every atom.

"What would you say right now," he asks, "were you in love with me?"

"I'm not," I instantly reply.

"Yes, we are only practicing." He pushes in deep, so goddamned deep, grinding against me. "Someday you'll be in love. Someday a man who deserves you will whisper his secrets into your mouth and you'll light up like you've swallowed starlight."

He kisses me slow and sultry, and my legs wrap around him, greedy for every inch. How did he know I was feeling lit up from inside? There's nowhere to hide, and if I weren't a minute from coming I'd push him the hell off me and go back to my room without a second glance and finish things myself.

Or would I? Um.

"I might say—" The words stall in my throat. I turn my head again, closing my eyes, shutting him out and chasing the orgasm creeping up to claim me.

"I know what I'd say, if I were holding the woman I love in my arms."

Cosmin pushes deep again, and I moan. He kisses my shoulder, my neck. His fingers move in my hair, and the sliding on my scalp is an added splash of pleasure, compounding the sweet ache pushing me to the edge.

"I would tell her that her face is the first image which comes to me in the morning—her plump lips, bewitching freckles, forest-green eyes..." His hands tighten in my hair, and I suspect he's close too. "The way her smile detonates in my heart like a Roman candle, the way I want to kiss away her little scowls and pouts."

A ripple of something both blissful and pained dances across his expression, and he lays his full weight on me—my God it's fucking heaven—and slides his hands down my arms to dovetail our fingers, moving our joined hands above my head. The delectable thrusting of his cock is driving me half crazy, and my locked ankles flex at his lower back.

"I'd tell her she lives in my soul, and I in hers." His voice is ragged, and with a broken sound he grits his teeth, trying to hold back for me. His movement pauses before he clearly loses the battle with self-control and surges into me hard and high, crying out.

Something about his surrender is so touching that my chest prickles with unexpected emotion, and as I feel his hot release, the golden net around me closes and lifts me high.

My legs drop and splay wide as I churn my hips to meet his last shuddering thrusts, surfing a wave of a climax that leaves me breathless. But not *quite* breathless, because—*what the holy hell? Is that **me** speaking?*—I hear myself saying, "I love you...oh fuck, I do..." and how is it both so right and so wrong? Have I lost my mind?

I jerk a hand from his and clap it over my mouth, and he pulls it away and kisses me hard. Once I get a breath, I back-pedal like mad.

"I didn't mean... Seriously, that's... Oh, Jesus Christ, Cos. I only meant that's what I'd say if I was in love—"

"I know, dragă. Nu-ţi fie ruşine de tine. There's no need for shame."

"I really didn't—"

"Please." His hand covers my lips gently. "Don't say you didn't mean it." He moves off me and gathers me against his chest. "Let me enjoy this lie," he whispers into my hair.

As our heartbeats align and settle, I listen to the steady music of his breathing, and wonder if it's a lie after all.

16

ROMANIA

MID-JUNE

COSMIN

The Ardelean Foundation children's home, Vlasia House, is midway between Balotesti and Snagov. It's a lovely, forested area near the water, with trails and small meadows.

The building is fifteen thousand square feet and sits on thirty acres. The ground floor has the kitchens, a massive dining room to fit sixty children and staff, and the administrative offices. The second floor has twenty bedrooms for the boys and girls, in addition to those for staff. The upper floor contains classrooms, a recreation room, and a library. The building is plain but surrounded by lavish gardens—both flowers and food crops—maintained by the children, which lends a softening effect.

When Viorica and I pull slowly up the driveway in her silver Dacia Duster, I see kids squeeze against the classroom windows upstairs. A head of white-blond hair bounces up and down in the crowd of children like a pogo stick—nine-year-old Crina, who made the bookmark Phaedra commented upon in Montréal.

A group of the first-year students stands in the south garden with their teacher Domnisoara Petrescu, gathering early vegetables. Warmth floods my chest at the sight of their faces, chattering and pointing at us.

"I am happiest here," I say, almost to myself.

"As am I." My sister shuts off the car, quietly watching the children with me.

After a minute, she reaches for my hand and squeezes it. The tension that has hovered throughout our half-hour drive, after an earlier quarrel, eases.

When Viorica told me I needn't rent a car because she could pick me up in Bucharest, I was surprised—typically she's far too busy to meet me at the airport. But she said she'd been in the city on business, about which she was evasive.

It was a further surprise to see her in a dress and heels, hair loose, wearing lipstick and jewelry. Working with children as she does, her attire tends toward sensible and stain resistant, without cosmetics to be smudged or accessories to be snagged by little hands.

I thought she'd had an afternoon date, the way she frowned self-consciously when I commented on her outfit. When I picked up a thick manila envelope on the passenger's seat as I got into the car, she snatched it away and tossed it into the back seat. My anger coasted in on a wave of suspicion as I realized she'd been to see Grigore Lupu about the donation.

A heated argument in the parking lot followed, in which respective accusations of deception and selfishness were thrown with the merciless precision only siblings can wield. She threatened to walk away and leave me to drive to Vlasia House alone if I wouldn't drop the issue, and a stiff silence rode north with us.

Viorica releases my hand now, giving it a pat.

"I can see Irini Petrescu's blush all the way across the yard," she murmurs with amusement. "She fancies you, Cosmin."

"Rubbish." But I return my sister's smile, relieved to be back in her good graces.

"She'd make an ideal wife. Smart, pretty, devoted. An excellent seamstress and cook. Lovely singing voice."

"These would be selling points in another era. Just how old *are* you, Rica?" I tease.

She jabs me in the ribs and I recoil, laughing.

"Imp!" she mock scolds. "You could do far worse than a good woman like Irini."

"It would be unprofessional," I protest, not having the heart to say the truth—that Irini Petrescu is sweet but timid and would be a poor match for me.

I watch her out the window and note the honest delight on the young teacher's face as she allows little Nicu to place an earthworm on her palm.

"Relia and Spiridon are married," Viorica points out, mentioning our head cook and mathematics teacher.

"Their positions are lateral. You and I employ Irini."

I look over at ginger-haired Ursule, her fingers laced through the wire fence that keeps deer from the vegetables. She grins and sticks out her tongue when I catch her eye.

Popping the door open, I tell Viorica over my shoulder, "Also I am currently pursuing a relationship that might have potential."

I close the car door and wave at the children, calling out a greeting. Irini offers a shy smile, then smooths the non-worm-holding hand through her dark hair to arrange it. Behind me I hear Viorica exit the car.

"Cosmin, wait." She trots around to loop an arm through mine. "What's this? 'Relationship'? I've never heard you use the word. You must tell me more."

"When there's more to tell."

Irini opens the gate and a dozen children flood out, tumbling toward us with laughter and questions. Curly-haired Radu launches himself at my legs and scales me, climbing to my shoulders for a ride into the house.

«*Hello to you too, young mountaineer!*» I tell him, draping my hands over his shoes to stabilize him. Twisting toward Viorica, I say in English, "We should install a climbing wall for the children."

Raising her eyebrows significantly, she replies, "We can have that, and many other things, given enough money. That is all it takes, Cosmin—*money.*"

The little ones caper around us as we stroll to the wide front steps, and Irini joins us, Ursule riding on her hip. Walking like this—Irini and I both carrying children—I can imagine another fate where I might have had a gentle country wife with soft eyes and strong hands.

But in my mind the fierce green fire in Phaedra's eyes yet burns, and echoing in my ears is the sound of her crying out *I love you!* as she fell apart in my arms.

▚▚▚▚▚

Țuică—a plum brandy—is usually served before a meal, but there are strict rules at Vlasia House about alcohol consumption: only after the children are in bed, and a single glass for those who wish to partake.

Of the twenty-two staff members, a dozen including myself are gathered for a late toast, games, and conversation. Viorica is discussing a library expansion with our language and history instructors, a group of four are playing whist, Relia and Spiridon are bent over a game of backgammon, and Irini is seated with me on the balcony.

She's wearing a summer dress, blue with flowers. Her legs are propped on the railing, and light shines through the fabric, outlining the contour of a pair of attractive legs. Her hair is gathered at one side of her neck, loosely tied with a ribbon, and pearl earrings she didn't have on earlier sway from her ears.

Her profile is girlish, with a small, sloped nose and fringe of bangs cut short. She's near my age, twenty-seven or twenty-eight, and I've noted an Orthodox cross on the wall of her room in passing.

During our conversation, she looks over her shoulder several times when she hears Viorica laugh. I wonder if she's worried about being caught flirting. Though if that's what she's doing, it's so subtle as to be imperceptible.

We finish our brandy, and the group inside begins to disperse. Through the open French doors I hear my sister bidding people good night. Viorica appears in the doorway, holding it with one hand. Her head is relaxed, tipped to one side, and her golden curls glow in the lamplight. It lifts my heart to see her happy.

I stand and offer my chair, going to lean against the balcony railing.

Viorica's gaze shifts from Irini to me. *«You two should walk down to the lake,»* she suggests. *«The irises are in bloom, and it's a full moon.»*

I give an easy smile to hide my annoyance at her matchmaking. *«That sounds enjoyable,»* I reply, hoping my words aren't a disappointment to Irini, *«but I am very tired. I was moments from going to bed.»*

Irini's eyes brighten, a reaction I don't expect.

«I could use a walk—I'm a bit restless.» She meets Viorica's eye. *«If you'd like to go see the lake...»*

Viorica swallows the last of her brandy. *«I am tired as well. It's been a long day.»*

Irini nods, twisting the stem of her glass where it sits on the chair arm. *«I should sleep. There is much to do tomorrow.»* She stands, and in a faltering gesture extends a hand to shake with me. *«Always a pleasure to see you.»*

She turns to Viorica and offers her hand. Viorica opens her palm and Irini lays her own atop it for a moment, then pulls it back and hurries inside.

I settle into the chair she vacated. Viorica is resting her

eyes, and takes a slow, contented breath. I tap the back of her hand with a fingertip. "I suspect I am not the Ardelean who makes Domnisoara Petrescu blush," I say just above a whisper, switching to English.

Her eyes snap open and she pins me with a stunned look. "Don't be absurd."

"I can't believe I never noticed." I shake my head, smiling. "It's obvious."

"No such thing."

"Rica?"

"Mmm?" She examines the interior of her empty glass.

"Look at me."

She rolls her eyes. "What?"

"I think this is not news to you—Irini's affection."

"She's lonely," Rica mutters. "That's all."

"That doesn't dictate one's romantic preferences."

"Truly, I thought her admiration was pointed at you, until moments ago."

Throwing a glance over my shoulder into the vacant room, I ask, "Now that things are clear, how do you feel?"

She closes her eyes again. "I'm flattered."

"Flattered and interested?"

"Cosmin," she says with a sigh. "Even if I were to...what is the word?" She waves a finger back and forth between us.

"Reciprocate?"

"Yes. *Reciprocate* such feelings, she is too young for me. And you know I don't date—I've no time for such nonsense." She lifts her hands. "My life is Vlasia House."

I recline in the chair, staring at the bright stars overhead. Summer breeze rustles the trees, and the crickets saw out their music.

"Viorica. If you might find love—"

"*Enough*." Her voice is hard, final. "I have a foundation to run. I'm too short on time for a social life." After a pause, she quietly adds, "Short on time, short on money."

I open my mouth to speak, defensive, but intuition tells me Rica is about to say more. I silence myself, waiting.

"Do you think we have magic elves here like Saint Nicholas?" Her tone is bleak. "The investments, grants, your money from Emerald...it keeps the ship sailing. But we lack the capital to expand." She pauses. "It's the reason I spoke further with Grigore."

I glare at her. "Ce pușcă mea? I knew it! That fucking monster Lupu."

"Calm yourself," Viorica snaps.

"I thought we were in agreement that—"

"Yes, *you thought*," she cuts in. "And I let you think it." Covering her eyes with one pale hand, she adds, "He is not quite the monster you see him as. Your perspective is uninformed. Not everything is black and white, little brother. You don't know the whole story. That man *saved* me, and yes, it's complicated. But I need you to stop pitying me because the real monster was our uncle. And you were the one who had to remain with *him*."

She stands and goes inside, the click of the shoes she wore for Grigore Lupu fading as she walks away.

17

AUSTRIA

LATE JUNE

PHAEDRA

I'm at a two-top table on the hotel patio—scrolling through track data on my iPad, about to slice into a nice salmon Benedict for breakfast—when brown suede high-heeled boots step into my peripheral vision.

Assuming someone is going to ask for my unused chair, I glance up and am stunned motionless by the sight of Natalia standing over me with a tentative smile.

She lifts a hand and waggles her fingers. "Um. Hi?"

I leap up so fast that I bash the table with my thigh and almost tip it over. Nat's hand shoots out to stabilize it, and she laughs—a sound that strangles off into a cough as I tackle her in a crushing hug.

"*Holyfuckingshit!*" I squeal.

She hugs me back hard, and I haven't been this happy in

two months, aside from when I temporarily stop thinking about the rift with Nat because Cosmin is naked.

We draw apart, and I hold her upper arms in the gorgeous burnt-orange dress she's wearing. A pair of fancy sunglasses sits atop her sleek brown hair, and she looks like an ad for expensive shampoo. A small Louis Vuitton purse hangs off her elbow.

"Sorry for not replying to your last email for a couple weeks," she says with a wince, pulling out the opposite chair and sitting. "My life kinda blew up the day you sent it, and I was a wreck. That's no excuse—I know."

I settle across from her. "Not to split hairs, but it's been *three* weeks since I sent it. And unless I missed something, you *still* haven't replied." I take a sip of iced coffee, cautiously studying her.

"Semantics," she says with an airy laugh. I think she realizes it sounds dismissive, and tries again, her face going grave. "I actually tried writing back several times, and it just kept sounding all wrong, and I'd delete it, then get more anxious and emotional and ashamed of myself. I know I screwed up, Phae. I'm sorry, honestly."

I wait, punishing her a little before allowing a wan smile. "We both screwed up. I was hitting below the belt with that stuff I said in Shanghai, so I'm sorry too." I gnaw at my lower lip. "I've missed you a ton—not gonna lie."

"Same!"

In the deep V of her neckline hangs a heart-shaped emerald pendant. I squint and lean forward to inspect it, then meet her eye. She touches it lightly as if just remembering she's wearing it, then jerks her hand away, fiddling with the clasp of her purse.

"Hm, quite a rock you're sporting there," I note with a cheeky faux aloofness, going for humor. "With the earrings I'm surrendering to you, you'll look like a Christmas tree."

I take another long sip of my coffee, then stir it, giving Nat space in which I hope she'll pick up the thread I've thrown out and start a conversation about Klaus—I suspect he bought her the necklace. I mean...an emerald? It's pretty on the nose.

Instead, she deflects again, and I decide to let her.

"No no no, don't give your grandmother's jewelry to me, silly. I was teasing with that whole bet thing." She leans forward with a conspiratory smirk. "Giving me the gossip about what the Randy Rookie is like in bed will be adequate payment."

A waiter comes over and I order Nat's favorite drink and pastry. "Could we get an oat-milk half-caf latte with a dusting of cinnamon," I request, "and a scone with seedless raspberry jam?" I'm trying to show that I know her preferences because I'm a top-notch friend. I'm not sure why even our best impulses toward each other are a little on the competitive side, but it's how we roll.

The guy doesn't bother hiding an "Oh, you're one of those customers" eye roll, then gives me a supercilious nod before breezing off.

"You're sweet," Nat tells me.

"No, *you*." My eyes roam the severe angles of her upper

body in the clinging dress. "This isn't a dig, but you look like you could use some breakfast—you're thinner than you were in April."

She twists the handles of her purse, not meeting my eyes. "I've been...struggling. And considering the subject matter during the spat you and I had, I didn't need an 'I told you so.'"

"Nat, I wouldn't."

She shoots a flat look my way that says, *We both know you would, and routinely **do**.*

I amend, "Okay, I mean I *won't*."

When she roots in her purse for a tissue and dabs under her eyelashes, I can't tell if she's legitimately distraught, or playing it up. "It's over, and it didn't even really begin," she confides. "I know I've said it before, but this seemed like it was going to be different."

Her shoulders draw up, and I know better than to say anything negative *or* positive, as much as I'm tempted to spill out some unhelpful bullshit like *It's for the best* or *Are you sure?*

"Do you want to tell me what happened?" I venture.

A dance of about four different emotions flits across her face. Finally she looks up, everything stilled into determination. "*No.* And that's enough of my BS anyway—let's talk about *you*. I'm so sorry about your dad. How is he?"

I prod my breakfast. "It's...he has a rare kind of brain tumor. And detected late, because he's a stubborn old Southern boy who let the symptoms rage for a year until he couldn't hide them." My throat catches with fought-back tears, and I swallow. "He's got a few months left. He's only *sixty*, Nat."

"Oh, God." She takes my hand. "I know there's nothing I can do, but—"

"I still need you." I risk an embarrassingly vulnerable moment, adding, "Please don't go away again. I promise I won't be an asshole."

"You aren't! And I'm not going *anywhere*."

As the waiter delivers the drink and scone, something catches up to me: Why didn't Nat seem shocked about the specifics?

"Hey, Nat?" I clear my throat. "Did Klaus tell you about Mo before my email? Or is there some kind of press leak?"

"What? No! As if that ice sculpture Klaus Franke would tell me anything." She breaks off a chunk of scone, crumbling it into smaller and smaller morsels without eating any. "You weren't kidding about him having a thing against journalists."

I drag my fork through some hollandaise sauce. "Yeah. I love Klaus and everything, but he's kind of an elegant luxury car you should only lease, never purchase."

I'm tempted to ask Nat if Klaus said anything about buying the team, but if she's to be believed about him not discussing my dad's illness, the subject wouldn't have come up. It sounds like he didn't trust her. I'd want to be loyally indignant about that for her sake if it weren't for the tiny, wary part of me that's hesitant to trust her either right now.

"I'm sure I don't have to say this to you," I begin, trying for casual, "but everything I've told you about Mo is off the record. That's obvious, right? I know you wouldn't—"

Her hands have frozen in the act of lifting a piece of scone to her mouth, and I fall silent when I see the unmistakable hurt on her face.

"I'm your friend, Phae. Would I betray you—or anyone—for . . . *a scoop*?"

"Of course not. I know that." I jab at an egg yolk, trying to hide the uncertainty prickling my gut. "Wouldn't even be much of a 'scoop.' He might be in hospice care in weeks—there'll be no keeping it out of the public eye then."

She makes a noise of pained sympathy through the bite of scone, nodding and doing her gesture that's so familiar to me, pressing a hand briefly over the center of her chest with the fingers flexed, like she's trapping her runaway heart in a cage. In this moment, everything about her is the Natalia I've known fourteen years, and I wonder how things got so off track with us.

Is this my fault?

We became inseparable in college when I was eighteen and she was twenty. I was sure I saw a future in which we'd be weird old ladies together. Has it only been the physical distance, all these years I've been working for Emerald, that allowed us to sustain an untested "besties in name only" status?

Hoping to put the subject to bed, I unwisely make it worse, because of course I fucking do. "Anyway, if you keep it under your hat for now, I'll ask Reece if we can give you an exclusive. Uh, when the bad thing happens."

Nat sets her coffee cup down with such pointed gingerliness that it feels almost louder than a slam. She studies me for a full three blinks before speaking.

"You don't think I'd keep my word without a payoff?"

"Oh, shit. Nat, I didn't—"

"It's painful, being punished for working in journalism. You're being just as weird to me as *he* was."

"Fuck." I put both hands over my face and slide them off. "Can we—"

"*I'm a person*," she interrupts with crisp emphasis. "I'm not my job."

"I totally agree, and I'm sorry. Let's pretend I didn't phrase that like a tacky bribe. My head isn't working right. I'm all fucked up over the, y'know, Mo being sick."

I'm not sure if she's really sympathetic, or just understands that according to the social contract, when someone plays the Cancer-Dad Card, you stop what you're doing. Nat has always been a little selfish—she can't help it because she had a neglected early childhood—but she has a good heart.

She fusses with her cup, rotating it. "It's fine. I know you didn't mean it the way I took it."

Now I feel guilty because I absolutely *did* mean it the way she took it.

"Of course not," I assure her.

I slice a triangle of my salmon Benedict and eat it, keeping an innocuous "I'm just so content to be sitting here with you" expression on my face, even though I'm actually worried things aren't settled between us, but for our own reasons we're feigning that they are.

She eats a bit of scone with a microscopic dab of jam on. I point at her little plate while swallowing my own food, then ask, "How is it?"

Her polite smile is affected, and I have to take my hat off to her. She's good at pretending to pretend something.

"I think the butter was too warm when they cut it into the flour," she says with a careless wave. "The texture's off. But that's totally not your fault—you're *absolutely the sweetest* to have ordered it for me."

I give her a radiant smile anyway, delivering the line we both know comes next.

"No, *you*."

18

ENGLAND

MID-JULY

COSMIN

The British Grand Prix holds a special magic. It's historic, fast, challenging, and the English weather can be a bit of a wild card even in the middle of summer. I'm especially excited to be in England because Phaedra's family owns a small home in Towcester, a few miles from the Silverstone Circuit, and I'll be staying with her there alone. No sneaking, no pillow-muffled cries, no panicked alibis.

On Tuesday of race week as I drive my rented BMW up the A5, I feel light and buoyant. Bowie's *Diamond Dogs* plays through the speakers, and I sing along, remembering when I saw Phaedra playing the album after she left the gym in Bahrain.

I've told everyone I'm staying with friends in Milton Keynes so there's no suspicion about why I'm not in the motorhome.

During European grands prix, drivers typically stay in luxury motorhomes that travel from country to country, and hotels provide our home base during races on other continents.

Six uninterrupted nights with Phaedra. A podium finish could scarcely please me more.

I pull into the drive of the Tudor-style house and see the curtains twitch. Phaedra comes out barefoot, in baggy cut-off jeans and a lacy white blouse. She wears white often now, and it makes my heart skip every time, remembering that first conversation about it, and how it stunned me breathless when I saw her in the bar in Melbourne.

I'm pulling my travel bag from the trunk when she walks up, hair tumbling over her shoulders in a mahogany waterfall. I loop an arm around her waist and go in for a kiss, and she veers back.

"Nosy neighbors," she whispers. Flicking a glance across the street, she deposits a dry peck on my cheek. "There," she says, stepping back with a wooden social smile.

I give her a wink. "I'm sure the neighbors will be fooled, considering I'm holding a suitcase and your nipples are hard enough to be visible from a block away."

"Smug bastard."

"You love it."

I maintain an appropriately platonic distance as I carry my bag inside, resisting the urge to lace my fingers with Phaedra's.

The truth is, my feelings for her are starting to make me reckless. I almost wish for a leaked photo or gossip-site murmur to force our hands.

✽✽✽✽✽

Wednesday evening, I'm in the large bathtub with Phaedra, soaking the tension from my muscles after a long training session with Guillaume. There's a faint dappling of sweat on her upper lip, which I'm imagining licking off.

Her arms stretch to drape along the edge of the tub where she reclines across from me, and her breasts rise above the waterline, tempting pink nipples breaking the surface. Our legs are entangled. My phone is on the floor beside the tub, connected to a Bluetooth speaker on the counter that plays Slowdive's *Souvlaki*, the dreamy buzz echoing in the tiled bathroom.

Phaedra drags aside a tendril of hair that has escaped the pile on top of her head. I cannot help but marvel at even the smallest of her details—right now I'm admiring the way the wet tip of the lock of hair is dark, with threads of copper.

I've never felt this before: a near reverence for mundane personal detail. Everything about this woman seems miraculous, from the tiny toast-colored beauty spot on her left earlobe to the pale moons of her fingernails. I want to hoard her like rare books.

"Let's play the game," Phaedra says, her eyes sparkling.

She's referring to something that has become part of our careful non-relationship idiom—telling each other what we *would* say, were we in love.

I flex one foot and caress her thigh. "Were I in love with you, Miss Morgan, I would say your every particular—right down to the most seemingly insignificant minutiae—holds me in thrall. Heats my blood, makes my imagination light up, and inspires a tenderness I never thought possible for a jaded tomcat such as myself."

"Hmm," she replies, lifting her eyebrows. "If you were in love, you'd be a really poetic guy."

"Thank you," I say, swinging an arm out as if bowing.

Phaedra tips her head back against the tub, studying me with a faint smile.

"If I were in love with *you*, sir—" She pauses, and her face gets serious. "I'd ask why you've looked sad since your last trip to Bucharest. I'd tell you I want to comfort you."

"Ah. Well then." I pull in a deep breath through my nose. "My sister is compromising her principles to accept a donation for Vlasia House from a very bad man. She's forgiven him for something she shouldn't. It's beneath her—*he's* beneath her. I'm angry and disappointed."

Phaedra blows a bit of hair off her forehead, appearing to wrestle with her reply. "Oh my. 'Beneath her.' That's quite, um…"

"Quite *what*?"

She shrugs. "Hate to break it to you, but 'doing such and such is beneath you' is bossy-shamey language. And whether she forgives someone is up to *her*."

"You're defending her reflexively in the absence of information."

"Look, I just can't tell you how many times, professionally, I've had a dude say basically 'I'd have expected better from you' to bully me into doing it their way. Believe me, the 'How is someone so smart doing something so disappointingly stupid?' approach feels like shit."

My foot drifts away from her leg.

"First point," I reply crisply. "This is what I've said to *you*—because you asked, please recall—and not how I phrased it to Viorica."

"Are you sure about that?"

I hold up a finger to stop her from interrupting and immediately feel like a domineering bastard for doing it. "Second point: I believe you said you wished to comfort me. If that's the case, you're doing a piss-poor job."

She sits up straighter, and I refrain from looking at her breasts, as much as I wish to.

"I'm asking a legitimate question, Cos! Not accusing you."

"I heard nothing in the form of a question."

She makes an impatient sound. "Okay, it's *perspective*, based on my experience. Is that not okay or something?"

I fold my arms. "It's fine. Proceed."

"Wow, thanks, Your Eminence. Anyway, news flash: comforting you doesn't mean I always say you're right. Aren't we supposed to be, like, practicing relationship crap?"

"Yes."

"Well, sometimes 'comfort' means pointing out mistakes so people can *fix the problem*. Do you want me to be honest, or just jerk you off?"

I lift an eyebrow.

"Okay, lemme rephrase—"

"I understand, yes," I concede. "What would you suggest?" I stop myself from adding *in all your womanly wisdom*, because I know it would start a full-scale battle, and justly so.

"Ugh, Cosmin." She rubs both wet hands over her face. "You're being snippy."

I'm ready to be even *more* snippy until her hands drop away and I see she genuinely looks upset. A flare of ache spreads in my chest.

"I apologize. Uita-te la ochii mei, draga mea."

She peeks up. "I recognize that one—*ochii*. 'Eyes,' right? Look at you?"

"I value your perspective very much. I'm being defensive, and it's uncalled for. The situation with Viorica is upsetting, and I feel quite at sea." My foot moves back to her thigh. "Were I in love with you, I would ask in earnest that you advise me, and I'd listen without behaving like a sullen jackass."

She rewards me with a grumpy smile.

"That's better. I'm just saying, have you, uh...*asked* your sister how she feels? About the forgiveness thing? Because I know your take-no-prisoners attitude, and I'd bet dollars to donuts you *decided how she should feel*, without letting her talk."

My brow furrows. "Why donuts?"

She pauses and is opening her mouth to explain the phrase when she sees my mischievous smile. She slices her hand through the water to splash me.

"Enough with the cute 'I do not know this word'!" she scolds, dropping into an imitation of my voice.

I sit forward and grasp her behind the knees, pulling her toward me. She rises and turns, sitting back between my legs, gathered into my chest, and I kiss her shoulder.

"This man—the donor," I say against her warm, damp neck,

"is a villain. He should not be allowed to purchase absolution for his sins. I'm frustrated that Rica sees only the money."

Phaedra sketches a spiral on my knee with a wet fingertip. "Actual *crime*? Like, it's drug money or something that could get you guys in trouble?"

"No, the man's business is transport equipment—machinery. His offense is of a personal nature."

Phaedra is quiet for a minute. "Forgiveness frees the person who's offering it, Cosmin—not just the one who receives it. I think you need to trust your sister. The world isn't black and white. And I know how you can hold a grudge."

Viorica's words were nearly identical: *not everything is black and white.*

I idly stroke Phaedra's hair, enjoying the warmth of her against my chest.

"I will discuss this with Viorica," I concede. "You're an impossibly stubborn woman. But wise."

"Aw, thanks, Legs. You're a stubborn prick too, but learning."

She tips her head to grin at me, and I kiss her temple. Just then, my phone chimes. I peer over the edge of the tub and view the screen.

"Fuck. It's Reece."

"Why is that bad?" Phaedra asks with drowsy amusement, trailing her fingers back and forth through the water.

"The message is all caps. She asks if I'm staying with you, and demands I text her my location immediately."

19

ENGLAND

PHAEDRA

Ordinarily, the sight of Cosmin stalking around my bedroom naked would have me swimming in lust, but this is a code red–level crisis. I jab my arms into a green kimono bathrobe and follow him to the bed.

He perches on the edge, staring for a long time at his phone in grim silence.

"What the fuck do we do?" I prompt.

"I am thinking."

He turns the phone sideways to type, then sets it on his lap without writing anything, muttering in Romanian under his breath.

"How the hell did she figure it out?" I groan.

"I don't know." He stares at the phone. "Scratch that—I *might* know. I said something to Guillaume this afternoon, and I'm not sure if I made it adequately clear that the information should go no further than his ears."

"Cos!" I flop back on the bed. "Fuck, Reece has no choice now but to tell Klaus, and this is just the excuse he needs to toss me out the air lock."

Cosmin scoffs. "He would do no such thing. Why do you—"

"The hell he wouldn't! This is the perfect excuse to muscle me out. He'll use this to convince Mo to sell. This whole... *entanglement*—it doesn't make me look professional." I cover my face with both hands. "I want to yell at you for blabbing to Guillaume, but this is really my stupid fault for starting shit with you in the first place."

I stand and stride to the window, and Cosmin follows, winding his arms around my waist. "This isn't a disaster. We can fix it. Reece may have gossip, but no proof."

"I wish it were that simple."

"It *is*. We deny everything." He kisses my neck. "*Deny, deny, deny,*" he whispers against my skin, his tone playful in an effort to ease my anxiety.

Despite his attempt at distraction, the reality hits me that this time bomb is going to go off eventually. We might stay under the radar now, but what about next week, month, year?

My shoulders sag. "I should just quit now and have the dignity to jump before I'm pushed. Lars can take over as your race engineer—Emerald doesn't need me. This all ends with Edward J. Morgan. Not his daughter."

Saying it out loud hurts more than I expected it to.

"What the shit? *No*," Cosmin insists. "Emerald needs you, as do I." He turns me in his arms and cradles my face. "Not only as the woman I love, but as my race engineer. Yes, Lars could man the comms during a race if necessary. But you and I have a specific dynamic."

As Cosmin's words catch up, my eyes burn with unexpected emotion. "Wait, did you say '*love*'?"

"You live in my head on track, and in my heart everywhere. Phaedra Morgan, my beautiful girl. When I get to that podium, we will be there together."

It's the first time I've heard that smooth, deep voice form my name, in the lilting accent I've imprinted on.

"Say it again," I urge, weaving my fingers into his damp hair. "I've never liked my name, but it sounds so right on your lips."

"Phaedra," he whispers. "*Phaedra.*"

I devour his mouth in response, and the warmth of him dizzies me. Overwhelmed, I tuck my face into the crook of his neck, savoring our combined scent in a deep breath like I'm waking from sleep.

"Te iubesc atât de mult...ah God, I love you," he says, picking me up and carrying me to the bed.

I want those fucking words like oxygen.

My heart pounds loud in my ears.

"Cosmin?"

"Don't ask me to rescind what I've said." He lays me on the bedspread and kisses me hard, as if afraid to free my lips and hear my rejection. "I won't fucking take it back."

"Cosmin."

"*No*—we don't need to speak of it."

I cradle his jaw. I know every curve and angle, and my heart trips over the crowded landscape of all his details I've come to treasure.

"I love you too," I confess.

The inevitability of our love closes around me like I've fallen into a pool of it.

I take a deep breath and let myself sink.

Cos and I agree to confess nothing for now. After our mutual declaration, I think we both see this has become too big to keep under wraps indefinitely. But an admission of contract violation—while Emerald's upcoming transition is still unstable—could torpedo everything for me.

I wanted a sexy secret, and...yeah, be careful what you wish for.

I feel selfish for being relieved that Nat's spark with Klaus fizzled, because otherwise I'd worry that she'd let it slip.

Reece demanded to know the next morning why Cosmin never replied, and he claimed he'd been in a game of pub trivia with friends in Milton Keynes until it was too late for a text. He bristled with convincing indignation when he told her he could supply any number of people who would vouch for his presence in the pub.

I advised him to go no-holds-barred shameless flirt all weekend with every ovary-bearing human to throw Reece off our trail.

Out of necessity, Formula Fuckboy is back.

On Thursday, Cosmin told a reporter she looked "delicious." After Friday practice, he told Francesca—the baker who works in Emerald's dining room—that her muffins were the best he'd ever put in his mouth, with a rakish wink that made her blush. After Saturday quali, a fan asked Cos to autograph her hand, and he suggested her thigh.

Classic.

The day of the grand prix, the weather is pleasant but overcast at sixty-eight degrees Fahrenheit. Due to an unavoidable gearbox replacement on Cosmin's car, he's got a five-place grid penalty and has gone from starting in third to eighth.

Jakob's in fifth, so Cos is behind him. He was surprisingly sanguine about that fact when I saw him earlier in the garage. The thing that chafes him is João Valle in seventh.

I'm sitting on the pit wall—all seven of us hunched over the monitors with our headsets—and my stomach feels flat against my spine with anxious anticipation as we watch the red lights over the grid flick on in sequence, then fall dark to signal the start.

I never speak to Cosmin in the initial moments of a race while he navigates the chaos of the field, the cars spreading out and finding their early placement.

"Very clean," Lars murmurs in approval through our channel, scrutinizing the pack as it breaks away.

Seconds later, I see the same thing he does on the monitor—catastrophe striking so quickly I'm only intaking a breath to speak when all hell breaks loose on track.

As Valle blatantly crowds out Cosmin approaching Abbey corner, their wheels make contact. I gasp, the instinctive knowledge hitting me that *this one is going to be bad*. A stuttering cry escapes me.

Cosmin's car spins and flips, sliding upside down before careening into the gravel and executing another three-sixty-degree barrel roll, launching over the tyre barrier, and coming to rest wedged between it and the catch fencing.

I'm on my feet instantly.

"Cosmin?" My fingers pinch the mouthpiece of my headset hard. "Cosmin, report."

Silence.

I look over at Klaus, whose lips are compressed into a line.

"Cosmin. *Report*, please," I try again, attempting to keep my tone pragmatic.

My gaze is riveted to the monitor where cable-camera footage offers a clearer angle. There's no way Cosmin can exit the car, and I'm scanning for signs of impending fire. It feels like I've spent a lifetime waiting to hear his reply, though it's been only seconds.

The FIA medical car is already on track, speeding to evaluate the situation. João Valle continued unscathed, and a vicious part of me wishes for that inept moron's car to vaporize. How fucking *dare* he keep driving?

"Cos? Babe, I need you to answer me. Please? Oh, God…"

Shit. Did I actually say that into the radio, or just in my head?

Moments later, the race is red-flagged.

I don't realize my face is running tears until Klaus turns

my shoulders away from a nearby cameraman, who's so close he might as well be X-raying my teeth. Klaus waves the man off with a scowl.

What the hell am I doing? "Race Engineer Crying" will be the next viral F1 meme for sure, with amusing things photoshopped onto the monitor—I know how this shit works. I wish I could care, but all I want is to hear Cosmin's voice.

"*Klaus,*" I falter.

"He's protected by the halo and roll hoop—you know this, Schatzi," he tells me sternly. "Pull yourself together."

"Why isn't he answering?" My voice is strangled with panic.

"Likely because he is unconscious."

"Or—"

"Stop," he interrupts with a glower. His voice softens. "Look at the glove biometrics."

I inspect the monitor, and of course he's right: the biometric reading from sensors in Cosmin's glove shows his heart is beating. When I look back at Klaus, he makes the gesture I know so well: chest tap, palm raise, forehead tap. *Your head is above your heart.*

The pit wall team unblinkingly watch the feed from the crash site as cars return to the pits. Things are oddly quiet, aside from the ever-present ambient crowd sound and the chuckling bawl of a helicopter.

Then I hear him.

"I'm . . . I'm all right." Cosmin's shaken voice in my ears makes me light up inside like New Year's fireworks.

Oh fucking thankyouthankyouthankyou, my brain blathers.

"Copy. Good to know, Legs," I reply, businesslike.

There are a hundred other things I want to say. His living, breathing voice is like water, and I needed it so desperately that I now sag onto my seat with relief as I'm quenched. I watch as track marshals move the car enough for Cosmin to climb from the wreckage. He's a little unsteady as the medical coordinator walks him to the medical car for assessment.

I dig at my irritated eyes, focused on what's happening, wondering if an ambulance will be called. They decide he's stable enough to ride to the circuit medical center in the car he's sitting in and take off.

Finally, I breathe.

I look up at Klaus and remove my headset. "I'm gonna head over."

There's a pause before he nods, and I jog to an Aprilia scooter we have nearby and hop on, latching the helmet and then wending my way toward the medical center. When I pull up, Reece is arriving, riding on the back of a scooter driven by a garage mechanic. She jumps off as I set my helmet aside, and we converge at the doors.

"We'll talk later about your public outburst," she says stiffly, holding the door open for me.

I trip to a halt. "We have bigger things to worry about. Let's focus on Cosmin."

"I wonder what Mo thought when he got an eyeful of your little display."

"He'd think I'm a human being! Why are you losing your mind over my business?" I demand.

"You and Cosmin clearly *lied to me*," she snaps. "I had no desire to be saddled with your tawdry secret, but you two made it my concern. And here we are! No one bloody listened to me, and now you're *compromised*."

A bitter shred of laughter escapes. "'Compromised'? What is this, a Cold War spy movie?" I stride away, headed to where I hear voices.

Cosmin sits on an exam table and is being attended by a doctor and nurse. His race suit is peeled down to the waist, draped behind him. He sees me and lifts a hand. His eyes are tired, but he's wearing a faint smile.

"Draga mea," he sighs out. "Vino aici şi sărută-mă."

This one I know—*come here and kiss me*—and I suspect it's freely rolling off his tongue because he doesn't think anyone else in the room will understand. Which is why his eyebrows jerk high when Reece walks in after me.

Ignoring her, I open my arms and go to Cosmin, hugging him hard.

"Holy shit am I glad to see you," I say against his neck.

When I pull back, he cradles my cheek with one hand, feathering the thumb under my lashes. His eyes move from my face to a point behind me where I know Reece is standing. With obvious reluctance his hand drops, forgoing the kiss.

She knows, I mouth at him.

Reece's phone chimes and she swipes it open. "Track is nearly clear—restart in a few minutes. Valle got a ten-second penalty for causing a collision."

"Ten seconds?" I snarl, suddenly furious as I'm reminded

of Valle's existence. "I've got a 'penalty' for that incompetent pipsqueak—how about ten seconds in a room with me and a baseball bat?"

"*Control yourself.*" The words carry a subtext, and Reece's eyes narrow as she delivers them. She addresses the tall man with a thick walrus mustache. "Doctor, might I get a video of Cos to post for fans?"

He steps back with a wave of one arm, and poor Cosmin ruffles a weary hand through his hair like the twenty-four-seven show pony he is. His expression is resignation, clearly knowing he's a product that needs to appear undamaged.

"Can we give him a fucking minute?" I ask Reece as she's lifting her phone.

She cuts a stern glare at me. "Oh, let's do wait. Meanwhile half the world's women are collapsing on fainting couches. There's already an 'RIP Cosmin' hashtag, and it's not been a half hour."

I turn to him, combing my fingers through his hair and smoothing his eyebrows. On impulse, I drop a kiss on the tip of his nose. He captures my face with both hands, brushing my lips with his own.

So much for discretion.

I step back so Reece can shoot the video. She taps the screen and nods. Cosmin affects a bright smile.

"Hello, all," he says. "Thank you for your concern and kind wishes. Owing to the skilled marshals and medical team here at Silverstone, I'm in good nick and looking forward to the GP at Hockenheim in two weeks. Cheers!"

His expression flattens immediately, and he rubs a hand over his face. He's trembling, and I look at the doctor with a question in my expression.

"He's fine," the man assures me. "It's the adrenaline rush coming down. Causes a drop in blood sugar."

The nurse hands Cosmin a pouch of glucose gel.

Reece looks up from her phone when I say her name, and I nod sideways toward the hallway in a suggestion for us to go. Clearing my throat, I try for a veneer of professionalism as I walk backward.

"Glad you're okay," I tell Cosmin.

"I will see you at home, draga mea. Te iubesc."

He knows full well that Reece just heard him say he loves me. As I turn away, a private smile creeps over my lips. My heart lifts, feeling for the first time as if this is real. I always seem to forget: the anticipation of a thing you're dreading is far worse than the reality once it actually happens.

Reece is silent as we make our way to the exit.

I'm both elated and terrified, wondering what will happen now that the cat's out of the bag.

20

ENGLAND

PHAEDRA

By the end of the race, the #RIPCosmin hashtag has slacked off, owing to the video Reece posted. But a particularly nasty group of sexist dickwads—the type who bitch on social media about how "annoying" it is to hear a woman's voice in the broadcasted race comms—have begun promoting exactly the type of hashtag I feared:

#CryingEngineersBeLike

Followed by—yep, I guessed it!—jokes about my period, or that I'm out of chocolate, or I just watched *Titanic*, or broke a heel on my Louboutins.

Awesome.

Cosmin is under observation for the rest of the day because he did technically lose consciousness. When he asserts that he's fine and insists on leaving, he's given a warning by the race stewards. Personally, I'm glad they threatened him into staying.

Hours after the race, I get a text from Klaus asking me to go to one of the paddock meeting rooms. My stomach is doing the un-fun type of cartwheels, and as I make my way down the hall, I tell myself it's probably fine—maybe he just wants to have a little chat. A friendly ol' chin-wag where he puts an arm around me and calls me Schatzi and boops my nose with a warning to keep my shit together better in the future.

This goes straight out the window when I'm met with grave looks on either side of the table—Klaus and Reece—and a monitor that appears to be set up for a video call I'm praying won't be my dad.

"Take a seat," Reece says, flicking a wave at the empty chair.

It's late and I'm exhausted—most team members are passing the twelve-hour mark for being at the track. I drag the chair out and sit, fingers twisting in my lap beneath the table.

"I hope that screen isn't about to be filled with Mo's face," I say. "He doesn't need this bullshit. I get that a poorly timed show of emotion isn't ideal in our business, but—"

"We have spoken with Edward already," Klaus cuts in, getting straight to the point. "I feel it might be wise for you to step aside for the remainder of the season."

A bitter note of laughter escapes like a messy hiccup as the news gut-punches me. "It 'might be'? As in this is a suggestion?" I shrug. "Yeah, okay—declined."

"Stronger than a suggestion, Schatzi," he clarifies, his voice low and soft.

"You would still have a role for now, of course," Reece adds, folding her hands and donning a sympathetic voice. "Though less hands-on."

"What, because I was so gauche as to break down a little when I thought our driver might be dead?"

Reece rubs her forehead below her small, feathery bangs. "We all know why we're sitting here," she says with a sigh. "Let's be adults and not turn this into an utter farce."

On the heels of my defensive reply, the phrasing of her previous comment sinks in. "Whoa whoa whoa." I hold up a hand. "What do you mean I have a role 'for now'?"

I lock eyes with Klaus, whose face holds the combination of grim resolve, reluctance, and sorrow one might see on a person who has to put down a dog infected with rabies.

It hits me hard that he absolutely *can fire me*, unless my dad were to override it. Mo is technically Klaus's boss, sure. But this is why team principals exist: to manage every moving part of the team. The buck stops there. A racing team *owner* is more like the person who owns a racehorse—he doesn't need to get his boots too dirty, because other people have been hired to wade through the shit.

Just as my panicked brain is bleating, *Deny everything!* I remember that Reece will certainly have disclosed what happened on the yacht in Barcelona—an event that neither Cosmin nor I denied when confronted.

The jig is up, as they say.

I'm replaceable; Cosmin isn't. I'm out and he stays.

A flood of panic rises in me as I imagine a decade's career destroyed.

Sitting upright, I hide my despair with calm defiance. "What I do in my free time is no one's goddamned business," I insist, sweeping them both with a cool glare.

It absolutely *is* the team's business—I'm straight-up bluster-ing. I was so caught up in the momentum of this thing with Cos that I was thinking with my pussy. If anyone else on the team had done it, I'd be calling for their head on a platter, but I can't let that show.

"Phae." Reece closes her eyes impatiently. "The situation all but guarantees you can no longer operate untainted by emo-tion. The ongoing nature of your little fling makes it clear that mature restraint is not forthcoming."

"*Why do you even have an opinion about this?*" I seethe.

"I have an opinion," she bites out, "because you hormonal delinquents made this my bloody problem."

"This is such bullshit," I growl. "Today was an unusual situation. *Everyone* was shitting themselves over that crash—it wasn't some girlie histrionics that only happened because I've seen Cos without his pants a couple of times." I cut a glare toward Klaus. "Was my performance off in Monaco? Mon-tréal, France, Austria?"

He sits back with a weary sigh, tapping his blue Montblanc pen against the tabletop and scrutinizing me. "Try to look at this objectively, Schatzi. We are working with thousandths of seconds' difference to win. Any emotion-based hesitation is a death sentence."

"My work is solid," I insist. "I fucking stand by it. And you know what? I'm calling y'all's bluff: if you were gonna shitcan me, HR would be sitting here with us."

Hoo boy. My dad's Carolina drawl only comes out when I'm at the end of my rope, and there it is. I pause, studying them both for a reaction, and see that I'm right, which gives me the confidence to press on.

"What'd Mo say, anyway?" I ask. "Does *he* want me out? Because his opinion is the one that matters most to me right now."

"Given your father's condition," Klaus says, "it would be a good time for you to fly home. Be with the family."

"That's not an answer. And Mo and I have discussed my coming home *repeatedly*. He's adamant that I stay here as long as possible and not let his—" My throat tightens. "Not let his health impact the season. He's firm on that point."

Reece and Klaus exchange a look I can't quite read.

"Shall I call him myself and ask?" I prompt.

Klaus pockets his pen, the gesture definitive.

"He's torn on the subject and doesn't feel he can address it impartially. So he gave me leave, as team principal, to make the decision I feel is best."

I'm frozen, eyes locked with his. A half minute that feels like forever passes.

"And I suppose," I say slowly, "there's no way that decision could be impacted by you wanting to buy Emerald out from under me, right?"

His expression is so genuinely offended that I immediately wish I could take the words back. As we stare each other down, I wait in vain for the gesture I hope is coming, our silent communication—*your head is above your heart*—to show me there are no hard feelings and he recognizes that I've just lost my temper out of frustration, as usual.

It doesn't happen, and I die inside a little. For years, Klaus has not only been my mentor and friend but something like family. This distance between us is horrible.

I look into my lap, frustrated tears prickling my eyes. "Okay," I finally concede. "I do trust you, Klaus—I always have. Make the call."

"I'd like to hear what *you* think I should do. Be honest."

Ah, fuck. It's a test.

I feel cold as I know what my answer has to be.

"Fine," I whisper. "Put Lars in my chair. I'll take a family leave and go back to the States, at least for the next race or two. And—"

The hollowness inside me is ghastly. If I have any hope of coming back this season, this *must* be done, and I need to make it look like it isn't killing me.

"I'll break off the thing with Cosmin. It's, uh..." I force the lie out. "It's nothing serious. A few weeks' absence will do the trick." I manage a crooked twist of a smile. "The guy'll be on to the next socialite or supermodel in days—everyone knows how he is."

Reece looks so relieved I almost pity her, mad as I am at her interfering ass. Klaus slides his hand across the table in invitation, and I clasp it.

"You will be glad you spent this time at home," he assures me gently. "There will be other seasons. There will be other *men*."

"Sure." I give his huge palm a squeeze and let go.

"You may soon have big shoes to fill as team owner. Be worthy of them."

I can't tell if he's mocking me, or possibly saying this to hide his true intentions from Reece. *Other seasons? Big shoes to fill?*

"Yeah, okay." I stand and rub my face, exhausted. Reece is already on the phone to Lars, calling him to the meeting room. "I'm gonna take off," I say, pointing a thumb over my shoulder. "You don't need me for the convo with Lars, right? I have stuff to take care of, obvi."

Klaus gets to his feet and comes to embrace me. "That's not only for you," he murmurs against my hair, "but for Edward as well. Please deliver it."

Fuck it—I'm letting myself cry. For me, for my dad, for Klaus, and for what I have to tell Cosmin tonight before I take a cab to the airport and leave him.

21

ENGLAND

COSMIN

After I climb into my hire car, I message Phaedra that it will be another hour before I'm cleared to leave—I want to surprise her with takeaway from the shop that has her favorite Indian food.

I stop and get palak paneer, chana aloo, and pakora, then drive the few remaining miles eager to be home with her after this emotionally fraught day. I ease the door open and nudge off my shoes. The only light is in the kitchen and as I walk to its doorway, I hear her sniffle.

She's bent over something at the table, turned away from me. The movement of her left elbow implies writing, and an empty glass sits near her right hand beside a bottle of scotch.

The takeaway bag crinkles as my hand shifts, and she startles with a yelp, whipping around.

"Fuck!" Her hand slaps against her chest. "Oh shit, I..."

She twists back to the table and folds a sheet of paper in half, tucking it between some books. "How are you home already?"

I chuckle and move toward her, lifting the bag in offering.

"It's been a difficult day for us both. I felt it would be a relief not to cook." Setting the food near the scotch, I lean to kiss her lips, which respond to mine a beat too late. "You seem almost disappointed to see me," I tease. "Should I check the closets for hidden Romeos?"

Phaedra rushes to her feet and flings her arms around me.

"Of course not. I just didn't know what—"

"Hush, sweet one. I understand. I was frightened too. I had a moment where I was certain I wouldn't survive the crash." I kiss her, relaxing into her familiar scent. "We needn't speak of it." My hands splay over her cheeks, which have the sticky feeling of dried tears. "I'm sure Reece scolded you for wearing your heart on your sleeve, yes? But I'm relieved we are done hiding."

"Cosmin…"

I press another kiss to her forehead. "Let's talk over dinner— I'm famished. I will go change clothes."

I take the narrow stairs two at a time and enter the bedroom. My feet trip to a stop when I see Phaedra's large suitcase open on the bed, untidily half-filled as if the clothes have been thrown in.

The unease in her posture comes back to me, and I recall her hiding a sheet of paper.

I walk down the stairs and into the kitchen, going straight for the stacked books and pulling the paper free.

She springs up. "Cosmin—no, give me that."

When she tries to snag the edge of the paper, I lift it over my head. "Why so unsettled, mmm?" I ask coolly.

She makes a small jump, attempting to reach what I'm holding, and I wheel my arm away.

"Please don't read that," she begs. "I'm...it's not..."

"Încerci să mă înşeli?" I murmur, eyes narrowing.

Hers are wide and glassy with tears.

"*Are. You. Deceiving. Me?*" I clarify, my tone frosty.

"I don't want you to read it like that, with me *here*." Her face is a map of grief.

With those words, her meaning connects indisputably: *she was going to leave.*

Icy anger floods me, and I stride out of the kitchen and into the powder room beneath the stairs, locking the door.

"Stop!" She knocks hard. "Not like this—I'm doing it all wrong!"

I lean against the door, unfolding the page.

> *Cosmin,*
>
> *Please don't be mad at me, but we can't do this any-more. We ignored reality because of our attraction. It's time for us to do* the thing that's right for the team *and call it off.*
>
> *Of course I like you very much. I've never had this much fun with anyone (and I don't just mean the sex). I'm going home for the next few races to be with Mo and the family. By the time I come back, this probably won't*

hurt anymore. You'll find some gorgeous German girl at
the next GP, and that'll ease the sting, haha.
I hope you

The letter stops there, apparently because I walked in.

I read it a second time, then open the door. Phaedra's not in the kitchen, so I go to the parlor and find her silhouetted in the shadows, framed by the leaded glass window overlooking the garden. My footsteps creak on the hardwood, and she turns.

I continue toward her, a hundred sentences tangling in my mind—angry, sad, pleading, sarcastic. I extend the arm holding the letter, crumpling the page and dropping it.

"This is bullshit," I tell her.

"I'm sorry." Her voice is wooden.

In the moonlight I see her cheeks sketched with fresh tears. My hands ache to cradle her face and brush them away, but I can't let myself.

"I don't accept this."

She gives a slight head shake. "You don't have a choice."

"'*Of course I like you very much*'?" I all but spit the words of her letter. "What the shit is that? Is this like the teenage romance movie we watched—the one that was your favorite as a girl? Now you will offer me a pen so I can write to you?"

"Please," she whimpers, trying to take my hand. I yank it away, and she puts her palm over her mouth with a stifled sob. "I thought you wouldn't be home for hours, and—"

My hands wrap around her upper arms, and she gasps. I wonder if she thinks I'll hurt her. The image of Uncle Andrei leaps to my mind—his dark outline in the doorway of my room, a belt hanging from one hand. My fear, because I've disappointed him again.

I relax my grip and walk Phaedra backward to the wall. "That you planned to leave me a letter...I don't know if you understand how much worse it is." I search her face, which is half in shadow.

Tears spill unblinking from her eyes. "I do understand," she whispers.

"Then *why*?" My voice is as cracked as my heart.

"I was scared."

"Of me?"

She looks down. "Of *me*. I was afraid if I saw you, I couldn't follow through."

"Don't you love me? Only days ago—"

"Please don't ask me that." She shuts her eyes tight.

I give her a small shake, and her eyes fly open.

"Pe dracu! I'm asking, dammit. Ce naiba zici!" I let go of her and cover my face.

"Don't curse at me in Romanian!"

I gather her against my chest. "My apologies. I'm frustrated." Leading her to the stiff Victorian-style sofa, I pull her onto my lap. She tries to struggle away, then settles against me.

"I should go. I'll leave you the key."

But even as she says it, she softens in my arms, fitting her head into the crook of my shoulder. We sit like that for a few minutes, our silence measured by the ticking of an antique wall clock.

"You *do* love me, Phaedra Morgan." My fingertips stroke the soft hair at the back of her neck.

"You're a smug, self-congratulatory egomaniac."

"And you're the brilliant, beautiful, ill-tempered minx who's in love with me."

She scoots off my lap and walks to the window, staring at the moonlit garden.

"Cos, I don't want you to be resentful and have it impact team dynamics, but everyone feels I need to step away and take an inactive role. At least until you and I can—"

"Not 'everyone,'" I assert, getting to my feet. "*I* don't agree. And you can't either. If anything, our communication at work has been *better*, owing to our relationship."

She says nothing.

"Or do you agree with them?" I ask.

"Yes."

"*No.*"

She puts both hands over her face and then slides them off. "Cos, they're *right*. This thing won't ultimately be good for anyone other than us. It'll implode. We caught it early, when it's still manageable to—"

She makes a gesture like cutting something out and discarding it, and it occurs to me that perhaps she's excising us because it was impossible to do the same with Mo's cancer.

I try another approach.

"If you could be satisfied with an inactive role, we're free to have a relationship. Or maybe…" I hesitate to say it, knowing how she feels, but offer the thought anyway. "Maybe it wouldn't be so bad if Klaus *did* buy Emerald. Then the problem is solved."

She shoots a murderous look my way. "For you, or for me?"

I lift my hands in concession. "I misspoke."

She stalks off to the kitchen, and I follow. Seeing the food sitting in the steam-softened bag gives me a jab of pain, thinking that not even an hour ago I was picturing a relaxed dinner together, likely followed by a shared bath and making love.

Phaedra pours out another splash of scotch, lifts it, then sets it down untasted with a look of disgust—I'm not sure with whom.

"You may not be used to hearing this, but just being your girlfriend wouldn't be enough for me. I'm an engineer, not a driver's bargain-bin arm candy. And Emerald is the 'family home' I grew up in. It *is* my family. I need you to understand that."

I tend to approach problems like a race. I excel at making instantaneous adjustments to respond to changes in the situation, finding the weak spot in someone's defense and pressing my advantage. But in this moment, something occurs to me:

With Phaedra, using this strategy feels dishonest.

I was about to say to her, *We can spend time apart while you're in the States but are still committed to the relationship. We will just be more discreet in the future.*

Instead, the next words to leave my mouth are guided by the memory of what she told me on Wednesday, when we discussed my sister.

"Phaedra."

She looks up.

"I won't tell you how to feel, my love. Instead, I am *asking*."

She studies me, gnawing her lower lip. "Really?"

"Yes. Whatever you want, I will comply."

"Okay. Good." She holds my gaze soberly. "I want to break up."

The last time I cried was when one of the children at Vlasia House died of leukemia. The sensation overtakes me now. My eyes burn, my chest feels as if crushed by a boulder.

"That's not what I'd hoped to hear," I manage.

"I know."

"You're certain?"

She pauses long enough that it gives me hope. Finally she speaks: "When Emerald signed you, Mo told me, *That's the boy who's gonna haul our butts outta midfield*. I'm not going to shit all over his dreams, like, *I know it could tank everything the team have worked for the past eight years, but the sex is really great*. This is bigger than you and me. Yes, I have feelings for you. But I owe my father everything—"

Her voice cracks. I take a step toward her, but she holds up a palm to warn me off, swiping at her tears impatiently.

"And the only gift I have to offer him," she continues, "is the security of knowing Emerald would be in good hands if he chooses to have me succeed him. Does that make sense?"

I lean against the sink, holding the edge in a death grip. "Yes."

She sighs so hard it's as if she's collapsing, deflating. I'm not sure if she's relieved or as brokenhearted as I am. I don't dare ask.

"I hope it was more than just 'the sex is great,'" I say, meeting her eyes. "Because it is for me."

"Absolutely," she agrees, her voice a rasp. "And I know it'd be more satisfying to end this with shouting—anger's easier than sorrow. You had my number in Bahrain on that: anger is my default. But more often in life, things end with a whimper, not a scream."

I give an anemic smile. "You're setting me up for a wicked joke about making you scream."

To my relief, she smiles back, equally wearily.

She picks up a napkin and pinches her nose with it. "We're not having goodbye sex, Cos. I couldn't do that and not break down. This is agonizing enough." She stands and tips a sideways nod toward the stairs. "I'm gonna finish packing. I need to be alone right now."

She walks out before I can reply, and I watch her slip around the corner. Creaking footfalls go up the stairs.

It's painful to be this far from her when I'm feeling so much—like a rubber band in my chest, stretched to its limit. But as I admit defeat and allow tears to flood my vision, I am glad to be alone too.

▪▪▪▪▪

When she comes out of the bedroom, I'm sitting on the top step of the landing.

"I'll carry your suitcase." I push to my feet.

She lets me take it, then follows me down the stairs to the entryway.

I meet her eyes. "Did you...?"

"I called a car, yeah. It's a couple blocks away."

Our helpless expressions are mirrored. I draw in a breath to speak, and she takes a quick step toward me and puts her fingers over my mouth.

"No last words. This isn't an execution or something. Let's be friendly about it."

There's little as frustrating as a thwarted declaration. I take her hands in mine, and she allows it.

"Promise me something?" she ventures. "Let's make this sacrifice *useful*. No moping. Put everything into racing. I want you on the podium as much as you want to be there."

"I will make you and Mo proud." The words feel like sawdust in my throat.

She takes a ring of keys from her bag and slides off two, pressing them into my hand.

I shove them in my pocket. "Can we still call?"

She shakes her head. "I'll see you during remote meetings— it's as much as I can handle." Her phone chimes, and she glances at it. "Car's here."

My heart twists, and my head is packed like crowded stands at a race—thousands of voices, blending into indistinguishable noise. I take her chilled hand. Grief is nearly undoing me.

"When you asked on Santorini," I tell her, "about my greatest fear and the missing scale on the dragon...*this* is it." I yank her hand toward me and crush it against my heart. "You shot the arrow, draga mea. Your aim was perfect."

My hands go to her waist, and she gets only one word in,

"I'm—" before my mouth claims hers. I lift her and take the last few steps to the wall, pressing her against it.

Our lips are feverish, hungry, open to the shape of our loneliness and trying to fill it with each other. Her hands clench my hair, and she moans against me.

After a minute we part. My face is wet and I'm not sure whose tears they are. She fumbles for the door and flings it open, grabbing her suitcase handle—pushing my hand away roughly when I try to help—and dragging it onto the walkway before pausing to look back.

"Like you promised in Barcelona," she chokes out, "you wrote your name in every room of me—it's indelible." Shaking her head, she directs, "Close the door, Legs. Don't watch me go."

22

NORTH CAROLINA

LATE JULY

PHAEDRA

The house at Holden Beach is the only place we ever acted like a normal family while I was growing up, so it makes sense that Dad would choose to die here. It's a beautiful beachfront five-bedroom, all soft white surfaces combined with cozy rustic shit.

As a kid, I had a conflicted relationship with the Holden house. It lacks the garage and workshop we have in our Charlotte home, so I sulked every year about having to be at the beach. When we weren't on the road, Dad insisted we spend half our time at the coast—it forced me to interact with the family.

Unfortunately, I usually ignored two-years-younger Aislinn in favor of my beloved textbooks. From ages eight to ten, I constantly had my nose in high school mathematics and physics books. From age eleven on up, it was college textbooks, which Dad would buy for me at a university bookstore.

My mother is pretending everything's the same, that Aislinn and I aren't cynical adults now, and Dad isn't weeks from dying. It's like she thinks if the throw pillows have the perfect knife chop, the floors gleam, and something's in the oven, everything is GOING TO BE JUST FINE.

Dad talks a bunch about old memories: funny and smart and cute things Aislinn and I did as kids, memories of his courtship with Mama back in the eighties (her hair is still incredibly high—I think that woman has stock in Aqua Net), memories of his boyhood in Fairmont, all the mischief he got up to with our uncle Skeet.

My whole life, Mo has been a big, jocular, "mostly muscular with a touch of middle aged spread" guy with sparkling eyes and charming laugh lines. Illness has shrunk him. He hasn't done chemo or radiation because he was told right out of the gate that it wouldn't help much and might just buy a handful of extra time. He was adamant he'd rather not have a few more months if it meant spending them puking and bald.

The guy is so fearless it freaks me out. Aislinn said Mama told her Dad's reaction when the oncologist laid out the facts: Dad was silent for about a half minute, then said, *All right— let's get on with it.* By which he meant dying, not treatment. Who *says* that shit?

Edward fucking Morgan, that's who.

"Girls," Mama scolds, lifting a steaming pan of striped bass from the oven, "put those darned screens away or I'll lock them in the liquor cabinet."

Mama's a teetotaler, and the liquor cabinet has always been where anything that causes bad behavior goes: fought-over toys, the Tamagotchi Aislinn wouldn't stop staring at when she was seven, my textbooks sometimes, flavored lip gloss (which she said was "trashy"), Dad's rare packs of Swisher Sweets.

Hard truths and unpleasant thoughts are "locked in a cabinet" with Mama as well. I thought we'd circle the wagons over Mo's illness—maybe she'd even call me to talk one-on-one sometimes, rather than just when someone pulls her into *their* call—but it hasn't happened.

I'm not sure if that's awkward or a relief. But any time I've tried in the past few months to make direct reference to Mo's cancer, she scowls and flaps a manicured hand, protesting, "Land's sake, can we focus on the positive?"

I look up now from where I'm slouched at the breakfast bar on the kitchen island, going over DiL simulator data on my iPad. Aislinn is at the far end, typing on her phone.

"Put away 'those darned screens'?" I can't help but sass. "I'm working, Ma—not playing *Minecraft*."

"And I'm…" Linn glances up, and I know that look, that pause. She's going to give Mama a half-truth and is crafting it to fit within the parameters of Technically Not a Lie. "It's a message from my boss at Charles Schwab."

Aha. So she's sleeping with him. *Gotcha, you prissy little twerp.*

I study her from the corner of my eye, and she catches me doing it and gives me an impatient look—green eyes wide, straight bleached-white teeth gritted in an attempt at fierceness. Her perfect honey-blond eyebrows would be indignantly high if it weren't for the Botox. (Who gets that shit at thirty?)

I smirk before sliding my focus back to the iPad.

"Y'all are on family leave and shouldn't be working," Mama insists, hands on hips in her polka dot Hedley & Bennett apron.

"Daddy *asked* me to look at this," I say. "I don't know about Linn's excuse."

"Oh, get stuffed," my sister mutters.

"Aislinn Augusta Morgan!" Mama snaps. "Language!"

"I meant like a turkey—not something rude."

I snort. "You don't think stuffing bread cubes and celery up my ass would be rude?"

"Phaedra Harriet Morgan, really now?" Mama clucks her tongue.

It just figures that not only did Aislinn get our mother's flawless C-cup tits and teeth that grew in straight without two years of braces like mine, but she got middle-named after our mother's hometown, whereas I—the lucky firstborn—was afflicted with a middle name honoring a dead grandmother I never met.

Mama stabs a potato to test it. "Phae, wake your daddy and tell him supper's on. Linny, set the table."

"Why does she get the easy job?" my sister whines, and you'd swear we were in middle school again. I'm always amazed at how being around our parents infantilizes us.

I flop the cover on my tablet closed and head across the big living room to the deck facing the ocean, where my father is napping on a cushioned lounger. The ocean breeze ruffles his thick, wavy chestnut-and-silver hair, and yesterday's Sunday crossword is mashed on his stomach under one giant paw, pen on the deck beside him.

I pause to watch him relaxed in sleep, carefree. I hate to drag him back into the world where he has terminal cancer.

I examine his face. Objectively, I know he's older, thinner, sick, tired. But I lack the ability to see him as anyone other than the person who carried me on his shoulders through the crowds at the track when I was little. I always felt like some powerful queen borne over an ocean teeming with life, and the mingled sound of engines and people was the roar of the tide.

With him gone, I won't be a queen anymore. It occurs to me with sudden horror that all these years of adulthood—as educated and skilled as I may be—I've only felt confident because I knew if things *really* got fucked up, my dad would be there.

His dark eyes open and slide my way, accompanied by an impish smile.

"Take a picture—it'll last longer," he quips. With a groaning stretch he scoots up in the lounge chair.

"Sorry to bug you," I tell him. "You seemed happy, sleeping."

"Happier now because I'm looking at you."

I sit on an Adirondack chair, rotating it to face him. "Mama's got supper ready."

He nods, taking my hand as he gazes out at the ocean.

After a reflective minute, he says, "I ask a lot of you, chickadee, but it's always been because I know you can handle it."

I give him a smile. "I know, Daddy."

"What I'm going to ask now is big, but you're so *capable*."

My stomach clenches. Is this it—he's going to tell me his plans for the team? I'm not sure if he's gearing me up to accept Emerald's sale gracefully, or become "head honcho," as he puts it. Or could it be about Cosmin? Mo's been silent on the issue and hasn't mentioned the video call with Reece and Klaus, which was over a week ago.

"First of all, the obvious stuff: take care of your mama and baby sister. Your ma will be lonely." He sighs. "Thirty-six years is a long time to get used to the way things are. The smiles, the *control*...She gives the impression she's okay when she's not. Dig deeper, you hear?"

"I promise, Daddy."

"Same with your sis. She needs you more'n I reckon you know."

I scoff. "I *don't* think Linn needs me. She's the one who's perfect."

He makes a comical raspberry noise. "Because she gets hundred-dollar haircuts, and I taught you how to cut your own backwards in a bathroom mirror? That don't mean shit. She's still your baby sister, and she wants your approval."

I nod, though I'm skeptical.

"Finally—and this is the biggie." He drops my hand and rubs the scruff on his jaw, staring at the beach. "I've made arrangements to be buried at sea. There's a place at Cape Hatteras that does it. The whole megillah—not just ashes. No embalming, no burning. That's what I want."

He folds his arms as if he expects resistance. I admit I *am* sort of shocked.

"Where I come from," he goes on, "they burn trash—not people. But I don't want to be buried. Out there, you're right back in the game. Free in a wide-open world, not tied to a little plot of dirt. Fish eat you right quick, and you're swimming. *Alive* again."

The thought of not having a fixed place to mourn him is paralyzing, but I recognize how selfish of me that is. Of course he'd want to be out there moving around. Mo's always been restless.

I gnaw at my lower lip. "That sounds like a good plan. But why's it a 'big ask'? Do I have to skipper the boat or something?" I joke weakly.

"Your ma and Linny hate it. They'll comply, but they don't understand my reasons. You're so much like me, I know *you* do. I hope you'll help 'em to be at peace with it."

I join him in his scrutiny of the long, gray horizon. I like the idea of him being a part of something so big—the ocean. Every time I go into the water and float on it, he'll be carrying me on his shoulders again.

My eyes are full of tears when I finally look at him.

"It's perfect," I assure him. "You'll be with me not only when I'm here, but when I'm across the Atlantic."

He smiles and stretches his arm to chuck me under the chin. "You wander on down to the water and talk to me any old time, chickadee."

We watch the waves together for another quiet minute. The whine of seagulls feels like an echo of my anxiety, but I keep a relaxed half smile on my face for Mo's sake. From inside the house comes the clink of dishes as Linn sets the table and the lilt of Mama's voice, directing her.

"For a second there," I say, trying to keep my tone light, "I thought you were gonna tell me about selling the team."

He swivels to look at me, but I keep my gaze on the shoreline, maintaining the neutral mood I hope will make him feel okay about whatever he needs to say. I know there's probably no chance he won't sell to Klaus now, with everything that's happened. It makes sense—I hate to admit it. Better to take the payout and set up the Morgan family with security after he's gone, rather than risk having his careless daughter ruin Emerald.

"Sell the team?" he says. "Who to? Is someone buying?"

I meet his eyes, and the shock he sees on my face elicits a laugh from him. He shakes his head as if it's the silliest thing he's ever heard.

"O-okay," I stammer, "but I mean, um—"

"I already talked to your mama about it and made the arrangements with Charlie and the rest of the legal eagles." A shadow of worry clouds his expression. "You don't *prefer* I find someone to buy us out, do you? I figured—"

"No—*God* no. Of course not. I just assumed it'd be, um, *Klaus*."

"Klausy?" Mo looks genuinely bewildered. "What would he want with that kind of headache—team principal *and* full owner?"

"Wait, for real? You guys haven't been—?"

"Hell," my dad says, cozying down into his lounge chair with a chuckle. "Klaus started talking about the transition— you as the new owner—the same day I told him I'm sick. It was just a foregone conclusion for him, no question."

I sink back in my own chair, stunned. Recalling Klaus's words after Silverstone, I reexamine them: *You may soon have big shoes to fill as team owner.*

I misunderstood the "may" and assumed it meant team ownership was up in the air. But it's now clear that Klaus was applying "may" to the *"soon"*—trying to soften the notion of Mo's death being close at hand.

Holy shit, I feel like an asshole, suspecting him all these months.

"K-Dog's in your corner, chickadee," my dad says, reaching to give my hand a squeeze and closing his eyes, the matter settled. "He's your first mate. He'll steer the ship all you need, but you'll be Emerald's captain."

■▪▪▪▪▪

It's Saturday night, and the German Grand Prix starts at nine Sunday morning, our time. Mo and I are going to stream it live, and I know any time there's a flash of the pit wall—Lars sitting in my place—or a shot of Cosmin's intense eyes staring out from his helmet during the prerace coverage, I'm going to want to scream.

I'm still having insomnia, even though the jet lag is far behind me two weeks after arriving in North Carolina. Chalk it up to grief over both Dad *and* Cosmin.

Cos and I saw each other in two remote meetings last week—exchanging coolly polite hellos—and Klaus later told me he wanted to relieve me of all work duties through the F1 summer break in August.

The day after the last meeting, Cosmin texted a heart emoji to me. I wanted to fill the screen with hearts back, but eventually went with a squid emoji, because squid are funny. I have no clue what I was trying to say—I panicked. I haven't heard from him since.

It's late Saturday night, and I'm sitting in bed staring at Duolingo on my phone. I've been doing lessons for three hours now, and if I ever happen to find myself in a Bucharest farmer's market, I'm all set—the emphasis on produce in this app is disproportionate.

I just wanted to hear the sound of the language—though it's not like I'm rubbing one out to it or anything. What started as curiosity hours ago has turned into a compulsion, as if acquiring *more words* will heal my aching heart. The "gamification" is sinister—I'm chasing points like a lab rat pressing a lever for cocaine.

In the adjacent room, Aislinn's voice has been droning on

for an hour on a phone call that launched with affectionate tones and giggles, then went off the rails. For the past fifteen minutes, my tinny Romanian recordings of «*The tall woman has an apple and a potato*» have been punctuated with tense outbursts from Linn.

I hear a thump against our adjoining wall, followed by what's definitely crying. I set my phone down, listening to the muted sobs. My father's words come back to me: *She needs you more'n I reckon you know.*

Ugh, fine. I'll give it a shot.

I stand on the bed, walk across it, hop down, then go out to the hallway, listening before tapping cautiously at the door.

After a pause, Aislinn calls out, "Mama?"

I stick my head in. "No such luck, Chuck. Just me."

"What do you want?" she demands, swiping her blond hair out of her face.

I try to lighten the mood with an absolutely terrible Jimmy Stewart impression—we used to watch *It's a Wonderful Life* every year, and I know she'll recognize the quote.

"*Me? Nothing,*" I drawl, hands in the pockets of my pajama pants as I saunter in like George Bailey, looking around. "*I just came in to get warm.*"

"Hilarious."

I pick up her phone—she must've thrown it hard, because the screen has a crack—and plop down on her bed, handing it over.

"Wanna tell me what happened?"

"Not particularly." She scowls at the damaged screen and sets the phone face down on the night table.

Yep, this was a bad idea.

I pop back to my feet. "All righty. See you at breakfast."

It's not a power move—I just genuinely have no clue what to do with her rebuff. But as I cross to the door, she calls, "Phae, wait." She points at the foot of the bed. "Sit."

I put my hands into a begging-dog pose. "I can balance a Milk-Bone on my nose too," I snark, going to perch cross-legged on the bed.

"Oh, eff off."

"Is this the kind of conversation that requires snacks? That's what they do in the movies. Should we be eating cookie dough straight outta the tube?"

"If we had any, I'd be all over it," she says with a wry look. "But you know Mama won't buy store-bought."

She rises onto her knees to stretch for a tissue box on the bedside table, and I glance at her impeccable yoga butt, encased in baby blue leggings I'd never be brave enough to wear.

"I'm shocked you'd consider eating cookie dough," I mutter, "and risk that perfect little size-two peach you're sporting."

"Yeah, well." She gives an unladylike honk into the tissue. "This perfect size-two peach didn't keep Remington from going back to his ex-wife."

"Please tell me you weren't actually fucking a guy whose parents named him after a gun." Of course I focus on the exactly wrong thing, because I am a garbage sister.

"Shut up." She smiles around the tissue, so maybe it wasn't the wrong thing to say.

I take the ball and run with it.

"It's not a name you could cry out in the heat of passion with a straight face." I flop my hand against my forehead like a swooning maiden and collapse back on the bed. "*Oh, Remington! Do me like a big funky sex machine!*"

She leans in to deliver a smack to my thigh, and I yelp. She shushes me, laughing, and to my surprise we're both cracking up now. I grab for her face the way I did when she was little, and finally she submits to my squeezing her cheeks into fish lips.

"Say it or I'll sit on you," I demand. "You know the drill."

Her eyes check mine for level of seriousness, and apparently she decides not to chance it. A sigh whistles from her protruding lips. "Teapot," she mumbles. "Teddy bear. Butter pecan."

I release her, and she massages her cheeks with a grumpy glare.

"We did have fun sometimes," I say, more to myself than to her.

Aislinn snorts. "*No*, you just found it entertaining to torture me."

Well, shit. She's not entirely wrong. Looking at her now, I remember the gangly, fuzzy-haired pest she was—back when I called her a "stinky little spider monkey"—and I feel bad.

"Sorry about that." I grab a pillow to put in my lap, and the way she flinches as if expecting me to pummel her makes the guilt even worse. "I wasn't around other kids. Spending all day every day with guys didn't train me well for, uh..." I clear my throat. "*Ladyhood.*"

She eyes me. "At least you probably understand men better than I do."

"*Psh!* I wish."

She twists one of her pearl stud earrings. "Guess we're both getting our hearts broken."

"How do you know about that?" A wave of paranoia goes through me. "Did you see something online? Gossip or whatever?"

She scoffs. "You're not exactly a Kardashian, Phae. The world doesn't give a rat's hiney about your love life."

I can tell she's getting a certain satisfaction out of taking me down a peg, so I let her have it as payback for the face squishing.

"I overheard some stuff the day before you got here," she goes on. "A video call with the, uh, who's that handsome older guy? The one who sounds like Arnold Schwarzenegger—"

"Klaus."

"And the short-haired British lady."

"Reece. Gotcha." I twist the corner of the pillow. "What'd they say?"

"I just heard the tail end, before they noticed I was around the corner. Daddy sounded tired when he hung up the call, and he said—" She pauses and shoots a look at me. "He said, 'I am real disappointed.'"

"Fuck." My stomach flops.

No wonder he hasn't said a word. I'm sure the last thing he wants to do with this pre-death family reunion is scold me about the Cosmin debacle. I've clearly shut it down, so there's nothing more to say.

"What else did you hear before they clammed up?"

Aislinn shrugs. "Mama just said, 'Was she havin' relations with that boy?' and Daddy said he didn't wanna talk about it."

I giggle. "You do a perfect imitation of Mama's voice. You have her drawl a little anyway."

"I do not!"

"Do so. Like how you sorta say 'tah-rd' instead of 'tie-urd.' I'd probably sound like that too if I'd spent more time at home with you guys as a kid."

"I *don't* have a Georgia drawl," Aislinn insists.

"Just a hint. But it's cute." I reach to prod her on the shoulder. "I'll bet Winchester thinks it's dreamy."

"*Remington*, you a-hole," she says, laughing and throwing a punch at my boob, which I block.

Her smile wilts, and I realize I'm being a self-absorbed dick. I came in here because she was crying, and I ended up grilling her for information that pertains to *me*.

"Hey, Linny," I say with an earnestness that I suspect catches both of us off guard. "Ol' Smith & Wesson doesn't fucking deserve you. You're gorgeous, you're smart, and most importantly you're a nice human being. Twenty thousand times nicer than me."

She flaps a hand, and I grab it and hold it.

"Seriously, Linn. I'm a shitty sister, I know. But I'm going to do better." I squeeze her hand. "I'm gonna, um, take care of you. I mean, if you need."

She twists a skeptical half smile. "Why? Daddy told you to? 'Cause I'm a fragile hothouse flower?"

Everything about her in this moment—her posture, her tone of voice—crashes into my memory banks, and the exact feeling of my childhood spills out. My heart wrenches and I yank her closer, flinging my arms around her neck.

"No. Because I fucking love you, you stinky little spider monkey."

23

HUNGARY

EARLY AUGUST

COSMIN

The fact that I was outside the points at Hockenheim last week created tension. Not to disparage Lars, who is a good race engineer, but after working hard to cultivate an almost faultless rapport with Phaedra over the first ten GPs of the season, adjusting to Lars's communication style is jarring. Add that to my emotional malaise, and it was a recipe for failure, resulting in my worst full-race finish for Emerald thus far.

Klaus came to my motorhome Sunday evening after the race in Germany.

"I have no patience with childlike sulking," he said. "Mistakes happen, but yours today were so uncharacteristic and numerous, I must conclude you're acting out."

I lifted my hands. "Everyone has an off race."

"No. Your petty temper hurt not just the few with whom

you are angry; you let down a team of nearly a thousand people." He pointed at me. "Don't be shit."

Apparently, despite nursing a sore heart and wounded pride, *Don't be shit* was the kick in the arse I needed, because this week I gaze down from the podium in second place.

Klaus surely assumes I've taken to Lars as my race engineer, but unbeknownst to them both, Phaedra is still the secret to my success. Many times during the race today, the phantom of her words and the memory of her skill visited me, and I responded as if she were there.

It's still true—perhaps now more than ever—what I said to her the week of Silverstone: *You live in my head on track and in my heart everywhere.*

I am unaccountably aware of my face when the national anthems are played during the trophy ceremony. Race winner Drew Powell fidgets with his hat as usual, raking his fingers through the regrettably thinning hair that matches his goatee. On the other side of Drew, Anders Olsson stands like a marble statue.

My gaze combs the crowd. Viorica is here somewhere—she told me there is a matter she wishes to discuss after the race.

The music over the loudspeaker dies off, and I'm relieved to throw myself into the distracting revelry of champagne spray. The person I want here more than anyone is five thousand miles away, and this long-anticipated moment feels anticlimactic.

The car is like an exoskeleton these days. It's the only thing holding me together.

A dozen of the crew go out to celebrate at Szimpla Kert, one of Budapest's iconic "ruin bars"—hip hangouts in dilapidated buildings. I texted Viorica an invitation to accompany us and have booked her a suite at the hotel where some Emerald teammates are staying, but she declined to leave her room.

«Come see me when you return, even if it is late,» she messaged before I left for the bar.

One hour and two cocktails later, I'm glad for an excuse to leave. I've glanced at my phone a hundred times, hoping for any message from Phaedra beyond her simple "Congratulations!" immediately after the race.

After telling Jakob and Inge that my sister isn't feeling well, I message Viorica that I'm on my way, then climb into a Bolt taxi to go to the hotel.

When she opens the door to her suite, she's still in her day clothes despite it being nearly midnight. Her only concession to the hour is a lack of shoes. Rica has always been a very controlled person, which is why it surprises me when I pass her in the doorway and smell liquor.

In the living room area, there's a bottle of Tokaj gin one-third empty with a tumbler beside it. She pours another centimeter and lifts the glass in offering.

"Thank you, no. I had a few at the bar." I nod at her slim black suit, joking, "Did you attend a funeral today?"

She shakes her head and drains the glass.

"What is troubling you, Rica?" I flick a hand toward the gin. "This is unlike you."

She sets her tumbler on the coffee table with a hollow click. "Two weeks ago," she begins, her voice tentative, "you asked how I feel about forgiving Grigore Lupu. I know what it took for you to ask me that without judgment or anger."

"That is Phaedra's doing." I sit on the sofa, a small, intimate smile overtaking me. "I've grown so much under her influence— her advice has been invaluable."

"Please thank her, in that case." Viorica twists a diamond ring on the third finger of her right hand. "I brushed off your question when you asked. But circumstances have changed." She sits near me, azure eyes serious. "It's time I told you about my son, Iosif. My son...with Grigore."

Bewilderment bursts in me like a rocket. My gaze jumps from the diamond ring to her belly—flat and seemingly unchanged.

"You're pregnant? And this?" I gesture to where her fingers twist the glittering band. "Does it mean you—"

"Cosmin. *No.* I'm not pregnant." She shifts closer on the sofa and takes my hand in both of hers. "It happened when I was seventeen."

"W-where is the baby now?" I stammer. "No, not a baby. He'd be twenty." I pull my hand from Viorica's grasp and clasp it over my forehead as if trying to contain the chaos within. "You're marrying Lupu—that devil?"

"Andrei Ardelean was the 'devil.' Grigore spared me, a lifetime ago, from what could have been much worse. Please let me explain." She covers her face for a moment, sighing. "What do you remember of our childhood home near Lake Oaşa?"

I shake my head. "The house was blue, with berry bushes outside. There was an old-fashioned rain barrel I liked to dip my hands into. I wish I could recall more."

"You were only four," she says gently. "When our parents died and we went to live with this uncle we'd never met, his first words to me—a fourteen-year-old child—were, 'You have eyes like frozen moonlight.'" She grimaces with disgust. "I thought it flattering. For a time."

She twists the ring again as if it's too tight.

"Your grief seemed bottomless, Cosminel. And Andrei had no patience with a little boy's tears. He said you needed 'toughening up.' Knowing what that might mean, I convinced him to send you away to school in the fall."

"That was your doing?"

"Yes. And please don't think I intend to provoke guilt when I tell you it was not without cost." Gravely she meets my eyes. "It was better that you were gone most of the time."

I push to my feet and walk to the window, close enough to the glass that a halo of my hot breath blooms on its surface.

"I assume you've heard the rumors of…a *purchase*," she says. "The truth was, Andrei owed Grigore an enormous sum—a gambling debt. It would have ruined him and beggared us. No boarding school, no karting."

I lean my forehead against the glass, a cold spot on which to focus. "*Rica, no,*" I whisper, shutting my eyes tight.

"Grigore knew how I suffered—it was an open secret. The

debt was cleared upon condition that Grigore would take me in. But before you think him the hero of this tale, it's best to be honest and admit his interest was not heroic. He lusted after a pretty sixteen-year-old."

My stomach boils with anger, but I do my best to keep my face impassive as I return to the sofa. Viorica rises to get her phone from the bedside table. She swipes it open and shows me a picture of a snapshot on glossy paper with one creased edge: an infant with dark blond hair and a faint smile.

"Until a few months ago, I had never seen a photo of my son. And I never thought I could forgive Grigore for taking him from me. Iosif went to a good family in Brașov, but that was no comfort at the time."

She settles beside me again.

"When I sought out Grigore in May, it was my intention to blackmail him into giving me money for Vlasia House. Instead, he wept and begged my forgiveness, took this photo from his wallet..." She fixes me with a level gaze. "Then asked me to marry him."

We stare at each other for a breath, two, three.

"Rica. A sentimental photograph does not negate what he did to you."

"I know."

"It doesn't make him a decent man."

"He's not. But his money will be mine one day—it's a condition of my accepting his proposal. I'm owed. And Cosmin, *it's not your place to judge my choice.* There will be no discussion. This is final."

As I turn to focus on the city lights below the window, jaw tense and my chest aching, I imagine Phaedra is with me. I can almost hear her saying, *This isn't your fight, Legs. Shut the fuck up and listen. Do better.*

My God, I don't want to say it, but I must.

"I trust you. I won't try to stand in your way. But can you love Grigore Lupu, Rica? A man such as that?"

She darkens her phone screen. "I may never love him, but I do love the memory of Iosif. It's enough."

24

NORTH CAROLINA

MID-AUGUST, EARLY SEPTEMBER

PHAEDRA

The first seizure is the hardest, at least for the family. We were peacefully watching *Doctor Zhivago* in the living room when Mama asked Mo *Am I crowding you?* because (she later explained) he'd suddenly tensed up, and next thing we knew he was in full-on convulsions and Aislinn was sobbing *Daddy! Daddy, no!* and Mama was begging *Not yet, Bear—don't you do this*, and I was fumbling with my phone to call 911.

I hadn't heard Mama call my dad "Bear" since I was a teenager and they were more affectionate, before life on the road started gnawing little holes in their marriage.

There's a hospice nurse living with us now.

We're in the middle of the F1 summer break. Mo told me yesterday, in a blithe tone I think he assumes will keep me from being totally shit-scared, that he "just wants to make it 'til Spa"—the Belgian Grand Prix—"and see how our boy does."

He means Cosmin. Jakob's a solid driver, but my dad has his hopes pinned on Cosmin more than ever since the podium finish ten days ago. The Spa circuit plays to Cosmin's strengths—it's fast and cerebral.

It'd be borderline poetic to have Cosmin win at Spa while we watch, then Mo peacefully drifts off to the great paddock in the sky in his recliner during the post-race interviews, a "big ol' shit-eatin' grin" (as he calls it) plastered on his mug.

The idea of him possibly not being here in two weeks is horrifying. Which is why, on a Wednesday night, despite knowing it's only five in the morning in Romania, I crack and FaceTime Cosmin.

We both start talking at once—I'm dithering apologies for waking him up, and he's telling me how pleased he is that I've called.

He's beautiful—sleep-rumpled and yawny, with that slightly scratchy morning voice that reminds me immediately of the stellar predawn fucks we had. It's still dark there, and Cosmin leans to switch on a bedside lamp.

"Don't apologize," he says, combing one of those big hands through his disheveled hair. "I'm delighted to hear from you. Though of course I hope it's not for a tragic reason."

"Nah, Mo's still kicking." I hope I don't sound callous, but it's the way my dad phrases it himself. I sigh. "Fuck, I'm really struggling, Cos. Nat can't be here—she tried to get away from work, but the magazine has her scrambling."

During the summer break, it's so-called silly season in Formula 1, when rumors fly and gossip gets hot about changes in upcoming driver lineups for the teams. Reporting on the sport shifts from facts and analysis to TMZ-like back-fence buzz.

"We talk on FaceTime," I say with a generous tone I don't really feel, "but…"

He waits a beat. "But," he states with quiet confidence, "you feel alone, even surrounded by family."

A melancholy warmth blooms in my chest. *How does he seem to know instinctively, always, what's in my heart and my head?*

"Yeah," I acknowledge in a whisper. "I told Nat I'm glad she can't be here because, y'know." I make air quotes with one hand. "Because 'things are so hectic.' But I didn't mean it, and was hoping maybe she'd read between the lines."

Cosmin stacks a few pillows and reclines, free arm behind his head, and I'm both thrilled and unnerved that he's shirtless. I hope he can't see the way my eyes travel the angles and slopes of his muscles. I don't want to remember how insanely hot it was to slide my hands over him while he was propped above me on those muscular arms.

One side of his mouth tightens in sympathy. "How can I help? Talk to me."

I'm just tired enough that an impulse takes over at his "talk to me." With a shy smile, I slowly say in Romanian:

«*Nineteen blue pencils are on the small table with my glasses, inside the heavy backpack.*»

As I fumble my way through the sentence, Cosmin breaks into a grin. He shakes his head, then laughs long enough that eventually I join him.

It feels amazing. Holy shit, it's the first time I've been unabashedly happy in a month. I'd honestly forgotten what it was like.

"Why did you choose this unusual sentence?" he asks.

"It's the longest one I know!"

We both dissolve into laughter again. I pull the quilt up to my neck, comforted.

"If you'd like to learn more interesting phrases," Cosmin teases, "I'm happy to accommodate."

"Hmm. I'll bet."

"Explain this course of study, dragă."

I pull my hair around to one side of my neck on the pillows behind me, and he watches me do it. This also is a feeling I'd all but forgotten—being admired for something other than my usefulness or strength.

I scrub one hand over my face, masking the prickle of tears I feel.

"This situation with Mo, there's no sense of control. I need something to—"

I almost say, "provide a distraction." With a swell of guilt, I remember having referred to Cosmin in that way multiple times.

"I need to decompress with something low stakes," I say

instead. "There's no garage here, so I can't work on an engine. I figured a language app might be a good focus. Also…"

Biting my lip, I sneak a glance at Cosmin, and the tender look on his face disarms me. The truth rushes out, useless as it is: "I miss hearing Romanian," I confess.

A sensation that's both painful and a relief, like stretching a sore muscle, spreads in my chest. *Oh, God. Why did I call? This is both the best and worst thing, talking with him.*

"How many lessons have you completed?" he asks.

"I've learned eleven hundred words. Twelve thousand experience points."

He pauses, watching me.

"Mi-e dor de tine în fiecare zi, și-mi simt inima frântă," he says, his speed and enunciation careful. "I wonder how many of these words you know."

His pupils look huge, but it might be a trick of the light, or the fact that my own eyes are shimmering with tears.

My lips part, and I can't speak for a moment.

"Inima frântă is 'broken heart,'" I almost whisper. "It wasn't in the lessons—I looked it up weeks ago."

We sit in this knowledge, surveying each other.

"What did Mo say about what Klaus and Reece told him?" Cosmin asks. "About us?"

I pull in a shaky breath. "He hasn't brought it up. But my sister was here the day of the video call, and she said he was disappointed."

Cosmin presses his lips together in resignation.

"But the good news is that we aren't selling the team." I

sweep my free arm up. "You're looking at Emerald's future Grand Poobah." Remembering his earlier unfamiliarity with Scooby-Doo, I ask, "Do you know that one?"

"*The Mikado*," he says with a smile. "Yes."

"Okay, major points," I concede. "But I was actually thinking of *The Flintstones* cartoon."

We both laugh, and Cosmin's lovely face goes serious as we trail off.

"I am relieved to know you'll be returning," he tells me gravely.

I shrug. "In some capacity, yeah." I swallow hard, nervous to ask the question screeching like a klaxon in my mind. "Have you, uh, are you dating anyone new?"

"What the shit? Phaedra. *No.*" A semi-hostile bewilderment flashes across his expression. "Are *you?*"

"For fuck's sake, Cos. Of course not."

His eyebrows dart up, and the memory comes to me viscerally—the way his skin smells. The warmth of touching his face with mine.

"It's 'of course not' for you, but expected of me?"

"A little bit," I admit.

His chin tips up. "I'm not that man anymore. I don't feel the same about myself. And I *do* feel the same about *you.*"

There are a hundred replies clawing their way to the top of the pile in my mind, and I choose the one that's necessary, even though my heart is breaking.

"That's why Lars is in my chair on the pit wall. So let's make this worth it, Legs. Give Mo a win at Spa—it'll be his last race."

Statistically, most people die in the three-to-four a.m. hour. I've been waking up around then every day, terrified and listening to the lingering night noises, waiting for the routine sounds of morning that let me know Mo is still here.

Today I overslept, having a very vivid dream. In it, I got up and my dad was already awake, sitting on the sofa watching the waves out the window.

How did you get out here without the wheelchair? I ask.

He shrugs, still gazing at the water. *I walked.* Turning to me, he says, *Let's go for a spin in the Vette. How fast can you drive?*

I grin. *I'll burn up the damned road. But Mama made you sell it years ago—remember?*

It's still in the garage, he tells me with a wink.

He stands and drapes one big arm over my shoulders, and he's solid on his feet as we walk down the steps.

The 1960 Corvette is black and white, fucking gorgeous. I was fifteen and went with Mo the day he bought it. He talked the guy from $100,000 down to $99,000, saying *Let's keep it at five figures so my wife won't shit a brick.* It's the car I learned to drive on.

We open 'er up on Ocean Boulevard, the wind churning our hair as I push the speedometer past a hundred, roaring along parallel to the beach where the sun is rising.

My mother squeezes my shoulder to wake me, and I'm mad because she's taken me away from him. Then I register the look on her face, and the mewling sounds of Aislinn crying in the next room.

"No." I sit straight up. "*Fuck* no." I shake my head hard, whipping the blanket off.

"Phae, honey. He's gone."

I won't look at her, and for some reason it becomes incredibly important to find my socks. Why am I stalling, instead of hurrying like I should? What the fuck is wrong with me?

I yank the socks on and storm into the hallway with the purposeful aggression of a woman about to correct a fuckup perpetrated by the less skilled. As I arrive at the main bedroom doorway, Aislinn is lying on the bed with her head on Dad's chest, and irrationally my hands shake with the urge to slap her.

I prepared for this. I did, I did, *I swear I did*.

But as I cross the carpet, all my preparation feels like a champion diver who perfected flawless triple flips, then discovered when it was time for the big event that there's no water in the pool.

I have the impulse to demand why Linn was awakened first. But she sits up and meets my eyes, and she's fucking ruined, so I let her have this. Because in that moment, I decide— since no one can ever prove it's not true—that my father was dreaming the same thing right along with me as he crossed the finish line.

Aislinn may have gotten the last hug, but dammit, I got the last race.

Mo didn't make it 'til Spa. He died on Wednesday the twenty-eighth, four days before the Belgian Grand Prix. Reece made an announcement at the press conference on Thursday.

Natalia unexpectedly flew back from Europe on Friday to be with me for the sea burial on Saturday, yesterday.

"You're *here!*" I gasped when I found her hauling a suitcase to the front door from her Uber. "Why?"

She paused in her climb up the wooden steps, giving me a baffled look. "*Why?*" Her expression went resolute. "Because we've both been stupid and stubborn, and I can't take this careful distance between us anymore. It's done, Phae."

"You didn't have to do this. I don't need—"

"*Enough.*" She stepped onto the porch and retracted her bag's tow handle with a smack, then pulled me into her arms. "We're not doing this BS anymore, the thing where you pretend you're too tough to need me, and I pretend—because my feelings are hurt about being rejected—that I'm too self-absorbed to *notice* you pushing me away." She pulled back and gave me a little shake. "No more hiding for either of us."

"But—"

"You're afraid our friendship can't be what it used to be. I get it; I'm scared too. But you know what? It's going to be *better.*"

She dragged her suitcase past me into the entryway.

"Now go take a shower. I'm gonna fry us up a foot-high stack of grilled cheese sandwiches, then we'll both have a boatload of carbs and a good cry."

I couldn't have gotten through the burial without her. The

useful thing about grief, I suppose, is it forces you to strip off your disguise and be real. I don't think I've ever felt closer to Nat than in the past twenty-four hours.

What a difference a day makes, as Cosmin once observed.

Today's the grand prix, and we're at the main house in Charlotte, in front of the monolith-size TV. In the open kitchen, Mama and Aislinn are deep in a project making brioche. They've been keeping busy and talking very little, dealing with the loss in their own way.

My coping strategy, per usual, is obsessing over data. My iPad is on my lap and I'm chewing black licorice, which Mo always said is good for focus. He and I were the only people in the family who liked it, and as I snap off bites and squint at my tablet, I can almost imagine he's here with me.

Periodically, I look up to inspect the prerace coverage, but I'm doing my best to pretend I'm more interested in the numbers. One of my peeks coincides with a shot of Cosmin sitting in the car, and it's like a backhand smack of anxiety and lust. I go stiff, and in my peripheral vision I feel Nat studying me.

"You're *for sure, for sure* about the breakup?" she ventures, her voice all sympathy.

I stop her with an icy glare, then—remembering we're committed to openness and honesty now—soften my expression.

"Nat? Not today. I can't talk about Cosmin, okay? We sent Mo on a permanent vacation to Davy Jones's fucking locker yesterday, and this is the first race he won't see, and—" My throat tightens. "It was practically his dying wish that I not tank Emerald by banging our star driver."

Nat's eyes flick toward the kitchen. "He didn't actually *tell* you that."

"He didn't have to specifically. Linn said he was disappointed." I jab at the iPad screen. "I know what's expected of me as owner."

The moment of silence for Mo before the race almost breaks me. Mama and Linn go quiet, coming to stand behind the sofa, all of us staring at the TV.

The coverage cycles through shots of the mechanics in the garage with heads bowed, the pit crew, crowds in the stands, the team members on the pit wall, and finally Jakob and Cosmin—solemn eyes framed by helmets.

As the tribute concludes, the camera is still on Cosmin. His dark gold lashes sweep up, and I die a little, missing him, seeing my own grief mirrored in his eyes thousands of miles away.

The camera zeroes in on Klaus, whose handsome, angular face is bleak. Out of the corner of my eye, I notice Nat press a hand to her chest in her caged-heart gesture.

"H-he just looks really upset," she falters when I give her a critical look.

She's not wearing the emerald pendant anymore and claims she's "over it." She even went on a date with a new guy— another journalist (who turned out to be a jerk), but something tells me the Klaus and Nat saga isn't quite done.

I don't press her on it. Part of being honest, rather than

saying everything, is knowing when to shut up and give each other a break. We're learning.

On lap 16 of the race, João Valle creates a disaster at the Eau Rouge corner and the ensuing three-car clusterfuck takes Cosmin out, along with Mateo Ortiz. No one is hurt, thankfully. In a sense I'm glad Mo didn't see this, because it would've been a shitty final race. Better that he imagined it as Cosmin's first number one.

The stunning dipshittery takes Valle up to twelve penalty points for the season, which will most certainly result in a race ban. There's a high probability Team Harrier will put their rockstar female reserve driver—Sage Sikora, the woman I begged for Emerald to hire last year—into Valle's seat.

I'm itching to see how she'll do. She's delightfully caustic— the only child of an eccentric West Coast dot-com bazillionaire. I can't wait to watch her crash the sausage party.

Shit just got interesting.

Emerald may not have a woman driver this year, but two-thumbs This Bitch owns the team now, and I have no plans to shake my metaphoric pom-poms on the sidelines like a simpering F1 cheerleader while the big boys go racing.

I text Klaus and tell him I'm coming back.

25

LATE SEPTEMBER

PHAEDRA

I'm in Sochi for race week, finally with the team again after a month of bullshit dealing with the business-y parts of the transition after Mo's death. Also Aislinn guilted me into sticking around North Carolina longer, because she was worried Mama would think I have no use for them now that Dad is gone.

Some Russian government muckety-mucks (as Mo would've called them) are throwing a bash to ensure there will continue to be grands prix in Glorious Mother Russia. Invited: FIA bigwigs, drivers, team principals, and owners.

While many may assume a fancy ball universally appeals to women, I'd rather get dysentery. I had to go shopping yesterday with Nat, who insisted neither of the skirts I own would work. She bullied me into buying the strappy midnight-blue gown I'm currently wearing.

Even I know better than to pair Converse with this, so I'm in heels, which means I'm about as graceful as some flailing B-movie alien. It also explains why I've been parked at a table all evening, poking at a plate of food that probably cost enough to feed a Chechen village.

Cosmin is here, of course. I've never seen him in a tux before tonight, and he looks annoyingly fuckable. I've had too much to drink to deal with this fact. I'm attempting to enjoy caviar (and failing) when two long, bare woman's legs stop beside my chair, and my first tipsy thought is *Who let in the naked chick?*

My eyes travel up. One side of my face unglamorously bulges with a mouthful of caviar and toast while I struggle to swallow.

Sage Sikora is wearing a friendly smirk and a dress that makes her look like a dominatrix—all straps and buckles. She pulls out the chair beside mine and sits, leaning an elbow on the table like a bored kid, and I love her already.

"All this shit they're serving is nasty," she says, flicking a hand at my plate. "Personally, I was hoping for tacos."

I choke down the caviar and take a mouthful of the pricey wine, somehow managing not to swish it before swallowing, like the class act I am.

"Same." I extend a hand to shake. "Phaedra Morgan, with Emerald. I'm kind of fangirling big time over you right now."

"Aw, shucks," she says as we clasp hands. "Thanks. And I know who you are. You're not 'with' Emerald—you *are* Emerald. Sorry to hear about your father."

"Thank you."

My throat tightens with the still-fresh grief, and I worry that a convo about my dad—combined with the bottle of Château Lafite Rothschild I've commandeered—might make me weepy and fuck up the eye makeup Nat so painstakingly applied.

I sweep one hand to indicate the crowd. "You figure about half these guys are Russian mafia?" I joke.

She wrinkles her nose and narrows a pair of mischievous, coppery-brown eyes. "They'd better not find out you're on to them, or someone'll poison your drink."

"Ha! Why do you think I'm guarding it like I'm at a frat party?"

Sage laughs. Her dark-rooted, wavy hair is dyed aqua, piled on her head in a messy updo, and she has safety pin earrings. If she weren't nearly a decade younger than me, I'd want to be her when I grow up. She has a *neck tattoo*, for fuck's sake—a life-size peacock feather tipped with realistic-looking fire.

"You know I'm a fangirl of yours too, Boss Bitch," Sage tells me with a chuckle, squeezing my knee. "You're eternally my hero for smacking down the Coraggio team boss with that hilarious butt plug shade on social media last year."

I lift my glass in a toast. "The snark heard 'round the world. It'll outlive me."

"And rumor has it you are or were fucking Cosmin Ardelean, and wouldn't we all love to break off a piece of *that* snack."

Her words are like a splash of ice water hitting my gut, but I give an indifferent shrug.

"Oh, you could break off your own piece—he's historically promiscuous, and you're like some gorgeous punk rock, race-car driver Bratz doll." I grab an unused glass and pour her a generous serving of the Château Lafite. "Shoot a well-timed wink in his direction, and you'll be playing seven minutes in heaven in the coat closet."

She accepts the wine and takes a sip. "Over between you two, huh?"

"Yeah." I pick up one of the toast points, then set it back down, sighing. "Still stings—I'm drunk enough to admit. But I have no claim on him, so don't worry that I'm being territorial. Feel free to shoot your shot."

Her face is compassionate, small full lips pushed into a sympathetic pout, dark brows together. She touches my knee again, and in my wine haze, I'm not sure she isn't flirting.

"Tempting, but I don't sleep with other drivers—that'd be crazy. If I hesitate a hundredth of a second because some jerkoff from a rival team has seen me naked, I might as well hang up my helmet."

"Wise words, girlfriend. It's why I got scraped off the pit wall." I gulp the last few inches of wine and release a showy sigh as I set the glass down. "I'm not getting within one dick length of Ardelean again—I'd like my old job back."

As if I've summoned Beetlejuice by saying his name, the man who essentially canned me and sent me home to North Carolina appears at the table.

"Miss Sikora," Klaus greets my companion. "Lovely to see you. What a fetching ensemble."

"*Miz*," she corrects good-naturedly, giving him a once-over that seems to speak volumes. "And you're looking pretty fly too, Franke. Nice suit…and everything in it."

Holy balls, have they fucked? Is there anyone Klaus hasn't sampled?

"Sage is making that shit-ass Li'l Rascals go-kart of Harrier's look like a McLaren MP4/4," I drawl pointedly.

His lips twitch in amusement. "Indeed."

"If they have any sense, the team'll jettison Valle and make Sage permanent, even after Valle's femur heals from the snowboarding accident." I squint one eye at Klaus. "Yooooouuu fucked up, buddy boy—you and Mo both. Coulda locked down this little lady like I recommended, but y'all passed like sexist twats."

Definitely too much wine. I'm getting punchy, and just accidentally called my dead father a twat. *Time to pack it in and go home, kids!*

"You appear to have been satisfied with Cosmin's performance nonetheless," Klaus quips.

"*Ooh, touché*," I whisper. "Ouch."

I pour myself the last of the wine, holding the inverted bottle aloft until every drop trickles into the glass, then gulp it down two-handed like a toddler with a sippy cup. Sage and Klaus fall into light conversation, which I tune out.

I suck my lower lip and scan the room for a roving waiter—y'know, because I definitely need more booze—but don't see one. Instead, I catch sight of Cosmin. He's talking to some FIA douche who has a woman half his age clamped under one stout arm.

Standing near the trophy wife is a curvaceous blonde in a black-and-white gown. She's riveted by Cosmin, twisting a lock of hair around one red-taloned finger, and it rolls over me like a dark cloud at a picnic that he'll probably take that chesty penguin-looking floozy back to his hotel room and do all the things with her he used to do with me.

I hate her so much.

Would it cause a fatal stampede to the exits if she suddenly burst into flame?

Sage stands and extends a hand to shake goodbye with Klaus, and he gets all gallant and brushes his lips over her knuckles. I frown, which he completely misses. But Sage catches it. She looks worried, and *damn my stupid drunk ass*, she probably thinks I'm annoyed because of some weird jealousy.

In reality, it's because I loyally want him to be sadder about missing out on Natalia rather than cavalierly trying to pull Sage.

Really, Klaus? Sage wasn't good enough to offer an Emerald seat, but a seat on your lap is another story?

I mercifully don't say my boozy thoughts aloud for once.

She holds out a hand to me to shake. "I hope we'll get a chance to talk more."

"Oh God, really? That's a relief. I'm not usually this much of a disaster, I swear. Please don't remember me as a drunk, trash-talking idiot. It's been a rough few months."

She pulls me into a hug. Near my ear, she murmurs, "Don't let the fuckers get you down, queen honeybee. Keep ruling."

She smells amazing, and part of my brain wants to make babies all over her. This woman is a triple threat—gorgeous, talented, smart. My arms tighten for a moment.

"Thank you," I breathe into her hair. "I needed that."

She touches my cheek before walking away.

I remember Klaus is still standing there. He raises one eyebrow and pulls my chair out, gesturing for me to sit. I can't tell if he's being courteous or bossy—the wine is making me paranoid, and I'm afraid I'm in trouble for something, though I haven't even talked to Cosmin all night. I lower myself unsteadily to my chair.

Klaus unbuttons his jacket and sits, stretching his legs out. "Aside from in meetings, you seem to be avoiding me since your return."

"Yeah, maybe." I look into my lap, running a finger along a tuck in the silky fabric stretched over my legs. "I guess I have a bone to pick with you, Klausy." My father's nickname for him spills out, possibly surprising us both. "Your 'will they or won't they' flirtation with my best friend—jerking Nat around for months—it not only hurt *her*, but it put me in an uncomfortable position. Whether you two had cooked up a romance or not, it meant I'd have to pick sides at some point, with two of the most important people in my life."

His tone is cryptically smooth. "It wasn't about you. And I was unaware it was subject to your blessing."

"Wow." Little nettles of frustration and embarrassment sting in my chest. "Okay, perfect. Thanks—good talk."

Two unexpected tears fall to my lap. I watch the pattern

with mathematical fascination as they bloom on the blue fabric.

Klaus sighs. He reaches for the front legs of my chair, just below my thighs, and pulls me closer, then tips my chin up with one finger. "Forgive me, Schatzi. I seem to be making every conceivable mistake, both with Talia and with you."

It doesn't escape my notice that he has a nickname for Natalia. A tiny smile flickers across my lips and fades. *Yeah, I called it—they're not done.*

"The thing with Nat isn't the biggest reason I'm mad at you though." My throat tightens with awful emotion. "Why didn't you come to the sea burial?" I demand in a rasp. "I needed you! I had to *put him in the water*, Klaus. In…the… fucking…*ocean!*"

He reaches for me and I do a wussy two-handed punch to push him away, but he ignores my flailing and pulls me to my feet, wrapping me in his arms. My body sags into him.

"You're a coward!" I accuse, voice muffled against his jacket. "You weren't there for me *or* for Mo, probably because you were afraid to see Natalia after treating her like shit." I pull back, glaring. "And you said the thing with you and Nat 'wasn't about me'? Well guess what, dipshit? My dad's burial *wasn't about you!* Maybe you could've—"

My words strangle off and I hide my face again, rubbing my cheek against Klaus's suit and not giving a shit that I'm staining it with mascara.

"You're not wrong—it was cowardly." His arms tighten.

"I'll never forgive myself for failing you. I knew I would cry, and I was afraid for you and Talia to see me like that."

Suddenly Cosmin is beside us, and the balm of his voice, that accent, is something I've been longing to hear, though he sounds angry.

"Why is she upset?" he demands of Klaus. "What did you say?"

I pull back and meet Cosmin's eye. I know I look disgusting—my makeup's ruined—but according to his expression, I might as well be a desert oasis spring spewing out Dom Pérignon and Bitcoin. Jesus Christ, if he really wanted to see me this badly, why has he been ignoring me all evening while he flirts with some fake-titted penguin?

"I'm just having a rough night," I tell him. Sniffling, I survey him up and down. My gaze settles on his green pocket square. "Nice outfit. You look like a leprechaun's pallbearer."

Welp, I'm nothing if not consistent. *Backhanded compliments: just add booze!*

One corner of his scrumptious lips tugs upward. "Mulțumesc," he says to me, and I'm sort of pleased with myself that I understand his "thank you," simple as it is.

I grind a knuckle into one eye, and it comes away smudged black. "I need to sleep. I'm turning into a pumpkin on so many levels."

Cosmin steps close, whipping out the pocket square and cradling the back of my head as he swipes under my eye. "No, the dress is quite flattering," he assures me.

Oh God. He doesn't get the pumpkin reference and thinks I'm saying I'm fat, and everything about this moment makes me simultaneously want to throw myself into his embrace and scuttle away like he's plutonium.

Cosmin—damn him, why does he have to be so adorable?

I push his hands away, slow, like we're underwater. "I'm gonna get a cab."

"I'll walk you out," he insists.

I slide a look over at Klaus. "See you tomorrow." I tilt a tired-but-sassy smirk at him. "Unless I fire you first. *Asshole.*"

He mirrors my smile and does the gesture I've been waiting for—*your head is above your heart*—before giving a pleasingly deferential little bow and excusing himself.

When Cosmin walks me out to wait for a car, we don't even talk. His arm is loosely around my shoulders, and the smell of him is driving me crazy. There's a pulse between my legs making me want to climb him like a Wichita lineman shimmying up a telephone pole.

We reach the edge of the curb and stand quietly. Cosmin adjusts the white faux-fur jacket Natalia lent me, popping the collar to keep my neck warm, though it's not really cold. The thrill of his fingers grazing my neck makes me almost whimper.

Please don't kiss me good night, please don't kiss me good night. Oh fuck almighty—please kiss me good night.

The venue door behind us opens and closes, and as it does, a ripple of laughter leaks out, and I remember the blonde who was ogling Cosmin earlier. I sidestep away from him. A dark sedan turns into the drive and coasts around the curve—I'm pretty sure it's my ride.

"Okey dokey," I tell Cosmin, planting a hand on his chest and giving him a hearty pat. "See you at the paddock."

He tucks a loose tendril of hair behind my ear. "It's a pleasure to have you back."

We stare at each other for too long, and the car glides up and stops at the curb. I deliver another pat, just as an excuse to touch him—I'll admit it.

"Have a good rest of your evening. There's a busty blonde in there clamoring to talk with you. A room *full* of women, really. You've got your pick."

He shakes his head and places both hands on my cheeks, and holy shit he's going to kiss me, and I might be even more excited than the first time it happened in Santorini.

But nope. He tilts my head down and grazes his lips against my forehead. *Ugh, a pity kiss.* Is anything worse?

He says with a melancholy smile, "When you're not in the room, it may as well be empty, draga mea." He looks down at my left hand, holding the green pocket square, and closes my fingers around it. "Keep that, please."

In the dark of the car on the way back to the hotel, very discreetly, I reach under my dress and tuck the handkerchief into my panties, and a shiver tears through me.

26

EARLY NOVEMBER

COSMIN

When I was a child, the American TV programs I saw were mostly old family sitcoms and dramas that were cheap to broadcast in Europe. Because of this, the mid-century American aesthetic has always appealed to me: the huge cars, white picket fences, fathers with briefcases and mothers in heels and pearls, diners and ice cream parlors.

And the food. I've eaten in the finest restaurants in the world and sampled nearly every cuisine, but something like a checkered-blanket picnic circa 1962 holds a special glamour.

In July, Phaedra and I talked about the US Grand Prix in Texas, and we planned to enjoy a day trip driving around early in the race week. Sitting in my hotel room last night after arriving here in Austin, staring out at the city lights, I felt quite sorry for myself.

The six races since my P2 in Hungary have been a mixed bag, with podium finishes at Monza, Sochi, and Suzuka, and various disappointments elsewhere. There was Valle's disaster at Spa. A gearbox failure in Singapore. Botched pit stop in Mexico.

I've three races left to get my win, and the focus on that—strategy meetings, brutally intense training sessions, DiL simulations—has mercifully kept me from thinking about Phaedra every waking moment. But this race week in her home country is especially difficult for me.

Which is why, when I awoke this morning, I decided to risk clearing my day to reclaim some semblance of the outing I'd once so eagerly anticipated. I canceled the endurance run scheduled with Guillaume, made a few phone calls to arrange details, and put on the shirt Phaedra has mentioned is especially flattering.

In the elevator on the way down to the dining room, a young woman with an elfish face, rose-gold hair, and brown eyes steps in from the floor reserved by Team Easton, two levels below Emerald's. We're alone, and she drapes herself coyly into the corner after I greet her. She blows a bit of stray fringe off her forehead, lips in a sensual pout, and eyes me.

"You're Owen's friend, right? Cosmo?"

Her voice is low and a touch raspy, something to which I've always been partial. She's in a sleeveless shirt and spandex shorts, standing in her stocking feet with a pair of trainers dangling by the laces from one hand—on her way to the hotel's gym, I presume.

"Cosmin." I extend my hand to shake.

"I'm Peach—Brooklyn's friend." She nods at the ceiling. "Staying with 'em this week."

I raise an eyebrow. "Ah! The infamous Peach. From Los Angeles, yes? Your reputation precedes you."

"In the flesh, babyboy," she singsongs, opening her arms. Her gaze prowls me in assessment. "You should come to our party tonight."

"A party?" I reply, warming to her game. "I've not heard about this. Who is coming?"

"You and everyone else, if we do it right." The elevator chimes, stopping at the dining room level. As the doors glide open, she adds in a whisper, "It'll just be the four of us."

Her eyes move from my face to something behind me, and her smile falters. I turn to find Phaedra standing with one hand in the pocket of her favorite jeans, the other holding a half-eaten croissant. She chews, leisurely, her expression sardonic. As the door begins to close, she stops it with an elbow.

"Going down?" she asks, the pun apparent.

"I am," Peach replies. Her brows lift in feigned innocence, and she adds, "To the gym, that is." I don't think I imagine her superior look as she eyes the croissant.

Phaedra laughs and takes a huge bite, saying around the mouthful, "Cool, have at it. I'll catch a ride on the way back up." She points her middle finger at the floor. "Off you fuck, sweet pea."

My lips are clamped together, stifling my mirth, as I step from the elevator.

"This is my floor," I tell Phaedra. "I was looking for you."

"Huh. Ya don't say." Her triumphant gaze angles past me.

Peach ignores her, focused on me. "See you tonight, baby-boy?" She taps her chest with a fingertip. "Peach—like the emoji."

Phaedra maintains her composure until the elevator doors slide shut, then bursts out laughing. Her hair is in a messy braid draped over her shoulder, pointing at one of her perfect little tits, which strain the writing on a tight gray T-shirt with a picture of an engine, reading STILL PLAYS WITH BLOCKS.

"Like the fuckin' emoji?" Phaedra cackles. "Oh, that is priceless. Not 'like the fruit,' mind you, but *the emoji*." She shakes her head, laughter condensing into a groan. "These Gen Z kids slay me—seriously."

"Wicked girl," I tease, "to engage in a battle of wits with someone so poorly armed."

We move aside as a group comes to wait for the elevator, and without realizing it, I've put an arm lightly around Phaedra's waist, guiding her toward me. She glances pointedly at my hand on her hip, and I remove it before taking a step back.

"What do you need, Legs?"

"Your company for approximately three hours." There's a glitter-size flake of pastry on her upper lip and it's all I can do not to lick it off. I reach with a thumb and brush it away.

She takes another slow bite of the croissant, examining me with suspicion.

"Yeah, sorry. I'm busy. I've got…um, a thing."

"What kind of thing?"

She casually sweeps a crumb off her shirt. "Are you my PA now?"

There follows a silence into which my hope stumbles, like a hidden hole in the terrain.

I'm not ready to give up. I touch her chin, tipping her face to meet my eyes. Hers go wide, and I see the pain there—she feels as wretched as I do.

"The only person," I tell her quietly, "who understands how much this hurts is the other. You and I, draga mea. Perhaps we cannot go back, but we can commiserate at least—as friends—on how unfair this is." I touch her lower lip with my thumb. "I'd like to be friends."

"That's dangerous," she replies immediately.

"So is racing. So is life."

There's a long pause in which she considers this.

On impulse, I add, slowly and clearly, "M-am gândit la tine toată ziua."

After processing the phrase, she ventures, "You think of me every day?"

"Toată ziua—all day. But also în fiecare zi—every day." I smile. "You're still studying."

She shrugs. "Little bit."

I sense her thawing, and try, "Consider it a belated birthday gift to come with me today."

"I sent you a swanky bottle of pinot noir."

"And no one with whom to share it."

She takes the last bite of pastry and chews, eyes narrowed. Her tongue darts out to touch one corner of her mouth.

"If you still have the wine," she says, "I'm pretty sure the horny 'emoji' from the elevator would be game to share."

I can't resist taunting her.

"And you would have no problem with that—my seducing another woman with the gift you gave me?" I step closer and drop my voice. "Licking the wine from her lips, undressing her, filling her pretty cunt?"

Phaedra freezes, lips parted, brow pinched. "That wouldn't make me happy, no."

"Nor I. Which is why I've no plans to accept her invitation." I reposition Phaedra's braid as an excuse to touch her. "I've accepted *no* invitations since you left me in England."

"Sure, buddy. July thirteenth is the last day you got laid."

I open my hands in a gesture of honesty.

"*Sixteen weeks*," she emphasizes. "For a guy who walks around with puss thrown at him like a perpetual cafeteria food fight. At the very least, I know you must've taken that Chilly Willy penguin-ass tramp back to your room."

I have no idea what she's talking about, but the characterization is so delightfully Phaedra that I burst out laughing. I grab her in a spontaneous embrace—arms pinned to her sides—and my laughter trails off into the warmth of her hair.

Bracing her arms between us, she wriggles to escape. "Knock that shit off, Ardelean."

"My apologies." I can't hold back the smile that creeps up.

She gives her T-shirt an indignant swipe as if I've wrinkled it. "You smell really good," she grumbles.

"Phaedra."

With a huff, she meets my gaze.

"Join me out front in…" I slide my phone from my pocket to check the time. "Forty minutes. I've something to show you. If you're not interested, you are free to walk away."

Scrunching her mouth to one side, she grants me a tight nod. "Fine."

She walks to the elevator and prods the button.

My heart aches—she's so reluctant, it seems there's little hope of a friendship ever developing. But before the doors open, she pivots back to me with the grumpy smile I treasure.

"This had better be great. Impress me."

▓▓▓▓▓

When she comes out the front doors of the hotel, her arms spread in slow motion, as if she's afraid she'll faint. She walks toward the car with dreamlike steps, eyes only for this nearly eighteen feet of glossy black, chrome-kissed mid-century beauty.

She puts one hand out, laying it flat on the warm metal as if shyly petting a powerful animal. I watch, hands in my pockets, enjoying her reaction. She throws a lovestruck look over her shoulder at me—though it's clearly the car she's fallen for.

"Holy shit! A '61 Lincoln Continental." She lifts her arms and drapes herself comically against the passenger-side window and roof with a moan. "Come here, you," she tells the car. "Have your way with me."

"O Doamne," I say with a laugh. "I'd have rented one of these ages ago, had I known it would so enrapture you."

Her hands glide down to the side-by-side door handles. "Mmm, suicide doors." She begins a slow walk around the Lincoln, trailing her fingers along the car's body.

"You like it?"

"I haven't seen anything this gorgeous since your clothes were on the floor." She says it so matter-of-factly that I almost laugh—she's not even flirting. "Can I pop the hood?"

"Anything you like. She's ours for the next six hours."

Phaedra looks at me over the top of the car as she opens the driver-side door. "No shit? Oh my God."

She ducks in and releases the hood then walks to the front to lift it, arms stretched over her head, gazing at the engine as if it's a banquet. My eyes trace the contours of muscle in her arms and shoulders, the pert swell of her breasts, the womanly curve of her lower belly.

She's wearing the same T-shirt and jeans as earlier, but with a man's oxford shirt over the top, rolled to the elbows. With a ripple of warm surprise, I realize the shirt was once mine. I cannot help but notice she's put on a touch of makeup. Her hair has been loosed from the earlier braid and is now held back by a pair of tortoiseshell sunglasses.

I'm drawn to her like a magnet, standing beside her as she surveys the engine.

"A 430 V8," she murmurs. "Three hundred twenty-five sexy-ass horses in this baby. The car's a goddamned beast— weighs over two-and-a-half tons."

"Will you drive?" I pull the loop of three keys from my pocket and jingle them.

Her hand closes around the bundle, then lingers. The pressure of her fingers is electric, and when I look from our touching hands to her face, her plump lips are parted, and her pupils are puddles of black that shine like the car.

I force myself not to check, but I'm fairly sure between the intimacy of the moment and her love for the car, her nipples are hard. I myself am glad my jeans are a bit snug, as my cock asserts itself with a twitch.

"Hell yeah," she breathes, clutching the keys. There's a pause while emotions fight for dominance in her expression. Then she stands on the toes of her untied Converse and presses a kiss to my cheek. "Thank you."

I almost lay my hand over the spot like a bashful boy as she walks away to get into the driver's seat.

"Let's blow this popsicle stand," she tells me with a radiant smile.

<hr />

We roar northward at nearly ninety miles per hour, the gray ribbon of highway parting the landscape.

"Open your window all the way!" Phaedra cries.

I crank the window down, and her hair becomes a lush storm churning around her shoulders. Her cheeks are pink with exhilaration; I cannot take my eyes off her.

"It's a shame they didn't have the convertible model," I say. "Though in my experience, women don't like them. It ruins the hairdo."

"Ha! Hairdo-schmairdo—you know I'm trash." Phaedra

throws a look at me, cocking one eyebrow. "You've been hanging out with some fussy little princesses. Did the penguin throw a tantrum when you messed up her 'do?"

I shake my head with a baffled smile. "Again, this 'penguin'?"

She chews at her lower lip. "That chick at the dinner in Sochi. The one with the, uh, 'bountiful bosoms' spilling out of a black-and-white dress."

"I'm sure it makes me a bad man that your jealousy charms me," I tease.

"That's not the only thing that makes you a bad man."

"She did make her interest apparent. But truly, I don't even remember her name. I did nothing to 'muss her hair,' rest assured."

"*Hmph.*" Her hands glide up and down the steering wheel restlessly.

"You must think very little of me, sweet girl," I say gravely, "to believe I would say to you what I did outside as we waited for your car, then make love to another woman."

She shrugs. "The person I thought you were back in March would do *exactly* that."

"And we were wrong about each other," I say simply.

She shoots a glare my way. "How were you wrong about *me*?"

"You thought me incapable of love. I thought the same of you, for different reasons."

Phaedra is silent for a long minute, and I don't press her.

"Hey, wanna know something about my Romanian studies?" she finally asks.

Assuming she's changing the subject, I hide a sigh. "Yes, of course."

"I learned something about myself. According to the app's analytics, I've got over two hundred hours of practice. And I'm getting pretty damned good at reading it. No surprise there—it's mechanics. Patterns, data. But the skill where I totally suck?"

She waits for me to say it. Because we both know.

"Speaking," I supply quietly.

She points sideways at me without looking. "*Ding ding ding! Winner!*" Shaking her head with a wry laugh, she adds, "And also listening. I'm shit at talking and listening—the symbolism couldn't be more fucking apt."

There are many things I wish to say. But with a defeating weight, the reality of our situation crushes them out of me. It doesn't matter that we were improving these skills, "practicing" with each other, and it doesn't matter that we fell in love by pretending. The die has been cast, and we must now move on.

"It didn't make me a very good girlfriend, Cos. But I'm going to be a good owner. It's what Mo wanted, and he obviously expected me to make sacrifices for it. Which is why..." She throws a pained glance my way.

"Please, tell me."

Her hands tighten on the steering wheel, the knuckles going pale.

"I need you to get used to Lars as your race engineer. I shouldn't be back on the pit wall. I'll be working as a non-trackside developmental engineer next season. Unless, uh, *circumstances* necessitate a more business-focused role as owner. In which case I'd be working from the US offices."

The boundaries have been drawn. And what hurts me the most, perhaps, is that Phaedra was the one to choose them. The distance between us will only increase.

I reach for her hand and squeeze it briefly. "I understand."

She starts to squeeze back just as I'm pulling away. I almost take her hand again, but don't. Our timing seems destined to be wrong in every respect.

For the next mile we ride in silence, pretending to examine the scenery while reflecting on the futility of our situation. Our feelings for each other are still there—I doubt even Phaedra would deny it, however pragmatic she's trying to appear—and like the aftermath of a flood, the landscape cannot instantly revert to what it was. Friendship will take time.

The diner is everything I hoped it would be when I looked it up online this morning, and for a moment after we've parked, all I can do is stare.

"Jesus, Ardelean," Phaedra teases. "You look like a kid who's spied Santa from across the mall and is going to sit on his lap for the first time. It's like..." She leans back with an assessing squint. "A combination of starstruck and disbelief and greed."

I angle an impish smile at her. "You know me too well."

As I begin to open my door, Phaedra does too, and I lay a hand on her shoulder.

"Please wait—allow me. I want to do this exactly how I imagined."

Her eyebrows lift in perplexity, but she pulls her door closed. I get out and walk around the huge car, then open her door, extending a hand. Her eyes glint with amusement as she pauses before accepting. I tuck her fingers into the crook of my elbow and lead her to the front door of the diner, opening it to usher her through.

A middle-aged woman behind the counter pivots to call through the service window, "Carl! It's the guy. The one you showed me the picture of."

A sturdy man with a mustache hurries from the kitchen.

"I'll be smoked," he says. Steering the woman our way, he offers a hand to shake. "Carl and Debbie Moore. Real honored to make your lunch today." He points one thumb over his shoulder toward the kitchen. "Found a basket and the right kind of blanket and everything."

His wife pinches her lips into a line. "You 'found' it? In my craft room, along with one of my best—"

He stops her with a squeeze. "For a *thousand-dollar lunch*, baby, we can buy another basket for your knitting, and a whole stack of plaid blankets." He gives us a toothy smile. "She don't mind—honest."

"Would you like a pass to the race on Sunday?" Phaedra offers.

The man's eyes go wide as the woman's narrow. He's about to reply when his wife cuts in, "We have to keep this place humming on weekends, but thank you kindly."

Phaedra looks at me, and I know exactly what she's thinking.

"How much does your restaurant typically make on a Sunday?" I ask.

The woman's expression softens. "Aw, just listen to that pretty accent. Where'd you say you're from? You sound Eye-talian."

"Romania," I tell her. "But you have a fine ear; the languages are a bit similar."

The man leans toward his wife. "Deb, we don't—"

She shushes him. "On a busy Sunday, we can make twelve hundred," she tells me.

"Deb..." the man ventures.

"Get the basket, Carl."

He pauses only a moment before slipping into the back.

The woman steps behind the cash register. "Cash or card?"

"Card, please." I withdraw my wallet.

Phaedra exchanges a smile with me, and it's the happiest I've felt in months.

I hold the card out. "Please run it for twenty-five hundred. Twelve for lunch and gratuity, and thirteen for Sunday, so you can close and attend the grand prix." I tip my head sideways, indicating Phaedra. "This is team owner Phaedra Morgan. She'll arrange for your pass."

The woman swipes the card, eyeing Phaedra. "Lady business owner, eh?"

"You and I *both*," Phaedra tells her. "Your diner is adorable." She looks up at me, eyes shining. "The perfect slice of Americana."

We drive to a small lake nearby and spread the blanket beneath a tree that looks straight out of a cowboy film. Phaedra insists on laying out the food while I lounge and watch.

"If you're gonna go legit *Mad Men* on this," she tells me with a saucy wink, "the lady needs to serve you. It's just a shame we don't have the right outfits." She removes the first plate and unwraps it.

"You look lovely in anything you wear," I tell her, leaning back on my hands.

"*Psh!* Whatevs." She pokes her tongue out at me and extracts another dish from the basket. "Apple pie, potato salad . . . holy shit, they really committed to the 'classic picnic' script—they even wrapped the sandwiches in wax paper." She examines them. "Tuna, egg, good ol' PB and J." Peeling the foil off another dish, she laughs. "Awwww! Precious. Your appetizers, sir." She hands me a length of celery stuffed with a white paste and raisins. "Ants on a log."

I take a bite and consider while I chew. "What is this substance?"

"Cream cheese."

I inspect it. "What flavor of cheese is it meant to be?"

"It doesn't technically have a flavor. *Milk*, I guess?"

She sets a filled plate between us, then flops onto her stomach. Her long shirt flips up as she lands, and I can't resist admiring her round ass.

"I'm not fond of this item," I say, laying the celery aside. "But the view would make anything palatable."

She pulls the shirt down. "Hilarious."

We eat our lunch and talk business, and the conversation is surprisingly comfortable despite the clear-but-unacknowledged fact that we'd be undressing each other on this blanket under different circumstances.

I finish a glass of lemonade and lie back, hands behind my head.

"I've been meaning to tell you," I say to Phaedra, "that your advice concerning Viorica was very intuitive, and much appreciated." I study the patterns of branches over us, and the gray clouds that have crept up. "She is marrying the man I mentioned. Grigore."

"The 'villain'?" Phaedra asks cautiously.

I nod. She rotates to lie down perpendicular to me, propping her head on my chest in an amiable way.

"Is she, like, happy?"

"I believe so. Grigore agreed to everything she requested: a small ceremony at Vlasia House, lavish food and gifts for the children and staff, and for construction on the new buildings to begin immediately."

I brush a bit of Phaedra's hair off her cheek.

"Things between Rica and me could have been very different, had I not heeded your advice and learned to listen better. I owe you a debt of gratitude."

"Meh." She shrugs and chases my fingertip away, but then

clasps it as I'm withdrawing. "You're welcome. Hope it works out well for them."

My heart is beating hard from the way she's grasping my index finger, and I'm sure she must hear it with her cheek pressed against me. A little smile flickers at one corner of her lips.

"Thank you for today," she says quietly.

"It's entirely selfish."

"Bullshit, Ardelean. You not only made my day with the car and the picnic, but between the money and the race pass, that couple at the diner will never stop talking about this."

She's still holding my forefinger, so I use my pinky to trace a line down her nose. "You gave them the tickets."

"We worked together on it."

"A good team."

Her mouth scrunches to one side, rueful. "In some ways." She brings the tip of my finger to her lower lip and makes one quick touch that isn't a kiss. "Not in the ways we wished."

"I don't know if I agree." I touch her lip again. "It worked well, but life had other plans."

A tense minute passes as I continue to touch her face, and she allows it. Her lips part and I can't resist putting my finger inside to the first joint, sweeping her tongue as her lips close around me for just an instant.

She pushes upright and backs away, on her knees on the blanket.

"Cosmin."

"I know…"

I'm about to apologize when the clamor of sudden rain hits the leaves above us, and we both look up.

"Fuck!" Phaedra begins scrambling to pack everything into the basket, and I help.

As we reach for a cup at the same time, her forehead hits my cheekbone, and we both recoil with a yelp and a laugh. I bundle the blanket and follow as Phaedra dashes for the car. By the time we put the picnic things into the trunk, we're half soaked. The rain is so fierce, the surface of the nearby lake boils dark as a stormy sea.

I jerk the back door open. Without hesitation Phaedra dives across the bench seat and I leap in after her, dragging the heavy door shut behind us.

She rakes damp hair away from her face, then presses her fingers to her forehead.

"Ow," she says with a wince. "You okay?"

I touch my cheek. "It's tender, but I doubt it will bruise."

Phaedra reaches into the foot well and pulls off her sneakers, followed by the socks. "If it does, I can tell everyone you put the moves on me and I decked you."

She rises onto her knees and comes toward me across the massive seat, turning my head toward the light.

"Yeah, you're fine," she pronounces, inspecting.

I trap her hand against my cheek, and her smile flattens into something grave.

"Hey, Cos?"

"Yes, sweet one." I snake one hand around her thigh and shift her to straddle my lap.

Her other hand joins the first, cradling my jaw. She licks her lips, and we watch each other for a long time.

Her gaze darts from one of my eyes to the other.

"What happens in the car stays in the car, right?" she murmurs.

"Agreed."

She's already peeling her clothes off before I've finished the word. She strips, then climbs back onto my lap and twists the buttons of my shirt apart. I'm wrestling with my jeans to free myself and arch up to push them out of the way, lifting her in the process.

"Nice core strength," she jokes, clinging to my shoulders.

When I set her down, she reaches between her legs and her chilled hand wraps around my cock. I gasp with both the pleasure and cold. Her icy touch is replaced by slick heat as she impales herself with a moan, then throws her arms around my neck, pressing her tits against me.

She goes still, panting shallowly, one fist tangled in my hair. Her delicious little cunt is a hot vise, and I slide my arms around her and hold her tight, burying my face in the curve of her neck, savoring her scent.

My hands weave into her hair, tipping her head so our eyes meet. "We aren't leaving this car," I tell her.

"That"—she bites my shoulder—"is a brilliant but impractical plan, as someone once told me."

I drag my fingertips along the warm valley of her spine, and a shiver goes through her. She tightens on me, and I groan.

"There's enough food in that basket for days." I slide my

hands under her ass and begin to guide her up and down, staring into her eyes as we roll against each other in hot waves. "And it will take me at least that long to fuck you every way I want."

When I dip to lick one of her nipples, she pushes against my mouth, raising her arms over her head and bracing her hands on the car's ceiling. I suck and flick until her soft whimpers are rhythmic with our movement.

The sweet juice of her pools around my cock, and her head is tipped at an angle, lashes swept closed, lost in arousal. Everything about this woman is irresistible. I never want to stop looking at her.

Reaching for me, nearing her peak, she goes quiet in the way I recall well—a lull so intense that to me it's a symphony.

"Are you going to come for me, gorgeous girl?"

Her hands tense, the right fisting my hair while the left digs into my bicep.

I drop a hand between us and massage her clit. She bucks against my hand, her muscles seizing me inside as a gasp escapes her.

"Uita-te la ochii mei," I say, directing her to look at me.

She shakes her head, brow furrowing in resistance. I pinch her clit between my fingers and she cries out, then shivers.

"Eyes on me if you want to come. Or should I keep you at the edge while you tremble and beg?" Her lips are parted and I grasp her chin, putting my thumb against her lower lip. "Shall I stop? How much do you need it?"

She takes my thumb into her mouth, stroking it with her

tongue, reminding me exactly how good she is with my cock. Her eyes open, locking on mine, and I smile.

"You're enticing me, hm? Making promises with your hot, wet mouth like the shameless girl you are?" I pull my thumb from her lips. "Two can play at that game." I rub her clit upward, feathering against her favorite spot. "I could hold you down and taste this sweet fruit until you sob for release."

I pinch her clit again and the hand she now has at the back of my head all but tears my hair. I give one side of her plump ass a smack and push down on her thighs, freezing her in place, my gaze riveted on hers.

"My God, how I've wanted you always. Since the first moment we met." My hands splay, and I move both thumbs to tease her where she's stretched wide around me. "I cannot give you up, draga mea. You say it doesn't leave this car, but you're everywhere with me already—in my head, in my heart, in my fucking soul."

Her thighs tense as she tries to rock against me and find her climax. With a cruel grin I shake my head. I stroke down her arms, move them behind her back, and manacle her wrists with one hand, then tuck my other between us again, gently teasing her swollen flesh.

"The price?" I taunt. "Your mouth on mine when you come. Don't think it's escaped my notice that you haven't kissed me."

"No." Her reply is so quiet over the drumming of the rain that I only see the shape of it.

I squeeze her wrists, and she sucks in a gasp through clenched teeth.

"I know your games—how you hold back, how you hide." My voice is dark, and I realize that as intensely as I love her in this moment, there's anger too. Anger for everything she can't give and at myself for wanting her to give it anyway.

Her nostrils flare and her eyes glitter. "No kissing."

My temper breaks, and I hate myself as I throw the words at her. "Is it because you don't want to, or because you *do*? Not brave enough?"

Her look is murder. "Fuck you, Ardelean!"

She rips her wrists from my grasp and starts to climb off my lap, and I wrap her in my arms. After one half-hearted shrug of resistance, she softens.

"I'm sorry," I whisper into her hair, stroking her back.

"We can't take it with us, Cosmin—it has to stay here. And we can't keep flirting with danger, finding excuses to be alone."

She pulls back and clasps my face.

"And yes, I shouldn't kiss you, because *I fucking want to*. When we're like this I'd wreck everything for you. And that's exactly what terrifies me. Don't you understand?"

"Yes. Forgive me."

She watches my eyes intently for a long minute, then begins to move on my cock.

I touch her again at our juncture, asking, "Tell me what you want. Your desire, your command. Anything, everything."

Her eyes flutter closed again. "It's too good," she breathes. "Why do you have to feel this good?" She presses close and slides her nipples up and down my chest as she thrusts against me.

"We're this good together. It's us—it's always been us…"

She tucks her forehead into my shoulder, and I know she's afraid to look at me. Her body is curved like a bow as she moves faster, panting. Her thighs tremor and her frantic thrusting slows into near stillness as I feel the tide of orgasm crash through her, milking me hard with spasms as she gasps out, *"Fuckfuckfucknoooo…"*

To my shock, she slides her cheek along mine and positions her lips to kiss me hard—I feel the moaning tail end of her words in my mouth. I open my lips with a joy and sorrow that bewilders me as her tongue searches for my own.

Her hips rock back and forth, and I'm not sure if it's another climax or a lingering continuation of the first, but a fresh cry—louder—vibrates between our mouths, and she sucks my lower lip with a groan as the final shudder rattles through her.

For a minute she catches her breath, face buried against my neck, and I graze a hand up and down her back. When she finally looks at me, her eyes are full of tears and her teeth are clenched as if she's cold.

"Cos," she begins, shaking her head as if in apology.

I cradle her face and kiss her. "Sweet one."

Her look is panic. "I can't stay. I have to go home. *I'm going home*, Cosmin. If I don't, this'll keep happening, and it *can't*."

"No."

"I'll fly back to Charlotte tomorrow. Klaus is right—"

"No!"

I flip her onto her back on the seat and re-enter her roughly. For a moment I'm terrified I've crossed a line, but her legs wrap around my waist and she claws at me, squeezing her eyes shut with a groaning "*Yes, more…*"

I fuck her hard, bracing both hands on her head to protect her as my angry grunts punctuate each thump of her pounding against the door. She gasps and cries out with every brutal thrust, writhing against me. Her legs open, one pressing the back of the front seats as she splays herself greedily, raking my ass to pull me in deeper.

Her little tits jostle between us, and I'm barely human, lost in something almost like animal bloodlust, nailing her in place with my cock. My jeans, halfway down, bite into my thighs.

The litany of things I babble in Romanian is so filthy that I hope she never learns such words. I'm owning her completely with my body as my voice tightens a net of rage and desire around her so she'll never escape.

With a desperate roar I spill into her, slamming deep and docking there, grinding her into submission. My fists are in her hair, and I crush a kiss to her mouth.

"You're not leaving—do you hear me? We earned each other, for good or ill."

Tears are sliding back along her temples, and she nods, eyes wide. I press light kisses to the salty tracks and lick her grief from my lips.

"I'm yours, draga mea. Ruin me if you must, but *never leave.*"

She chokes out a sob, covering her face.

"No tears, my love." I gather her in my arms and twist so she's lying on top of me, where she goes limp, melting into my every contour so our bodies are seamless. I breathe in our combined scent.

The next morning, I discover she's checked out of the hotel and flown home.

27

NORTH CAROLINA

MID-NOVEMBER

PHAEDRA

Interlagos, the track for the Brazilian Grand Prix, is tricky for multiple reasons. It's bumpy as hell, full of hilly bits that follow the natural terrain rather than having been built flat. The circuit runs counterclockwise—one of only a handful that do—so it's especially physically demanding because the strain on the driver's body is ass-backward. And finally, *the damned rain.*

I'm watching the race from the Holden Beach house, where I'm staying alone. It might make me a bad daughter that I was relieved when my mother declined to join me here. I did stay with her for a week before heading to the coast, so I'm not entirely garbage. But when I asked whether she'd like to come along, she said she wasn't ready yet.

Frankly, *I'm* not ready yet. Dad's ghost (speaking in a non-paranormal Cranky Science Nerd way) is everywhere. I see him gazing at the beach from the deck chairs, chuckling in the living room while eating ice cream in front of the TV, and I hear the comforting rumble of him talking with Mama down the hall as I fall asleep.

I'm not imagining I can smell him—Mo wore Brut by Fabergé my entire life, and it's permeated the fabric of his recliner, where I now sit. It's noon here when the race begins, and I wait until 12:01 before pouring a glass of scotch to make it acceptable because, y'know, it's the afternoon now.

The start is delayed because the track is so wet. Commentators are killing time, trying to find human interest shit to blab about, broadcasting footage from the garages, nattering about driver strengths and weaknesses, and so on.

I cheer and raise a toast when Natalia shows up on the screen. Unfortunately for her, she's standing next to that prick reporter Alexander Laskaris—the one she went on the failed date with. The guy's a dipshit who happens to have great bone structure and journalism-royalty parents rather than talent, but he draws a lot of water at the magazine.

I can't help my smirk when a commentator mentions that the weather conditions should be no problem for Cosmin because "Ardelean is fantastic in the rain." The memory comes back to me with a surge of heat, being in the back seat of that Lincoln while rain hammered the roof and Cosmin hammered me.

Fantastic indeed.

It may seem callous that I blocked his number before I even left the hotel in Austin to head for the airport. But I know my limits. I once again proved I have no self-control where he's concerned.

I haven't determined yet whether I'm enough of an undisciplined garbage-monster that I'll have to spend next season in the United States, or if I can set aside my unquenchable thirst for the infuriating asshole I'm in love with. Realistically, it'll probably require that one or both of us gets into a new relationship—a prospect that sounds about as appealing as sucking on cardboard.

Cos had a tragically poor showing in the US Grand Prix a few days after I left. He qualified sixth, made two stupid mistakes, and bitched over the radio about tyre strategy, which meant he not only looked like a passive-aggressive team-undermining dick but a whiner for implying it was a strategic issue when anyone with eyes could see he was driving like crap.

I get that his lack of focus may be my fault.

Our fault.

They just flashed a view of Cosmin in the car, waiting, and *my God*. Those intense, black-flecked blue eyes staring out from his helmet make me unconsciously stop breathing while he's on-screen, as if the flutter of my breath might cause the camera to pan away.

The scene changes to a pair of dazzling-without-makeup female eyes—Sage Sikora in the white-and-sky-blue Harrier HR77. That freaky witch has doubled Team Harrier's points in six races.

I'd be actively hoping for João Valle to be abducted by aliens and disappear from the sport to bequest Sage his seat, if it weren't for the shrewd part of my brain that wonders how much money we'll have to throw at her to lure her to Emerald.

It's my call now; that's *one* good thing. My heart is broken, but I can insist we court the driver I want. Huzzah.

Jakob is a sweetheart, but his contract is up after next year, and Sage Sikora would be a feather in our cap. Mad talent plus the X factor of being a woman has the entire planet watching her. Can a biblical plague be a *good* thing? Because if so, there's a biblical plague of sponsor dollars poised to deluge the lucky team that "puts a ring on it" with the F1 It Girl.

I get myself inappropriately day-drunk over the hour delay, watching track stewards use push brooms to clear water off the low spots, and metaphorically dumping sand over the coals in my aching heart every time I spot Cos.

I check the satellite weather for São Paulo again and it doesn't look good. Once the cars get going, there's a chance another wave of rain will hit before even a half-ass dry line forms on the track. Any further delays and the race will time out before the full seventy-one laps.

By the time it starts, I'm pickled. Enough so that I'm commenting out loud as if Mo were here watching with me.

"Olsson—track limits again! What the hell is this, amateur hour?"

"Two defensive moves! Penalty, you beaky fucker!"

"Unsafe release! Christ, can the race stewards wake up?"

Things look exciting for Emerald—Cosmin's chasing Powell for second.

He changed from full-wet to intermediate tyres at his last pit stop, which was risky. When he insisted on it over the radio, I literally growled in frustration. It feels too soon. If I were his race engineer today, I'd have questioned it. But Lars rolled over, so inters it is.

There's enough of a dry line forming that Powell's full-wet tyres are degrading fast—they need the water to avoid overheating. He's obviously gonna box soon. Which is why I cannot believe my eyes when it becomes clear that Cosmin is about to try overtaking.

I jump to my feet, arms flung out. "What the hell are you doing?" I rage.

Admittedly, the opening is tempting, but it's such maverick bullshit that if I could get my hands on him, I'd strangle the guy. Leaving the racing line, inters are rubbish—they shift only about 35 percent of the water full-wet tyres do.

Is he blind? What's telling him this move is smart?

I clench my hair as I watch the inevitable crash. The safety car comes out—Powell and everyone else must be throwing air-kisses at Cosmin for gifting them with basically a free pit stop.

Lovely. More points Drew Powell (who already has the driver's championship locked down) and Allonby Racing don't need, and which Emerald *does*.

Seeing Cosmin climb from the car causes one second of relief before I want to punch him in the back of the head for crashing out of a points-paying position that might've solidified us third place in the constructors' championship.

World champion driver status is great for the cock of the walk who clinches it. It's the public face of Formula 1, and what everyone thinks of when they hear "world championship." Drivers are the glamour and sex appeal of the sport, with their swaggering egos, seductive accents, and thirst-trap workout videos splashed on social media.

But what a team wants most is to bag the *constructors'* championship, because that's what determines the bottom line—prize money—and money makes a team run. The points for the constructors' championship are the same as those awarded to the drivers: dependent on where they finish during the race. But those points are combined, so if *both* drivers finish in the top ten, it can amount to a good haul for their team.

This is precisely why I'm throwing a drunk hissy fit in front of the TV, yelling at stupid Cosmin about how many millions of dollars he's potentially cost us. As I pace in the living room, ranting a shrill inventory of his crimes, I notice tears are running down my cheeks, and the rant has gotten very personal.

Slapping my hands over my face, I stomp blindly toward the recliner. I step on the edge of a party-size bowl of cheesy poofs, and it flips up, slamming me on the shin hard enough that I rage-shriek and collapse in front of the chair.

I let myself cry for a while, and as I trail off into whining and sniffling, I realize I have my arms draped on the recliner as if my dad were in it and I'm still the little kid who would sit on the floor and lean against his knees while we watched TV.

I grope for the remote and turn the race off. Silence descends.

I haul myself up and put on a coat and the rain boots I've had since I was fourteen. Dad got them for me because they have cartoon birds on them and he always called me chickadee, and that's what the birds sort of look like. The boots are too tight now, but I still love them.

I walk outside and down to the water's edge to talk to Mo, like he told me to.

"I don't know what I'm doing, Mo," I say. "Everything fucking sucks. You didn't want me to be, but... I'm in love with Cosmin and I'm miserable without him."

A wave races up and seethes around my boots, which sink into the sand an inch.

"If you were here," I go on, "you could tell me what to do. That's the one flaw in your 'Come down to the ocean and talk to me' suggestion—the conversation just goes one way, and I have to guess your replies." A grim chuckle escapes me. "Fortunately I know you pretty well."

I give a sheepish look at the waves.

"I'm the same with Cosmin. Even back when I couldn't stand the guy, we were in each other's heads from the first day. I never thought I could know a person who wasn't you this well. Weird, huh? And depressing, since I one hundred percent can't be with him."

I shake my head, lips pressed in a determined line.

"But I'm not going to disappoint the team—you'll see. I'll make you proud."

I stare at my boots, pulling them free of the sand.

"Dammit, Mo! I could use some advice. Maybe an email?" I joke.

I'm studying one of the cartoon birds when a crazy thought flashes through me with such a shock that I gasp.

Chickadee.

Email.

Fuck!

I pivot and sprint back to the house. I'm laughing like a maniac as I wrestle the boots off and drop them, then rush to my laptop.

Of course I don't remember the password for emerald-chickadee87@gmail.com, because I haven't used it in like four years. I basically use only my work email, because who the hell emails for anything *other* than work?

My dad did.

And it might not have occurred to him that I don't. If he had anything personal to say, he wouldn't have sent it through Emerald's server, because our IT has access to everything there.

I send a "reset password" to my work account, and my hands are shaking when I finally get it sorted out and log in.

I scroll through nearly three months' worth of spam, holding my breath as I make my way back to August's emails.

> **edwardjmorgan**
> **Hey there, chickadee**
> **Aug 23**

"Oh God!" I clamp a trembling hand over my mouth. The last letter from my father, sent five days before he died. I open the email.

> Reckon I'm a coward for not talking this out in person, but you know I'm better with action than words. It's part of why you and I are two peas in a pod. We're both allergic to mushy talk and have always understood each other without jawing about it.
>
> I've meant to tell you a dozen times since you got home about my feelings on you and Cosmin. But it seemed you'd quit him firm, so I didn't want to reopen any wounds. Still I have to say my piece, in case you're on the fence and hiding your feelings like you tend to do.
>
> That nonfraternization rule may or may not exist for a solid reason — I feel I can't rightly judge there. But I was disappointed in how Klausy and Reece butted into your business. Seemed to me you two kids were handling things fine and making good results on track. I told Klaus I wasn't gonna put my oar in because if word got around

about me dictating his handling of the matter, there'd be talk of favoritism, and I know how you feel about that.

You thought you were hiding your relationship from everyone, but I've actually known for months, ever since Kim in IT brought something to my attention: Cosmin's been writing you love letters for ages on his Emerald email and saving them unsent in drafts. Kim was concerned and forwarded the first batch to me in late April.

Early on you said that boy was a damned arrogant fool, though a good driver. But I've always had a hunch he runs deeper, and I wasn't wrong. Everything in those letters says he's in love with you. He's intelligent, observant, and has a generous heart.

Klaus may think you shouldn't be tangled up with Cosmin because it's bad for the team. But love makes people stronger, not weaker. It makes them fight harder for what they want. I've given this a hell of a lotta thought. If you have feelings for him, don't give up. You have my blessing.

It's been a real privilege being your daddy. I'm proud of you and I love you.

P.S. The next email is for Klausy, and I don't want to send it through the Emerald server but don't have any other address for him. Please print it out and give it to him on paper. (It's fine by me if you read it.)

By the time I get to the end of the letter, my tears could rival the rain in São Paulo. I am a sobbing, snurfling, handful-of-napkins-wringing mess.

I back out of the email and click on the next one.

Hey there Klausy,

I've been ruminating on it, and I think you're wrong about the risks in Phaedra and Cosmin being sweet on each other.

You know Phae is a damned fine race engineer — that girl is a wizard, and she takes her job serious. Her closeness with Ardelean is an asset, not a vulnerability. Hell, I about shit myself too when I saw that crash, so you all need to stop giving Phae grief over her reaction. Sure, the whole world poked fun at her for a few days. But you know what? They were focused on Emerald. Why? Because PEOPLE make a story interesting.

If the cars were twice as fast and the tracks twice as thrilling, but the race was driverless, would there still be seventy million people tuning in? You know the answer as well as I do.

The cars, the strategy, the tech . . . those are great. But fans love racing because of the human story: victory and defeat, heartbreak and heroism. Phae and Cos being in love makes Emerald's story more exciting. It raises the stakes, and fans are more invested.

It's also the decent thing to do, letting them be happy. I know how much you miss your Sofia — that was a hell of a love match. Let my girl have hers too.

And please take care of her for me. I trust you.

You've been a great friend, Klausy. I'll see you when you cross the bar too someday.

The first thing I do is cry with my head in my arms on the kitchen counter for a good fifteen minutes, until I'm empty.

The second thing: I watch the end of the race.

Third, I book a plane ticket to Abu Dhabi for the last grand prix of the year.

28

ABU DHABI

EARLY DECEMBER

PHAEDRA

I send the printed email up to Klaus through the front desk when I check in. On the back of the envelope, I write *Call me*.

Shuffling exhausted through the lobby, riding the elevator, and walking down the hallway to my room, my gaze discreetly sweeps the surroundings for Cosmin, not wanting to be caught blatantly hunting for him in case he spots me first. I'm as nervous as a middle schooler scanning the lunchroom for an eyeful of her crush.

My flight came in late, local time. It's dark—eight in the evening on Friday here, only eleven a.m. in North Carolina. The flight was fourteen hours, and I can't sleep worth a damn on a plane even in first class.

I'm lying on the bed in my suite on Emerald's reserved floor of the hotel—staring at the ceiling and trying to summon the energy to take a shower—when my phone buzzes.

Klaus
20:07
Meet me in the lobby, please. 15 mins.

"Oh, fuck a duck," I say, sighing and rubbing my eyes before remembering I put mascara on. "Phone call maybe, Klausy?"

I rub my black-smudged fingertips on the front of my shirt, then haul myself to my feet and hurry into the shower. Five minutes later my wet hair becomes a braid with a tip that drips onto the left boob of my CAMP SOH-CAH-TOA T-shirt, and I'm not getting any fancier than yoga pants (which—surprising no one—have never seen the inside of a yoga studio).

The Department of Culture and Tourism should hire Klaus for a side hustle in ads where he stands and looks regal in Abu Dhabi's priciest hotels, because if I didn't know he's naturally suave without trying, I'd swear he's doing a bit.

He's in a tailored suit, his wavy hair tumbles over an elegant brow, and he's holding a saucer while tipping a cup of espresso (evening espresso! so bold!) to his shapely lips, gazing pensively out the hotel's front window.

As he sees me walking across the lobby, he hands the cup and saucer to a hotel employee who gives a little bow before scurrying away. He's so thoroughly the embodiment of a commercial that he almost needs a string quartet soundtrack.

I walk up and am taking in a breath to serve up a helping of sass, teasing him for being a perfect handsome son of a bitch, when I see his eyes are red. My mouth freezes mid-snark.

"Schatzi." He pulls me into an embrace.

I stand with my arms hanging dumbly, unsure how to respond. Finally I give him a pat on the lower back—Klaus is like a hundred feet tall, so I only come to mid-chest on him. His cologne makes my heart ache because it reminds me of Mo, even though Klaus's cologne probably costs as much as a tractor trailer full of Brut by Fabergé.

He pulls back and, gently holding my arms, nods toward the door. "Shall we walk by the waterfront?"

"Uh, sure."

It's warm outside the climate-controlled hotel, and before we even get to the railing near the water, Klaus has removed his jacket and rolled his shirtsleeves to the elbows, displaying gym-toned arms. He slings his jacket over one shoulder and leans on the railing.

"Being shamed by the dead is humbling," he tells me. "And also defeating, because there is no way to tell them they were right."

I snort. "Most people would say that's a plus."

"The irony," he continues, staring at the water, "is that I would have agreed with Edward, had he made his opinion clear."

"Yeah, well. You know how Mo was. The same thing that made him a good father made him a good team owner—his leadership strategy was 'questions, not commands.'"

"I thought I was reading him correctly and giving him what he was reluctant to ask for: your return to North Carolina. I wasn't truly worried about you losing your head over Cosmin. It was an excuse to send you home, which is why I didn't bring HR into it. I always felt it was more of a personal matter than a professional one."

"I agree, but I could hardly stick a finger in everyone's eye and be like, 'Hey, the rest of you keep your lusty little paws off each other, but there are different rules for me.'"

Klaus gives me his "smize" side-eye. "As your business partner, it's my recommendation we omit that clause from contracts going forward. It was already in effect when Edward bought the struggling Montrose Racing team and changed the name to Emerald. Fletcher Montrose was a moralist. But that stipulation has no place in a team that treats its members as adults."

"For fuck's sake, Klaus. It might've been helpful for you to mention this a few months ago." I shake my head with a grim laugh. "But I suppose you had to buffalo both Mo and me a little to get us to do what we wanted to anyway."

We watch a yacht pass, each lost in our thoughts.

I lean over to nudge Klaus with my shoulder. "Well, as Mo would say, 'I don't know whether to shit or go blind.' Do I give it a shot now with Cosmin because I got Mo's posthumous thumbs-up and doctored the rules? Or should I let sleeping dogs lie?"

Klaus puts his arm around me, and I'm wondering if he's going to be more affectionate all the time now because of Mo telling him in the email to take care of me.

"What does your heart say?" he asks.

"I don't know if it matters what my stupid heart says. I was a dick to Cosmin in Texas. We sort of, um, 'had a moment,' and he was like, 'We're gonna fight for this!' and then I ghosted him. Didn't exactly do his pride a world of good."

"Men who allow their pride to get the better of them are failures. Successful men are resilient. Those who adapt become kings, and those who entrench themselves in bitterness remain peasants."

"Oh my God, you sound like such a rich bastard right now. *Peasants*! Did you hand Cos the same speech when he stank up the track in Austin and then sniveled about it?"

"I did." Klaus's lips twitch with a suppressed smile.

We're comfortably quiet for another minute.

"All righty." I stand up and stretch. "Maybe I'll lay my cards on the table and see what happens."

Klaus fixes me with a look. "I hope you end up as happy with Cosmin as I was with Sofia as a young man."

I scrunch my mouth to the side, feeling a prickle of tears and going for casual to hide it. "And I hope someday you're happy with Natalia, so I don't have to use you as a fuckin' speed bump. I admit you guys would make a great couple, if you can pull your head outta your ass."

I'm galumphing toward the elevators, the tongues of my untied Converse flapping, when I spy a group of four gorgeously dressed twentysomethings heading to the dining room.

Cosmin's best friend Owen Byrne—a talented but inconsistent driver from Team Easton—is in a jewel-blue suit, the color enlivening his ginger hair. His arm is draped around a tall, curly-haired goddess with colored streaks in her wild mane, who's wearing white jeans that are all but painted on and a metallic wrap shirt plunging between gravity-defying tatas.

Cosmin's wearing the green suit I teased him about in Melbourne, his beachy-gorgeous hair exquisitely styled aside from one perfect lock hanging like sexy punctuation on his forehead.

With two Pilates-toned arms threaded through the crook of his elbow is none other than the horny emoji from Austin—Peach.

He brought her to Abu Dhabi?

Her yellow dress is skintight with semicircular cutouts down one side, as if she's been nibbled like an ear of fuckable corn. What is it with this bitch and produce?

They see me, and Cosmin adjusts their trajectory to meet mine.

He has a faint smile of courtesy, but his eyes are cold. I'm trying to figure out the appropriate thing to say—my plans have been derailed in the space of an instant—and simultaneously throwing my defensive shields up, anticipating a blast of shade from the emoji.

Did I mention my heart is also breaking?

Because yeah, Cosmin has moved on.

Fuck. It. Sideways. I'm going back to North Carolina and

getting a condo and a dog, and once a year I can find some big-dicked Tinder moron to service me, because love is for chumps, and I lost the title by parking just shy of the finish line.

Cosmin Ardelean was ready to take on the world and fight for our love, and I gave up like a coward days before my dead dad sent me "permission" to love Cosmin back.

I deserve to have failed. It occurs to me with brutal clarity that running to Cosmin now, saying *I'm ready to love you— ghost-Dad green-flagged it* is the feeblest argument for love ever, and I'm an idiot who deserves to be alone.

The emoji and I are glaring at each other with such "bring it, bitch" energy that I can practically hear light sabers activating as we metaphorically crouch into battle position.

"Oh my God. Did you get mugged?" she asks with fake concern, eyes combing my outfit. "Did they take anything other than your dignity?"

I'm about to clap back, asking if she also lost half her brain in the shark attack that claimed half her tacky-ass dress, when Owen's date makes a giddy *squeeeeee!* noise and launches herself at me for a hug as if we're long-lost friends.

"I've wanted to meet you like *forr…evv…errrr.* You're a legend!" She jams her hand into mine, doing a sawing motion as if we're working together to fell a tree. "I'm Brooklyn Katz—this guy's old lady." She jerks a thumb over her shoulder at Owen.

I force a smile. "Nice to meet you. Cosmin mentioned, uh—" I nod in his direction, and something feels unnerving about referring to him at all, so I rephrase. "I've heard about you."

"*Lies!*" she faux-screeches, laughing. "Nah, it's probably all true." She shoots a look at Cosmin so ecstatic I wonder if she's coked up or just always like this. "You haaaaave to come to dinner with us," she insists, seizing my hands in a death grip.

Before I can take a breath to decline, the emoji cuts in.

"Brook, there's probably a dress code."

"So what?" Brooklyn retorts. "She can go upstairs and change and meet us."

I sneak a glance at Cosmin, whose nostrils flare that tiny arrogant bit I recognize so well. We haven't said a syllable to each other, and I think everyone other than Brooklyn has noticed.

"You're sweet to invite me," I tell her. "But my flight was the equivalent of four Zack Snyder films long and I'm dead on my feet."

"That explains it," the emoji pipes up, all sympathy. "You were sleepwalking!"

I'm gratified when Cosmin disentangles his arm from her tentacles and takes his phone out, glancing at it. I wonder if there's anything on the screen. Is he low-key putting her in her place for being ratty? Or putting *me* in my place by pretending to check the time, implying I'm wasting theirs?

I point at the elevators. "Sorry, but for real, I gotta hit the hay."

The emoji attempts to slither her arms around Cosmin's elbow again, and for a second time he avoids her, putting his phone in his pocket and straightening his cuffs. She pulls a pout and he offers her a stiff smile, plucking her hand up and hooking it on his arm. I'm not sure what to make of the exchange.

For some reason it hurts especially that I had a territorial showdown with her hours before being fucked deliciously half to death in that Lincoln. Her being here with him now makes it seem like the afternoon I spent with him, rather than being a transcendent moment of connection, was a detour in *their* journey.

How long did he wait before calling her? Was it the same day I left for North Carolina? She must've gone with him to São Paulo. I could spit poison, realizing that while I was reading my dad's email and crying during the Brazilian GP, this halfwit was waiting for Cosmin at the Hotel Emiliano.

Folding my arms, I back away from the group. "Brooklyn? Lovely meeting you. Nice seeing you too, Owen."

I flatten my lips in a regretful way when I look at Cosmin, unable to affect any pretense that I'm not dying inside.

Let the bitch savor her victory—there'll be no parting middle finger from me this time. The best I can manage is to ignore her, which is pretty weak sauce.

The only person I hate more than her right now is myself.

"Awwww!" Brooklyn whines, rushing to bear-hug me again. "Another time, right?"

"Of course." I pat her fashionably emaciated shoulder blade and disengage before shifting my focus to Cosmin.

Ugh, he's so gorgeous. I let myself unabashedly peruse his dumb perfect face—the marble-angel bone structure, the delicious lips I've felt everywhere, the eyes I've locked with as I came, the lush hair I've grabbed while his head was between my thighs.

"Good luck on Sunday," I tell him.

"Will you be there?"

"Undecided."

He extends a hand, and if there ever existed a more soul-punching door prize than a goodbye handshake from the guy you're in love with, I don't wanna know about it. I take his hand and hide the shiver that goes through me at his warmth.

"You're still the best race engineer," he says with a melancholy smile. "Lars is good, but you're the best."

"*Was* the best," I correct. I pull my hand from his and put it behind my back. "Bag a win for Mo this weekend, Legs."

I pivot toward the elevators because hell no I'm not letting the emoji see my tears.

As I walk away, Cosmin calls after me, "Noapte bună, dragă," and I wish I'd never learned a word of Romanian, because even a simple "good night" is like a beautiful curse, damning me never to be free of my love for him.

29

ABU DHABI

PHAEDRA

Thankfully the *squeeeeee!* shriek warns me a second before impact or I'd think I was being attacked and give Brooklyn a defensive punch in the tit.

She spins me around by the shoulders, and the guy in front of us in line scowls. Sometimes I really hate Abu Dhabi because of the glares I see men deliver to women when they "act up"—as in, make their presence discernible on any level.

This works in Brooklyn's favor, because my normal impulse would be to respond to her effusiveness in typical deadpan fashion, but to send a nice *fuck you, buddy* to the douche in front of us, I fling my arms around her and loudly exclaim back.

"Soooo nice to see you!"

Social merriment is so unlike me that I'm worried I'll sound sarcastic, but she makes a happy groaning noise and squeezes me. The dickhead in front of us moves off to collect his coffee, and I'm about to put in my order when Brooklyn stops me.

"Don't get the shitty coffee here. There's a place a cab ride away that you have to try. We can catch up!"

Technically "catching up" implies a history, but I don't bother pointing this out. The cashier clears his throat, taking exception to Brooklyn's valuation of the coffee.

"Don't hate me!" she begs him, digging in her purse. Whipping a twenty-euro note out, she plants it in the tip jar before manacling my arm and dragging me away.

She practically frog-marches me into a cab—the casual observer might be concerned I'm being kidnapped. After giving me a playful hip check, she slides into the back seat and directs our driver to wherever the hell we're off to.

"So, what's the verdict?" she asks. "Are you going to the race? I'm gonna head to the paddock after lunch."

"Meh. Things are weird—I feel out of place. I don't know how to do this without Mo."

"Hmm, yeah." She pulls a tin of pastilles from her bag. "Doesn't help that you and Cozzy are on the outs. Is that a real deal, or one of those things where you pretend to be mad and it turns into hot make-up sex?"

I hum a grim note of laughter. "Ha, no."

"Oh God, Peach was such a brat on Friday when we saw you."

I pretend to examine a building we're passing. "Can't say I noticed."

"I'd have told Owen to turn her over his knee, but they'd both love it. Not much of a punishment."

I respond with an ambiguous chuckle that works whether she's serious or joking.

"She's been such a sassy britches lately," Brooklyn adds with a sigh.

Super terrif. I'll bet she's all kinds of spicy in the sack, I mentally sulk. A younger, more fun version of me—the bitchy banter, minus the pesky intellect and existential angst.

"Between you and me? It's this," Brooklyn goes on, thrusting her left hand out to display a pink diamond engagement ring that'd easily cost as much as a McLaren 720S if it's real. "Owen proposed in Brazil. I told him to get Peach something too so she wouldn't pout—he bought her a pair of honkin' big Tahitian pearl and diamond Tiffany earrings."

"Clever lad. Never hurts to throw Tiffany at the problem."

"But then she goes, 'Shouldn't we all three handfast?' And I'm like *excuse me*? That's hippie crap. I love the girl—I do. But we are *not* throuple-marrying. This puppy is gonna be legally binding standard issue."

She digs a smooth candy from the tin.

"Can you imagine the press if Owen were a polygamist?" She pops the pastille into her mouth. "Like something from one of my dad's TV shows. Peach and I go way back, so she forgets that even though she's been my friend since boarding school, she's the extra where Owen and I are concerned—the bar in the letter *A*, you might say. Sometimes *literally*. There's a 'modified Eiffel Tower' sort of thing we..."

She trails off, because I think there's a weird expression on my face at the surprising news—I hope it resembles the confusion it is, rather than judgment.

The emoji is dating Brooklyn and Owen, not Cosmin?

Huh.

"T-M-I?" she asks, wincing at my long pause. "Or wait, do you not know what I mean? The sex act, not the landmark."

"I'm not *that* old, for fuck's sake. Yes, I know you mean the sex act." I give her a bland smirk. "Does it make me sound like a size queen that when I first saw the Eiffel Tower, it was way smaller than I expected? Unimpressed."

She cracks up, flinging an arm around me. "You should *live* on social media—I mean it, girl."

We both flail forward as the driver slams on his brakes and mutters darkly at another cab. Brooklyn says something to him in a language I don't recognize, and he flicks a glance over his shoulder, smiling and responding in kind.

She notices my raised eyebrows.

"Hindi," she explains as if it's nothing.

"Holy shit, lady. How many languages do you have under that technicolor hairdo?"

She works the candy around in her mouth, eyes moving ceilingward in thought.

"I'm only good at two: Hebrew and Swedish, because of my parents. But I grew up in Beverly Hills with an international cast of characters swirling around our place, so I picked up bits and pieces. Mostly if I ended up fucking someone who spoke it."

I can't help asking, "Know any Romanian?"

She chuckles, biting down on the candy with a loud snap and grinding it up.

"I haven't sampled Cos." She takes out another pastille. "Neither has Peach—I know you're worried about that." She puts the second candy between her lips. "Not that she didn't try to wear him down. But he's in love with you, soooo yeah. No." She shrugs.

My impulse is to say *Not anymore*, but her phone chimes and I hold back my reply and ponder her comment, gazing out the window at the city sliding past while Brooklyn sends a volley of messages back and forth with someone.

The cab pulls up to the curb outside a café with big windows, and Brooklyn pays for the ride digitally, then presses a fifty-euro note into the driver's hand despite his protests. This girl is such a star—she has style for days and is exactly the kind of well-balanced rich kid I rarely meet. She's generous without being showy about it, confident but not arrogant, and has a joie de vivre implying she recognizes her privilege and truly is happy and grateful rather than being a jaded monster.

I follow Brooklyn into the café and up to the counter.

"Their blended drinks are out of this world," she tells me. "Can I do the dude thing and order for you?"

She rattles off our order in (I think?) Arabic, and I no longer want to be Sage Sikora when I grow up. I want to be the love child of Sage and Brooklyn.

She herds me to the end of the counter and thrusts the cup of slush into my hand. "Try it," she urges, plonking a paper straw into her own.

I take an experimental sip. "That's fucking delicious."

"Right?" She grabs a white pastry bag and tips her head sideways for me to follow as she weaves through the tables.

"What's in it?" I ask.

We head for a row of stools facing the windows.

"Dates and honey. Really sets off the coffee." She pulls out the chair for me, then sits too. "Don't think I'm a stalker, but let's go shopping together and have brunch before sharing a ride back. Wanna?"

"Um." I sip the cool drink and swipe a shred of unblended date pulp off my molar with my tongue. "I'm flattered you seem to like me, but not gonna lie—I suck at friendship. I get quiet or crabby or just straight-up weird." Wiggling the straw to stir my drink, I add, "My bitch-tastic cleverness on social media can be misleading."

"Don't make me adore you more than I already do. Socially awkward people are my catnip—the yin to my yang. The fact that Owen and I are both extroverts is a fluke."

She opens the pastry bag and extracts a slab of baklava. She peels a flake off and lays it on her tongue, then points at the rest with eyebrows raised to share. I pull out the whole clove studding the top and suck the honey off the tip.

"You'll think I'm full of shit," she tells me with a sly smile, "but Peach is super insecure."

I cover my lips as I laugh with a mouthful of coffee slushy. "I *do* think you're full of shit."

"For real though. We became friends in boarding school because she was a disaster." She lifts another layer of phyllo and nibbles it. "Her dad's in jail for trying to have her mom offed. And the mom's a lush who's addicted to plastic surgery. Peach is surprisingly fragile." She examines me while chewing. "Not saying that to make you pity her. Just, people get a certain view of each other."

"Huh. Yeah, true."

I know Brooklyn isn't trying to make me feel like an asshole, but I do.

"Friday night she got morose because Cosmin wouldn't take her to his room. She cried when we got back to our suite and said, 'Why can't I be a science genius girlboss like that Emerald owner, so guys get obsessed with me, and I could take it or leave it like she does?'"

"Holy shitbiscuits, I cannot convey to you how thoroughly I do *not* feel like I could 'take it or leave it.'" I suck in more of my coffee drink, scowling. "I'm in love with him. But for fuck's sake, *don't* tell him that. I just can't—" I fiddle with my straw.

"Do go on," Brooklyn says in a comically fake British accent. "You just can't *what*?"

I eat a layer of baklava, considering how much to share. "Bottom line," I tell her, sucking sugary walnut goop off my teeth, "he's better off without me."

She laughs. "Literally no one means it when they say that. Is the sex terrible? It'd be a pity if those good looks are wasted on a guy who's lousy in bed."

"Oh hell no—he's a rocket. But, uh..." I angle a reticent glance at her. "You didn't sign on to be my therapist, but here's the skinny: I fucked up. You know Cos and I got into a thing, and the team found out and it was like 'Nope! Shut it down.' Which we did. Aside from a bit of an 'oopsie' in Texas, when—"

"The rainstorm in the car," she says with a serious nod.

My eyes go wide. I'm not mad Cosmin told her, because I'm certain he was doing his angsty Romanian thing and not gossiping. Still, it's uncomfortable.

"Oh. Um."

"Shit, maybe I shouldn't have mentioned that." She takes another sip of her drink. "But he said it was the most passionate sex of his life, and he hoped it was good for you too, but he was so in-his-head in love with you during it that he more remembers the emotional intensity."

Her words splinter me like a cannonball of sorrow. My fucking God.

What might things be like if I'd stayed in Austin? If the next morning we'd met up in one of our suites, made love again (that term…who *am* I?) and committed to going forward as a couple, damn the consequences, Bonnie and Clyde without the grisly parts.

"All right, but here's the deal," I insist. "*I gave up.* The thing that made me change my mind was a letter from my dead dad saying it's okay to fall for Cos." I cover my face, frustrated. "It doesn't make me a good candidate for managing the kind of commitment and struggle a life with Cosmin Ardelean would entail. I'm not equipped for this!"

On one hand it feels odd to be trauma dumping with a

near stranger. But my lack of history with Brooklyn is actually making it easier to confess things. Nat and I are still rebuilding the bridges we torched during our fight, and I haven't been willing to discuss much of this with her yet. Since Mo's passing, we've had lots of convos about family and grief, but have conspicuously avoided anything more than superficial relationship chat.

Brooklyn scrunches one side of her mouth. "You're being absurd."

"Are you hearing me?" My voice is panicky. "*I needed my dad to give me permission*, Brooklyn—a dead guy! I'm not a competent leader, I suck at love, and dammit, I don't know what I'm doing, but I have a hundred-million-dollar team to run!"

Crying in public is the worst. With my luck, there's a tabloid fuckface across the street getting it on film, and I'm off and running into humiliating-meme territory again.

Brooklyn's arms go around me, and rather than wanting to flap like a chicken to free myself, I sag into the comfort.

"You can tell me to mind my own business," she says, patting my back, "but I'm gonna put it out there anyway—being a nosy, bossy bitch gives me a blank check on saying things people may not wanna hear."

"Okay," I sniffle against her.

She pulls away. "This'll sound like a cheesy movie, but... do you love him?"

"I just said I did!" I squawk, my voice creaky.

"And has being an engineer taught you to analyze failure and make changes without getting pissy about it?"

"Obviously."

Oh, shit.

I see where she's headed with this, and I want to stop her, because dammit, she's going to make me take a gamble on love. And it's way less scary to tell myself it's already ruined. Loss has been the theme of my year, and I've gotten skilled at it, but sticking my neck out with Cos and having him shoot me down might destroy me.

She gathers my hands in hers and goes all earnest, and the cynic in me is hating this so much, while the in-love dork is hanging on her words.

"When people say 'The only thing that matters is love,' it sounds overly simplistic," she tells me evenly. "The practical asshole in all of us replies 'That's bliss-ninny nonsense. Difficult real-life shit is going to happen. The world doesn't run on love.' And that Practical Asshole is right, sure. But you know what?"

Her face is fierce, and she stabs her finger at an invisible foe.

"The difficult real-life shit is going to happen anyway. The thing that makes it bearable is love. We don't *forgo* love because bad stuff is going to happen, or because love might fail. We take the risk because when it *does* work, it makes the struggle worth it. It's why we wake up and keep swinging every day."

She gives me an almost grandmotherly smile I wouldn't expect on a manic polyamorous Hollywood kid with hair the color of Froot Loops.

"Now let's go buy you a cute outfit and get to Yas before the race starts, so you can tell Cozzy you're all in."

30

ABU DHABI

COSMIN

On Saturday night when I hear a knock, my heart briefly kicks into high gear, then stalls when I open the door of my suite.

"Wow—delighted to see you too," Brooklyn says with an eye roll.

She saunters past, a gold robe swirling around her legs, and goes to a white armchair in front of the huge windows, flops down and puts her feet—clad in slippers with curled toes, like a genie—on the coffee table.

"I don't wish to be rude," I tell her, closing the door and following, "but the night before a race I adhere to a routine, and—"

"Yeah, gotcha. Owen's the same way. But his routine is probably more fun than yours." Holding up her phone, she adds, "I made your moody Romanian ass a playlist."

I sit across from her on the sofa with a sigh. "Is the new playlist a pressing matter requiring a personal appearance?"

"Such a gracious host," she drawls, crossing her legs. "Where are my hors d'oeuvres?"

"Brook." I try to sound stern, but it just comes out tired. "I lack the mental resources for socializing tonight."

She ignores me, fiddling with her phone. Mine lights up on the table.

"Check it out," she directs, leaning back.

I scroll through the list. "Fleetwood Mac, 'Go Your Own Way.' Joy Division, 'Love Will Tear Us Apart.' The Police, 'The Bed's Too Big Without You.' Bon Iver, 'Skinny Love.' Sinéad O'Connor, 'Nothing Compares 2 U'—"

"Wait for the best one."

"'Coast to Coast,' Elliott Smith. 'Back to Black,' Amy Winehouse." I look up. "This is all quite depressing."

"Keep going," she says teasingly.

I scroll farther. Spotting the song she's likely referring to, I burst out laughing.

"You rickrolled me?"

"A little levity. Plus the lyrics fit."

She recrosses her legs and the robe falls open for a moment before she covers herself. I know she wants to talk about Phaedra, and I both dread and yearn for such a conversation. Buying time, I fall back on a wink and a bit of suggestive banter.

"Trying to tell me something with those pretty legs, iubi?"

She snorts. "Down, boy. Point your bogus flirting somewhere else. I'm impervious to your charms. Plus you're so messed up on Phaedra Morgan that if I full-on flashed the magic kingdom, you wouldn't do a damned thing about it."

I get up and walk to the dark window, eyes drifting over the glitter of the marina.

"If you understand that I'm torn over my feelings for her," I ask quietly, "why would you twist the knife in my heart with this music?"

"Don't be a drama llama." She puts her hands behind her neck and leans back with a comfortable sigh. "I know you, Cos. Gloomy music is exactly what you need."

"Oh?"

"Yep. Because it's decision time: either you listen to those songs and get sad—women can't resist a sad bastard, so that strategy would work—and go to her with your heart on your sleeve and win her back. Or—"

"I don't think she's still in Abu Dhabi. She wasn't at any of the meetings today."

Brooklyn lifts an eyebrow. "Did you *ask* anyone where she is? Don't answer that—of course you didn't. Men don't ask for directions."

"Some men don't need them," I retort.

She stands and stretches. "Sure. Anyway, the other option? You listen to the songs and get sad as hell and *walk through that fire and get over her.*"

I turn away in disgust—I'm unsure whether with myself or with Brook—and stare at the lights below.

"But you know what?" she concludes. "You need to pull the trigger one way or the other. Personally, I vote for trying again. Unless she's genuinely not into you, in which case... same advice I gave you in Monaco: don't mug yourself."

I scrub one hand over my face. "I can't think about this right now."

"Yeah, gotcha. I'll let you get back to your little prerace jerk-off ritual. Congrats on P2 in quali, by the way." She offers a mocking curtsy before heading toward the door.

My brow furrows. I said I don't wish to discuss it, but in truth, there's nothing I crave more than the melancholy of tasting Phaedra's name in my mouth. Brooklyn leaving without forcing the issue almost feels like a tease.

"Thank you for disturbing my fragile peace," I snap.

"Again: *draaaaa-maaaa*," she singsongs.

Annoyed, I follow her to the door and pull it open. "Care to explain why it was necessary to show up in person rather than texting the playlist?"

She pauses on the threshold and throws a smug look over her shoulder. "Maybe to remind you how much you wished it'd been Phaedra when I knocked."

▪▀▪▀▪▀

Jet lag is part of the job in this sport, and traveling eastward is especially hard on the system. The general rule is one day's acclimation for each hour's time-zone difference. Abu Dhabi is seven hours ahead of São Paulo, and I arrived nine days ago after a brief stop to see Viorica and the Vlasia House children. But the adjustment has been unusually difficult this time.

The morning of the grand prix, I give up on sleep at four thirty and go down to the gym to run on the treadmill. Guillaume will arrive at six o'clock for a short training session, then I will have a massage before breakfast and the strategy meeting.

I listen to the playlist Brooklyn made, running at a breakneck pace and wondering if Phaedra is still in Abu Dhabi. Is it possible she's asleep upstairs?

Over the course of a dozen songs, I change my mind as many times:

Yes. I must try one final time and make her see.

No. My job is demanding enough without a personal life that veers between euphoria and despair so routinely I almost suffer altitude sickness.

But if we commit to—

No!

We are too similar. We would become miserable within months.

I cannot win her if I don't take the risk. She must see! I will tell her—

Stop, you fool. You already did, and she walked away.

When Guillaume shows up, I'm all but scaling a mountain at the machine's maximum incline, my feet punishing the belt, thighs burning, arms swinging as if I'm delivering killing-blow uppercuts.

"Putain de bordel de merde!" he barks at me, jabbing the control panel to slow the speed and lower the ramp. "It is only flesh and blood, as they say." He throws a small white towel at me in disgust. "Imbécile. You push a car like this? It fucking breaks."

I pace on the treadmill as it slows to a stop, then twist my canteen open and take a long drink before mopping my face and neck. As I catch sight of myself in the window's reflection, hollow eyes stare back, and I wonder if I'm already broken.

"Killing yourself," Guillaume all but spits at me, "because you...comment dit-on? You are 'in your head' about this woman." He scoffs. "I 'ave some advice for you, mec. Say 'Je m'en fous' and move on. Why give a shit?"

He adjusts the weights on one of the machines and beckons me over to sit on the bench.

"You could have anyone. How many girls last year when you drove for Greitis? Every week, different one on the arm." He backhand smacks my stomach. "Assez de ces conneries— remember who you are and find a new one."

She's not at the morning meeting either.

Recalling Brooklyn's teasing, I consider asking Klaus for Phaedra's whereabouts. But how would it look for me to be moping over her when the most critical race of the year is hours away?

If I make podium and Jakob finishes sixth or better, Emerald nets third in the constructors' championship, securing a place in the "big three." I must remain focused on the goal. Any distraction could quite literally be deadly.

Draaaaa-maaaa, I seem to hear Brooklyn taunt.

Fuck!

I need my mind to be silent now, and instead there's a crowd in it.

I cannot forget Phaedra's expression on Friday before she walked away in the hotel lobby. What did she see on my face? Could she read the truth of how miserable I am?

I sat through a four-course meal with a ridiculous girl who doesn't eat and who chattered my ears off with vacant scraps. The whole evening, I was yearning for the rich conversation I share with Phaedra—whether the topic is music, books, history, or pure silliness, there is no moment she fails to captivate me.

I must stop thinking about this.

She's gone. All I can do today is give her a win, if possible.

I do some final preparation with Guillaume: breathing exercises, eye muscle exercises, reaction drills. In my darkened driver's room I lie down for ten minutes before going to the garage, attempting to relax and focus my mind, doing a mental walk-through to visualize the race.

Once I'm in the car and the pit lane opens, we head out for a reconnaissance lap. The E-19 is beautifully responsive, track conditions are near ideal, the weather is agreeable—everything on the outside feels perfect.

Inside me, all is chaos.

I have to admit to myself, I'm pained that she's not here. Certainly, my selfishness is at the tip of the emotion, but the larger part is knowing I may have driven her away when she came to Abu Dhabi to honor her father.

I allowed her to assume I was on a date with someone else. *And she left. End of story.*

We assemble on the grid, where Emerald's team of

mechanics wait. I climb out. Someone follows me with an umbrella to ward off the sun, attempting to keep in step as I pace, and I have to dismiss him so I can think.

Reporters mill about. I spot Natalia Evans and Alexander Laskaris from *Auto Racing*. Natalia is deep in discussion with Drew Powell, and Alexander descends upon me.

"Hey, mate!" he calls out.

"Mr. Laskaris," I return with a noncommittal smile. I've never liked the man. UK-born to wealthy and famous Greek parents, he affects a personality seemingly assembled from a half-dozen American archetypes—from hard-boiled detective to frat boy—in hopes of bringing an "edge" to his posh and pampered roots.

He flicks on a voice recorder.

"Today's your day, yeah? *Nearly* made pole. Weather's hot as hell, but of course you're prepared for that. Ready to net that number one for Emerald, *finally*—after all those almosts. So close to victory you could've touched it." A sly smile curls on his face. "But you're not a man to worry he's been 'jinxed' by, uh…"

His words die as I slide the phone from his fingers, fixing him with a cold eye and tapping the screen to stop recording.

"Miss Morgan's estimation of you is accurate," I say. "You like to play mind games."

He takes his phone back. "How's that, exactly?"

"'*Nearly* made pole,'" I repeat. "Commenting on the heat to emphasize it. Predicting a win as if it's assured, and in the same breath reminding me of the lingering stain of failure."

He shakes his head with a chuckle. "Are you superstitious or just easily rattled?"

"Hmm, and apparently you're still trying."

"Damn, you're touchy." He gazes theatrically into the middle distance, sketching out a pretend headline with one hand. "'Is the Paddock Pinup Boy Not as Confident as He Appears?' Now *that'd* make a fun article..."

I force an aloof expression in case anyone is taking photographs.

"Do you have any *journalistic* questions, or are you simply a nuisance? I know you sailed here on your little raft of nepotism, wearing the smart sailor suit Mother dressed you in, but perhaps you could look to your colleague Miss Evans for guidance on professionalism."

He tries for a smirk of bravado, but I can see the comment was a direct hit. One of his eyebrows lifts as he prepares his return fire.

"You *are* fazed. Big time. And it wasn't *my* doing—word on the street is Phaedra Morgan is the one gaming your mind. Got her hooks well into you."

"Laskaris," I warn.

His look is innocent. "Hmm?"

Weeks of frustration come to a head, and I can imagine viscerally how satisfying it would be to knock him down—the weight of my fist powering into his flesh.

My smile is malevolent, my voice a lethal purr, low enough that no one will overhear.

"I wouldn't risk injury to my hands minutes before a race.

But if you continue this line of discussion into disrespectful territory…the next time I find myself in your presence, I will beat some manners into you."

A flicker of fear crosses his face. There is fear in me also as I recognize the words my uncle spoke so many times.

My God. I'm even wearing his cruel smile. The mob in my head presses closer as Andrei Ardelean joins it.

Alexander puts his phone in his back pocket and holds his hands up. "I get carried away with the friendly shit-talk. Boys'll be boys."

"Some of them *remain* boys while others become men. And we both know you weren't being friendly. Now, if you'll excuse me."

"Holdonholdonholdon," he says, almost putting a hand on my arm. "Sorry, I can't help winding you up a little to see if I can get a livelier quote than, uh—"

I notice him glance toward Natalia, then stop himself.

"A better one than anyone else," he concludes.

I suspect the competition between them has ramped up since Natalia started doing a show for the magazine's YouTube channel. It's become quite popular.

"When you find yourself behind another car," I say casually, adjusting one cuff of my race suit, "bitterness won't help you overtake."

He pulls a wry face. "Yeah, well. Circumstances can make a win impossible sometimes."

"If so, you fight for the place you *can* achieve, accept it gracefully, and learn."

"Some days that place is a DNF." He extends a hand to shake. "No hard feelings?"

I glance at his hand before reluctantly accepting. I don't like the man, but making enemies in the press is unwise.

"Fine."

"Coolcoolcool. Incidentally—my advice, since you gave me yours—if you want to lock the girl down, *scare her*. Let the tabloids catch you cracking on with some hotties. Jealousy's a top-notch motivator."

He's such an absurd parody of a human, I can't even be angry this time.

"Mr. Laskaris, you were *this* close to being tolerable," I say, holding my fingers a centimeter apart. "But you've also given me something to think about. So I thank you."

Walking away, I pull in a deep breath through my nose as if savoring mountain air. Something settles in me, tranquil, reflecting upon Phaedra. Everyone—including this crass fool Laskaris—seems to have an opinion on the "strategy" I should employ with her.

Listen to sad songs and wear your heart on your sleeve.
Walk through the fire and get over her.
Find another girl—the hotel is full of them.
Jealousy is a good motivator. Scare her.

I cannot think of Phaedra in terms of strategy: she's not a car, a racetrack, a puzzle.

This relationship may be a DNF. But you cannot run a race

with the car you *wish* you had. Do your best with what you have, and—as I told Alexander—*accept the result with grace.*

I've been intent on asserting my position: the indisputability of our being right for each other. I've used my words, my will, my body.

Push push push.

It's time I accept that she will make up her own mind. Even if what she chooses is a future that does not include me.

Natalia heads my way. "Can I get a few words, Cosmin?"

"Certainly."

Her focus shifts past me and she waves enthusiastically, rising on her toes to peer into the milling crowd. "Phae—oh my God, you came after all!"

I wheel around, and Phaedra's smile envelops me.

I can barely feel my feet. Her eyes are wide, glossy, the new green of growing things. My arms lift, then drop, uncertain.

"You're . . . *here*," I say simply.

She's not dressed for work, but in white from head to toe: a tuxedo-style jacket with a longer, gauzy shirt beneath, skimming the hips of white trousers. My eyes travel to her feet, where I find her usual black Converse sneakers.

"Gotta do it my way," she jokes, pointing at the shoes.

We're still two strides apart. Eyes are certainly on us, given the persistent gossip since Silverstone, months ago. Not knowing what she's feeling—though I have my hopes—I don't dare move any closer. Then I notice the way she peeks at my lips in tentative invitation. I recall the first time I saw that shift of her eyes, in her room at Santorini.

The white noise of crowd chatter brings to mind the sigh of the Aegean outside the windows that night. Our words, like small pebbles dropped to test the depth of a well:

Afraid of losing those earrings to Natalia?

I'm afraid of losing more than that...

I narrow the gap between us by another step, unable to hold back my surge of emotion at the memory.

"Whatever else happens today, seeing you here...will have been the best part, dragă." My brow furrows at having let the pet name slip. "If I may call you that," I add.

She takes the final step, so close now. "I'd prefer draga *mea*. Because..." A smile—uncharacteristically shy, yet expectant—blooms on her lips. She hooks one finger into the placket of my race suit and pulls me toward her. "I'm yours."

Her words assemble my ruined heart and spur it into motion. I pick her up around the waist. A happy whimper spills from her, and it almost sounds like pain. Then my mouth is on hers. Sixty thousand spectators at the track around us disappear, the grim voices inside me fall silent, and we are the only two people on earth—dizzy and kissing as if breathing depends upon it.

The clicking of cameras pulses in the background, but I can't stop—I'm almost afraid if we part now, she'll change her mind. I put into our kiss the echo of every moment we've had together, and I sense she's doing the same. I devour her lips, an arm bracing her waist, crushing her against me, the other hand tangled in her hair.

The blast of a horn signals ten minutes until the race—time

to clear the grid of guests, journalists, and nontechnical team members. I set Phaedra down with one last kiss and a contented sigh, unable to take my eyes off her, and cradle her face, stroking it with my thumbs.

I know I should already be in the car for the systems check, and Phae knows it too. She plants one palm on my stomach and gives me a shove.

"Get in the fucking cockpit. What am I paying you for?"

"You'll still be here when I cross the finish line?"

She snakes her arms around my waist, looking straight up at me, and her expression is half teasing, half serious.

"I hope I'm with you when we *both* cross the finish line, at a hundred years old."

I offer a wink and a mischievous quip to head off the swell of emotion her words bring.

"*You'll* be a hundred, draga mea—I'll only be ninety-five."

"You'll be planted in the back garden if you don't watch it, you pain in the ass."

She steps back and lifts her hand in a small, static wave. Near my car, the chief mechanic calls out to me, and I trot off.

After donning my helmet and climbing in, we fasten the harness and collar-like HANS device. I can undo the safety harness but can't fasten it—a mechanic does the job. There's little opportunity to change it if it isn't perfect. During a pit stop, one doesn't want to be fiddling with the harness—a good stop is under 2.5 seconds. Emerald's pit crew is the best, averaging quicker this season than even the two leading teams.

At the one-minute signal, engines are started, tyre blankets removed, and the car is lowered from its stands. Mechanics are trotting away—each car's personnel and equipment must be off the track at the fifteen-second mark.

We go out for the formation lap, and my focus is concentrated like a live wire humming the frequency of every detail—the movement of other cars, the angle of light and shadow, the sound and tactile sense of my car, the connection of my own body, which feels plugged in—an extension of the machinery.

Right down to the most subtle scrap of minutiae, I'm present, living this process.

I weave to get heat into the tyres, responding to operational cues from Lars, his staid voice dropping effortlessly into my ear through the radio. I give the team firsthand feedback on track conditions, and we make a few last-minute setup adjustments.

Back at the grid, we line up again, and the starting sequence is initiated. As my eyes lock on the five red lights on the gantry, a thought spreads in my mind, smoothing and leveling everything: *if my focus is a live wire, seeing Phaedra minutes ago was the insulation around that wire.*

It's stabilizing knowing she's here, watching from the garage with the other engineers, crowded around screens of data, graphs, camera feeds, and circuit maps.

The lights go on one at a time and fall dark, and we're off.

Drew Powell is on pole, and we both get off to a clean start, running on soft tyres. Neither of us knows whether the other team will be using a one-stop or two-stop strategy. There are countless variables that could make each the better approach.

Responding to the decisions made by the other teams—in addition to evolving changes in track conditions, weather, and the myriad mechanical details not only of your own car, but your rivals'—is like a chess match played at 200 kilometers per hour. Anything has the potential to upend the game when one is playing with thousandths of seconds.

Eight laps in, Powell and I have pulled ahead of the pack. I attempt an overtake and fall back when he blocks.

"Pe dracu," I mutter in frustration.

It shocks me when Phaedra speaks over the radio.

"Ai grijă ce vorbești," she says with a smile in her voice, scolding me to watch my language. "What if the kids at Vlasia are watching?"

"Fancy meeting you here, draga mea," I reply. I'm silent while navigating the next few turns, then ask, "Where is Lars?"

"One seat over. Musical chairs—Klaus is in the garage. Ready to tackle this together, Legs?"

"Beautiful."

I can't resist teasing her, because she once told me it used to annoy her when I said that. Her hum of laughter in my ear harmonizes with the engine to produce the potent music I've badly missed hearing since July.

Our communication is so light and direct, as natural as gravity. She's part of me, present in every motion, look, breath.

Emerald's plan A is one-stop, with a single change to hard compound tyres around the twentieth lap out of fifty-eight. Things such as the safety car going out could change these plans at a moment's notice.

We're confident Powell's team—Allonby—is going one-stop as well when he sails past the pit entrance at lap 20, wringing everything he can get out of the aging soft tyres. Each team is keeping an eye on the other's pit crew for signs the car will box. Powell is known for good tyre management, and I'm feeling the degradation on mine.

"Tyres are holding up," I tell Phaedra, confident she can read the extra bit of information in my tone and phrasing.

"Copy—understood."

Powell pits on lap 21 and I fly past, finally enjoying the brief respite of clean air after chasing him at close range for so long. Seconds later Phaedra speaks up.

"Four-one," she comments, her voice light as a leaf.

It's all she needs to say, and it's almost conversational—the way one might note a cloudless sky and say, "Nice weather" to a stranger. Part of the beauty of our effortless communication is that I instinctively recognize the smallest changes in her delivery. It gives me as much detail as the words themselves.

"Copy," I reply.

Powell's pit stop was a bit long at 4.1 seconds—a gift for Emerald, if our crew sticks to the better-than-average time it's managed for most of the season.

"Box this lap, Cos," she tells me.

My stop is poetry—a flawless 2.3 seconds—and I zip through the tunnel section of Yas's pit lane exit and rejoin the track smiling inside, though my face is impassive, focused down to the smallest muscle.

My tyres are one lap fresher than Powell's—a negligible

advantage, if any—and I'm hunting for an opportunity to overtake. Neither of us puts a foot wrong as our cars dance with each other.

I tell myself I have a slight psychological advantage, as Powell already has the title locked up, and I'm ravenous for my first win and riding high on the euphoria of Phaedra's return and our effortless teamwork.

On lap 36, Powell lengthens his lead a touch just before turn 8, but I'm well within range of DRS—which opens a flap on the rear wing, thus reducing drag—as we shoot into the area between turns 8 and 9.

It's not enough.

As we wend our way through the marina section, Phaedra speaks up. "Plan C, plan C."

An added rush of adrenaline jets through me. *This could be it.*

We're pivoting to a two-stop strategy. It's a massive risk, but if everything lines up precisely right, it could mean victory.

First, we need the pit stop to be faultlessly quick. The outcome rests partly in the hands of my crew—the briefest delay could spell disaster. In this sport, one second may as well be an eternity.

Next, we need to gain at least one second per lap for the remainder of the race.

Every. Single. Lap.

The average full time expenditure of pitting—from entry to exit, not merely the span where the car is at rest—is just under twenty-two seconds at this track. There are twenty-two laps to go, and I'll have to work my way back up to where Powell is.

If I go in for fresh medium tyres, it may be too late for him to do the same. If he chooses to pit on the next lap, he most likely drops behind my position. He'll probably stay the course and take a gamble that I won't be able to gain a second per lap.

I slot into the pit box and, o Doamne, it's the best stop I've had all season at 2.1 seconds. I shoot away down the pit lane, riding the precise speed limit.

Her voice is there again.

"You should come out ahead of traffic in P6, Cos. Clear road ahead," she says calmly.

"Copy."

I glide back onto the track precisely as predicted. The tyres are still a bit cool, but the next lap should be phenomenal. I overtake Akio Ono at turn 5 and open up DRS on the straight, where I also pass Mateo Ortiz.

Owen in his Team Easton car and Anders Olsson stand between me and second place. Once there, I need only focus on plucking those precious seconds one at a time like ripe fruit.

I can feel how deliciously fast the car is by the time I'm halfway through lap 37—it wouldn't surprise me to hear I've gained three seconds. As if reading my mind, Phaedra is there again, and the way she says it—a cool and matter-of-fact, "Keep it up; this pace is good"—tells me I'm right. I've grabbed this race by the throat.

At the end of lap 38, she gives me the words I long to hear.

"Cosmin, you are the fastest man on track."

Her smooth voice all but vibrates with a timbre of profound-yet-calm elation, and the moment between us is as intense as sex. It feels *irrefutable*. So right, so real.

Fucking hell! *I've set fastest lap for the race.*

"Fastest *driver*, I mean," she amends with an amiable note of laughter. It's the first time she's been on the pit wall since Sage took over a seat at Harrier.

Owen gives me a good fight on lap 48 before I get past him at turn 9. At lap 51, Olsson is having some sort of struggle—his car is slowing—and I whip past him. I'm all but praying he won't end up in a spot requiring the safety car to come out. Moments later, Phaedra tells me he managed to limp into the pits, and I breathe a metaphoric sigh of relief.

This is it. A handful of laps to go, and I'm within striking distance.

Closer and closer each time around. Powell's tyres are nearly spent, but his ART09 is a faster car, were all other factors equal. Allonby took an aerodynamic risk this year and it paid off.

My E-19 is good, Emerald's strategy is strong, and my drive today has been potent. Still, without getting within a second of Powell by turn 8 of the final lap, there's little hope. I need DRS to give me the necessary boost, combined with my better tyres.

Even if circumstances line up perfectly, I likely only get one shot.

I just make it between turns 6 and 7, and we bunch up. The moment we hit the straight, I attack.

He blocks once, but a second defensive move would be weaving, and as I overtake him and see the gorgeous sight of clear track ahead of me, the crowd is in my head again, but this time it's all cheering.

"Foarte bine," Phaedra sighs into my ear. "Beautiful, beautiful."

I dive around turn 9, Powell in my mirrors, but with the shape his tyres are in, it's all over unless I make a mistake. As I twist through the marina section, I'm riding on air. Only a few turns to go and the checkered flag is mine.

Rounding the final corner is both unreal and the most concentrated reality I've ever experienced. The black-and-white churning of the flag plucks a cord of emotion that wrenches a tearless sob from me as I streak past, Powell mere yards behind.

I'm shouting deliriously, and through the radio I hear the team whooping as well. The crowd in the grandstands are thrashing like a field of flowers in the wind, and as I spy a wildly flapping Romanian flag—blue, yellow, and red—I'm laughing and crying all at once.

On my cool-down lap, a turn worker leans into the track with another Romanian flag, signaling me to stop and take it. I know it's frowned upon as a safety hazard, but I can't resist. I pull over and the young, dark haired man rushes to the car, shouting, "Ce zi glorioasă!"—*What a glorious day!*—and I feel like a king returning from battle.

I finish the lap, clutching the flag in my gloved fist, and head for the parc fermé area near the podium. Once stopped,

I take a moment to pull myself together with a few deep breaths, then remove the steering wheel and wriggle out of the car, climbing up to stand on top, the flag clamped in both hands in triumph.

As I display it over my head a final time, the roar of the crowd surges. I hop down and stride to the fencing to throw myself into the beckoning throng of team members.

Someone takes the flag and I remove my helmet, panting with excitement and exhaustion as I comb a hand through my hair. My grin, after ninety minutes of my face being nearly immobilized in the fitted helmet, seems to split me in half.

Cameras lift and hands wave, questions and congratulations are called out, and through all the commotion... *I see her.*

The formerly pristine white clothes are a bit wrinkled, her auburn hair is disheveled, and her cheeks are pink with wide-eyed thrill. I touch the anonymous hands being held out as I pass, but the only thing in my sight is Phaedra.

There's an expectant pause as I stop, and we survey each other.

"Nice driving, Legs."

I remove my gloves and pull her into my arms, each of us on one side of the fence. "I had help."

I kiss her twice, three times. Our aim is poor in our enthusiasm, overjoyed to be touching, however inelegant the execution.

"I have to go weigh," I tell her with regret, nodding toward where the scale is. "But I don't want to let you go."

She kisses me again. "Scram. I'll catch up with you after you're soaked in champagne."

Suddenly Klaus is there, in the crush of people.

"Congratulations," he tells me, pride shining in his dark eyes. "You've done Emerald proud. Thank you." He shakes my hand, smacking my shoulder firmly. "Edward would thank you as well."

My throat is tight, and the look Phaedra gives me tells me she knows what I'm feeling—that this is the praise I always wished I'd got from my uncle, had he been a good man.

Klaus's attention shifts to Phaedra. "A winning combination, you two. I'm glad you agreed to serve as race engineer today when I asked."

She chuckles. "Glad I could help. And did I have a choice? I *am* basically wearing the white flag of surrender." Eyeing me with amusement, she adds, "That was probably this guy's plan all season."

"It wasn't surrender I wanted," I assure her. "You're not easily overthrown, Phaedra Morgan. An equal partner, not a conquest."

"Well, on track a white flag means a slow-moving vehicle ahead," she teases. "But it still fits—I've been slow in admitting I can't live without you. Admitting it to myself, and to you."

"I love that you've challenged me to battle for my place in your heart." I take her hands. "Do you really have no clue why I imagined you in white after that first race?"

Her brows draw together and she offers a perplexed smile. Seconds later, her eyes go wide. "Wait, are you talking about—?" She bites her lip. "Do you mean what I think?"

"I do."

"That's crazy—it's so soon...isn't it?"

"A long engagement is fine, if you'll have me." I kiss her again. "Stay fierce and make me earn every moment." I shake my head with a helpless smile. "I know I'm not doing this properly. There's no ring."

She flings her arms around me. "It's far from being round," she says, her broken laugh half tears, "but we're technically standing next to a ring right now."

"Twenty-one rings a year, draga mea. And you are the jewel in each one."

Don't miss Klaus and Natalia's story in
COMING IN HOT,
available Summer 2025!

ACKNOWLEDGMENTS

Being a math and science geek, I tend to love rules and systems. That is, as long as they're either concocted by me in yet another bid to become organized or they're imposed by the laws of physics. (Okay, not gonna lie—I've had a bone to pick with gravity since I hit middle age. But *most* of the laws of physics.) The anxiety over "what order to thank people" had me freaked out until I decided I'd just pick a rule to follow. I went with chronological, because...y'know, we're all trapped in linear time. (Pretty angsty, right? I was a 1980s goth girl, so you get what you get.)

Massive thanks and love to my parents first, for giving me a childhood full of books, an obsession with stories, and unflagging encouragement in my writing. Mum, you were my first and most brutally honest editor, never afraid to scrawl a red-pencil "Yuck, I'm gagging" in the margins. Dad, you always told me I could do anything, and you helped to make my first newspaper job possible by paying half my rent that year so I could work my way up on a tiny salary. I am a writer because of you both.

To my grandma Josephine, for teaching me to read, laughing at my bad jokes, and doing the voices when you read me stories. The puppet shows you did without puppets taught me that it's possible to paint a vivid scene out of nothing but imagination. I miss you. I wish you could've seen this... though I know you would have said, "Why do you need all that swearing and sex in your nice book, honey?"

To my dearest friend since childhood, Amanda Nicolich North. Thank you for being the Princess Leia to my Flying Unicorn, for long letters and cassette tapes during the years we lived far apart, and for populating a world of characters with me in the Place of the Trees.

To SWQ, who was my great friend and first adolescent crush. Thank you for poetry, quiet talks in darkened after-hours classrooms, long walks, and teaching me how to flirt. A little of you is in every hero I write. I hope you're at peace, beautiful boy. "Have no guilt, feel no fear," as you once told me.

To author Julian Barnes, who showed me in "Parenthesis" what love is, and that it is not only essential but possible to describe. Your writing awakened my soul.

Jewel of My Felicity, Sean. Where do I start? You are everything. My real-life HEA, my most ardent supporter, best friend and partner, absolute inspiration. You and I will be tossing *Four Lions* quotes back and forth on our deathbeds at one hundred years old, cracking up. Holy shit, do I ever love you.

To my wonderful in-laws, Linda and Beau, thank you for your love and encouragement. I'm so lucky to have you. And to John, thank you for teaching Sean to love Formula 1, engineering, and cars, so he could teach *me*.

To my amazing fellow-writer friends, who have combed

over my manuscripts, talked shop, talked shit, and generally made this journey fun every day, even when I wanted to frisbee my laptop into a volcano. In alphabetical order (*because rules*, right?): Kate Cole, Elin Corva, Lisa Larkins, Heather McPeake, and Carman Webb—you're all goddesses.

To my unparalleled agent, Melissa Edwards, thank you eternally for believing in this book and in me. Your guidance, expertise, and absolute levelheadedness are invaluable. Half the sentences you've ever said to me qualify for being calligraphed on parchment and framed in gold. I want to get you a helicopter and a pair of white tigers.

To my treasured editor at Forever, Leah Hultenschmidt, infinite thanks. Your brilliance, eagle eye, warmth, sense of humor, and encouragement have made all the difference. You've talked me off the ledge countless times when I was losing it over this manuscript, and always make me feel that my questions are valuable, and that *I* am too.

To Caroline Green and Dana Cuadrado for the immense marketing enthusiasm, Sam Brody, Mari Okuda, and everyone else on the Forever team who have made *Double Apex* possible. Thank you so much for everything.

To Sarah Maxwell, who brought Phaedra and Cosmin to life with this stunning cover. I can't stop swooning over it—you're magic!

And that brings us up to this minute, and *you*, the reader. I'm so grateful to you for joining my characters on their journey. I hope I can show my love and appreciation by giving you many more stories. You are absolutely the reason I do this.

ABOUT THE AUTHOR

Josie Juniper is a Pacific Northwest native who has worked chiefly in mathematics and journalism. She writes romance featuring STEM, sass, spice, smart women, and angsty, wicked-talking men. She lives in Portland, Oregon, with her artist husband and a flock of rescue turkeys. In addition to weird loud birds, she's a fan of Formula 1 racing, prime numbers, tattoos, rain, crochet, and lost causes.

You can learn more at:
Instagram @JosieJuniperAuthor
TikTok @JosieJuniperAuthor